MW01503938

Paths of

Young Men

Matthew Chase Stroud

BLACK ROSE
writing™

© 2014 by Matthew Chase Stroud

All rights reserved. No part of this book may be reproduced, stored in a retrieval system or transmitted in any form or by any means without the prior written permission of the publishers, except by a reviewer who may quote brief passages in a review to be printed in a newspaper, magazine or journal.

The final approval for this literary material is granted by the author.

First printing

All characters appearing in this work are fictitious. Any resemblance to real persons, living or dead, is purely coincidental.

ISBN: 978-1-61296-319-8

PUBLISHED BY BLACK ROSE WRITING

www.blackrosewriting.com

Printed in the United States of America

Paths of Young Men is printed in Traditional Arabic

To the woman I love,
The women I've lost,
And to my father

Paths of

Young Men

I.

Michael

Coaxing the lock, the young nurse fought the door to the dormitories and ruminated over why she had returned to this place. The shouting had already started. Not a catcall like men of a salacious conviction would pursue, but a shout that had the weight of urgency came from overhead. It was Michael. She tried to ignore it, if only to concentrate on the door, and by-and-by she made her way into the lobby of the West Ward. Michael acted as a child would at times, throwing tantrums to demand attention and hollering until he went mute, and just the thought of Michael Corbin was enough to make her stomach roil.

"Caroline!"

The young nurse had returned from her morning break to start the afternoon shift. Michael slept through most mornings, proving the afternoon to be the most difficult part of her day, and this had become Caroline's plight as she started for the steps to the second floor of Stonebrook Hospital.

"Caroline!"

She could hear the echoes scratching their way down the hall. The calls softened, his voice breaking. He could hear her coming from the scuffling of her footsteps. She came to his door, straightened, knocked, and then forced the key into the lock.

"Yes, Michael. What is it?" said Caroline, coming into the room.

"Do you know what time it is now? The sky is starting to dim some outside. I would like to know what time it is."

"Two past," she said. "It's good that you are up. Is there anything I can do?"

"No, not of present. Did I receive any mail today?"

"Yes, a few articles."

"Can I have them sent to me? That is all I request for the day."

"I placed them on your bed stand before I left this morning. They must have been overlooked," replied Caroline. "It is such a beautiful day outside. I would hate for you to miss it before the storm. Do you wish to go out? We can have you about the yard in no time. It will be beautiful, just beautiful."

"Thank you, Caroline, but that will take a considerable amount of thought."

Michael Corbin sat his club chair, a shadow of legs and chair creeping across the floor to the other side of the room. He tilted his head sideways and watched the birds gather around the fountain in the courtyard. The grounds had been worked over, yellow leaves raked into tight rows resembling grave beds, and the groundskeeper kept at them with steady determination.

A rouse of movement gloated outside while the vivacity of life slowly drained from the cold silence inside of the ward. Michael sat with one leg crossed over the other and tapped his forefinger on the arm of the chair rhythmically. The young nurse rested her hand on the back of his chair, then plucked some lent from his shoulder. He flinched, coiled up his arms, and eased back into the chair. The young man could see his reflection in the glass, and it occurred to him that he had become nothing more than a confounded puzzle piece missing from the world's game board—a mirrored portrait of the phantom that roamed this place. And so were his thoughts that the greenness of everything became gray and flat and unappealing. He spoke.

"Do you know what happens to a bear cub when it becomes ill, or too weak to travel with the mother and the other cubs on their great forages?"

"No," she responded. "I do not."

"It can take a long time, as you can imagine, for this cub to get in such a shape that it cannot continue on. And for most of this time, the mother will tend to its needs and go slow so it can keep up."

"I imagine that the mother would want to tend to all of her cubs."

"So it seems ... take after the hurt cub. Though the other cubs are

8

indifferent to the lame one, the mother will help it survive as long as she can. They will travel and make their way to the salmon run, the more equipped cubs getting the better of the spoils, while the lame cub gimps along behind."

"Okay. Are you sure we can't get you outside for just a bit today? It is so nice presently."

"I want you to listen to everything that I am saying. Can you do that?"

"Yes. But I want you to do something productive today, so you listen to what I am telling you. That is as fair of a trade as I am willing to offer."

"That sounds marvelous, but listen to what I say, will you!" he shouted. "So, the hurt cub finally becomes so lame that it cannot handle the pain or the weakness from lack of food, and will just die on the journey."

"That is awful. I wish some of those poor animals could get medical help. If only someone could get out there to help them."

"Yes, wouldn't that be great. Interfere with the whole damn way of natural life. Would that help ease your conscience?" Michael Corbin agitated easily. "Sorry, Caroline. So, the hurt cub is now a dead cub, and the dead cub is now wolf chum, or so we would think. But do you know what really happens to that little bear?"

"No. I do not." Caroline's voice shook with suppressed anger. "And I do not appreciate the tone you have about you. Do you remember what we have said about this? Fresh air could help these outbursts."

"Yes. I comprehend what you are saying. Now, would you please …"

"Yes."

"Before any other creature can get to the rotted out little bastard, the mother bear and the rest of the cubs eat every piece of skin and meat off of its pitiful little body. Only a shell of bones will be found of that bear for future vultures to sniff. Can you believe that?"

"That is a horrible story. Those poor bears. Will you tell me what makes you think about things like that?"

"It is no damn story. You can look it up in any animal magazine or research done on the damn things. They are just as vicious as all of the depraved humans that roam this entire country, and all the ones of foreign seed. I just could not believe it when I read it, the cannibalism and the grotesqueness of it all."

"I understand. It is very terrible indeed."

"Then, I thought about it. I thought about all of us. I thought about that very beautiful world out there, and I could believe it. I could see it as clear as day, and how perfect it was, and how humans never think of things purely in the terms of survival anymore." Michael's face turned blank. "We just shove our loved ones in the dirt or burn them up. We give the maggots and the flowers fuel. They give the air fuel. We breathe them in. We die too and give others fragrance. But no one wants the fragrance. They just want the sustenance. They are hungry and greedy to be full every day they wake, every waking day."

"Don't you think that you are just making generalizations? You know it would be good for you to think positively every once in a while. It might help to get you out of here, and get you to where you belong."

Michael looked straight up at the woman, his eyes sullen and set back in his eye sockets like coals on a pit fire. His hair curled just above his eyebrows while his young face remained unspoiled by the strain of insanity burrowing deeper within. It seemed as though his physical form was trying to compensate for his deleterious mental state. The man's physical presence would not wither first, nor had it been the body that presently withered. Something desolate wandered in those hurt eyes, something illusory, an indication of a mind losing its sentience.

"Where do I belong? Can you tell me that from your deep well of wisdom?"

"I did not mean to get you riled. I will be going now."

"That is surely advisable."

She rested her hand once more on his shoulder and then turned and went for the door. The white dress she wore, freshly pressed, formed her young body well and her hat rested neatly on top of the bun in her hair. She wore black work shoes and straight-laced stockings that made her legs look very tan and arousing as she walked. Michael heard the unlatching of the door and then the sound of it creaking as it closed. He listened for the clicking sound of the latch when locked from the outside.

He sat in his chair for a time and waited until the sun fell past his window. A shadow followed and spanned the hills from where the clouds hid the light emanating from the west. It soon grew dark, as a storm was imminent and rapidly oncoming, and black clouds started to materialize like large bursts of cannonball smoke. Michael imagined a great war in the sky in which the heavens churned, screaming behind each crack of thunder. He wished he could open the windows, if only to feel the fury of the wind. He could see the gardeners and some patients about the yard start to scurry inside in terror of the developing storm and his mental state rose to great acuteness as he harbored the storm's energy. With this notion, he came from his chair and walked the room.

Mahogany served as the trim on all of the furniture with gothic creatures etched into the wood. The room resembling a sanctuary or archaic temple. In one corner of the room sat a typing table with a typewriter on it. Nothing written on the paper in its scroll. Some postcards sat, turned upside down next to the typewriter, and a bookshelf stood barren in the corner. Paintings of the institution's founders had been bolted to the walls and some of Michael's own paintings opposed them in their novice abstraction. All of the artwork now peered damningly from the ceiling down to the floor. As he walked the room he ran his fingers over the rough wood and his silhouette looked like that of a goblin lurking through the darkness. Lightning exploded outside and a truculent crash followed. Something sinister advanced across the land—a revelation eerily oncoming.

As he had attempted several times before, Michael turned to sit at the typing table adjacent his paintings, but had not come to write. His shaky hands felt their way to the clay lamp resting atop his worktable. Etched into the lamp was an engraving of three canoes floating vertically in a still blue pond, oars transecting at the bows. Slight carving around the rim and bottom of the clay vase. He turned on the lamp and his shaky hands emerged in the lamplight. Facing the large stack of envelopes stuffed into a mail slot at the top of the desk only galvanized the pain that grew abysmally in his brain, but he fought the small terrors of his affliction, the fury of his mind torturing him so, bringing him to such dissolution—the wretched, seething, spiraling pain that pulled at the fibers of his brain—those being tugged at so very often at the back of his skull—the fiery embers that were starting to fray the ends of his neurons returning, returning. "Do not punish me!" he screamed. "Not now, for I have no tears to give!" The thunder struck louder now and the room shook with Richter-scale tumult. He turned to look out at the intermittent pulses of electricity illuminating the sky. His hands settled and he felt for the wad of papers stuffed into the mail slot. The time had come for him to sift through this daunting pile of letters. In order for him to rehabilitate, he would first have to combat the anxiety of addressing his past.

He read the dates on the letters. Each one fell further and further away from the previous letter like blankets of time covering the stains of the past. The pain had started to go to work elsewhere in his body now and the bile in his gut lurched and he grew sick with anxiety. He read the return addresses and his breathing grew heavy when he got to the letter postmarked with the earliest date. It was from his brother, Carson. He fought every amount of discomfort that his body tried to exert and thumbed the envelope sleeve and split the glue completely free from the envelope and took out the piece of paper inside. With the sheet of paper in his hands he leaned back in his chair and turned to the window to regain control. The storm had arrived with the intention of persisting and his trepidation eased. He turned back to the paper in the lamplight. It was a one-sided note, for no ink surfaced on the backside of the paper to blur the words.

Mikey,

I wish this had been the life we all set out for. You know, the life where you became the ruler of your own town ... but even then, those around you would have driven you to insanity. I use that all very

loosely. I have faith in you. Chris is taking it all very hard as well, but he does it with that refreshing candor of his. There is good in all of us. Do not think that you are void of that. You are the one that the old man wished the best for, perhaps because you were the youngest. I know these words may get to you on your own time, but I will write and not expect a response. That is not the reason to tell others how you feel. All I can offer you of my own sentiment is that I hope you can eventually overcome it. Mom doesn't want you in there. She says you weren't born to be in a place like that, says Dad didn't raise you that way. I think that the two of you should swap places. You know that. I hope you know that. I understand that people need what they need. I am not sure how I will handle this business with Dad's death. I will probably do it in my usual fashion and move off somewhere for a bit. Maybe go to the mountains and get my head right. Maybe grow a long beard. I want to let you know that I think nothing different of you for what you are going through. I'll be there to see you as soon as you allow it. Dad would want you healthy, you know. Hold on.
    Carson

Michael Corbin sat back in his chair and let the letter fall to the table and watched as it curled up at both ends like some paper-thin boat gliding across a sea of oak. He thought of what his brother had written and a relief came over him, one he feared would never come. He'd assumed that the letters would purport nothing but ridicule. Because of his anxiety, he had allowed no visitors, no news of his family. Just unopened letters. He turned once more from the table before pulling the brass chain of the lamp. Outside the sky still grumbled, over laden with harsh darkness, and no stars flickered. Michael Corbin did not feel his usual loneliness and when he climbed into bed that night he assured himself that the heavens would fall with rain and bury his thoughts into the ground. A hoard of memories followed his sleep and pooled up into some cerebral reservoir far beyond reach. They would come to him in time, but only when his mental state could sustain them.

Christopher

On the day that the call came in and the coroner announced that his mother had died, Christopher Corbin wept for a short time, walked the city to gather his thoughts, and returned to his apartment with an exotic ambition. And now, no more than a week after they had incinerated her body and sealed her ashes, he had started the necessary preparations to act on that ambition.

In the stale energy of his apartment Christopher stood, hunched over his workbench, whittling away at a dry switch. He could smell the street vender's meats cooking down on the corner where cars passed and sputtered. The city had a much different smell to it than the hay-rich fields of his youth. He missed the sweet smell of coumarin extract that filled the women's perfumes. He missed the crickets chirping on a cool spring night. He even missed the way it felt when he was alone in bed in his childhood home next to the cemetery. Remembrance of one's past is always peculiar in its manifestation, as it is quite opposite from the memory that spurs it.

On a book labeled *Outdoor Lore* there had fallen some of the whittled pieces he had shorn. On those lay tiny splotches of blood—the slip of the knife followed by, "shit!" that had now left his index finger patched with gauze. Christopher had just finished constructing an animal trap when a loud hum came from the laundry room at the other end of his kitchen. Setting the box and knife on the floor, he left his workbench and looked out of the window as he passed through his living room. He considered the prominent features of the city; the tree tops barely visible above the high buildings, the pigeons flying and perching and dropping gray scat on cars, the ambulatory people starting to agitate and quarrel already in the dog-day afternoon. Something about his current condition granted him perspective over the individuals walking the streets. Christopher felt of himself a moral hierarchy, as though he could pick out treachery before it occurred—his own touch of Godliness.

His travel garb had finished drying and he brought the clothing over to his bedroom and set them on the bed. He began packing the trap, a few books and photos, his knife, a hatchet, some nylon rope, and his mother's urn into his travel bag and secured the items by using the clothing as dunnage. He sat on his bed for a while in the pale light of noon. Depressing it seemed, to be inside of the apartment with the curtains drawn, but he preferred it to the city's open wistfulness. He watched a few insects crawl over empty food wrappers, scurrying and reveling there in the residual scraps on the floor, and could feel his finger start to throb again. He took the wrap off, medicated it, and wrapped it once more before packing the gauze for good at the top of his suitcase.

Christopher walked, riverside, by nightfall and rounded his track toward Wrigley's Bar. One last drink with Jack-John and Howerton. The night had been cool and there were no lights in the sky save for the bright orbs of fluorescent glass bound to erect street polls, the hardened metal units ejaculating artificial light into perfect pools mottled on the pavement. On the corner of East Street he came to the sign that hovered over the entrance to Wrigley's. Outside sat a few youths smoking. They looked at him sharply as he passed and nodded. Wrigley's had a cavernous feel to it on the inside and the music playing sounded like that of a slow-motion car crash. An ensemble of horns wildly off beat. Cue balls cracked and sounded like glass shattering when he entered. Some grizzly-looking men gathered about the dwelling sipping long drinks of whiskey and bouncing the asses of their pool sticks on the floor. The beat of the rubber on cement sounded like a soft gallop. He could see Jack-John conversing with a woman in a black dress. A shimmer of sequins. The corner of the bar that they occupied was dark, making it hard for Christopher to see much more than the gossamer that was her blonde hair.

"Hey, Jack boy."

"See this'n here." Jack-John turned around and grabbed Christopher's hand as it rested on the back of his seat. A crack of a cue ball clicked from the other room.

"I thought you were headed on."

"Tomorrow. I figured I would come by and see you and Howerton before I headed out. Where is that old tick?"

"He was in here earlier. I'm not sure, directly, where he is now."

Jack-John glanced over at the skinny woman across from him. He turned back and gave Christopher a chinked smile and then grabbed the girl's hand and fawned over the skeleton-like structure of her wrist. He leaned forward to snag a kiss, but she did not concede.

"Who's this?"

"This is Jennifer. I met her in here earlier. She's been telling me about the college she goes to upstate." He retracted his hand from the girl.

She eyed Christopher inquisitively and twirled her hair from finger to finger. Something about her looked ripe with need. It quickly became evident that she would be easy to take home—just the kind old Jack-John liked and had always been able to find in the dark recesses of half-rate bars—She, a leech to misunderstood prophetic language and enigmatic conversation, was truly a target for men like Jack-John.

"Pleased to meet you."

"You too. What's your name?"

"Chris," he replied. "Listen, Jack boy, leave her be for a minute. Let's get a drink."

Christopher waved the girl off, irritating her at being dropped from the conversation. Jack-John tried to kiss her again, but she turned with an acrid grimace and pawed at him. He grabbed his drink off of the table and tipped hers over, as if on accident. She swept back in her chair pushing the ice from her dress.

"You ass!" she hollered.

Jack-John followed Christopher about the bar and soft lights held over them like plummeting giants stretching doggedly from some unknown beyond. Howerton sat in a booth by himself drinking some foul liquid that was tall and fat and dark, his face inchoate and childish. He had already started to mumble something as they neared.

"Come on in. Sit a while," he said enthusiastically. "Let me ask you something? Did you ever once drink so much, and for so many days in a row, that you woke up only to forget that you had slept at all? Like you were continuing some long stream of consciousness or delirium?"

"How long have you been here, Howerton?"

The two men slumped down into the vinyl seat across from their friend. Howerton looked at his hand and then at the paucity of drink left in the glass. "I have anchored myself to this very bench for three hours. I am like a damned stubborn barnacle. Oh, and I pissed once, contributing to nearly three minutes of elapsed time without my ass being stuck to this seat." The man tipped back his drink to let the thick liquid climb down his throat. If a drop of it remained, it would have been a miracle. "I sat and watched this group of flies linger over the same man for about two of those hours. He never even seemed to notice that the dirty things were having a fiesta atop that bald scalp of his. Boy, was he bald. He must have had some boils or something that they were interested in. Then, I watched numb nuts here," he said pointing at Jack–John, "flirt with that horrid creature for a while. Jack–John and Skeletor. I can picture the gangly little mutant kids right now. Jack, you have really got to start learning how to pick them better. This is getting out of hand."

Howerton's eyes had marbled over and were now glassy. A waitress came by and the other men ordered a beer like Howerton's. The girl went and then brought back the cold mugs, handles touching, and placed them in front of Christopher and Jack–John. They began to imbibe, same as their friend.

"I never see you do any better, Howey. Hell, I don't think I have ever even seen you with a girl. That might tell us all something," said Jack–John.

"Your attempts to humiliate me are pitiable at best, you ... you ... bone–bagging troll man. Keep on swooning over girls that still can't make the cut with the lights off."

"You are both idiots, and what the hell does bone bagging even mean?" said Christopher.

Christopher sat on the inside of the booth with one arm resting on the seat behind Jack–John. He looked at Howerton, searching for any sort of sobriety behind his sullen eyes.

"I think he is implying that I prefer skinny girls, Chris, if I can articulate for this drunken little leprechaun." Jack-John tipped back his beer.

Someone hit the jukebox. A lazy drone of sound came out that instantly enticed the now staggering bodies to commence dancing. All of the bar's inhabitants tottered about the poolroom arguing over pool shots and darts. A few bruiser brawlers got into arms with one another—ensuing acts of vileness incarnate—and it all happened under the cloak of black leather jackets and skullcaps.

"Well, Jack, Chris, this is pleasant, getting to see you. With both of you being so lost in your ways. And as I try to bring you to the light, you can't help but push away. Chris, I see that you have taken the opportunity to finally give in to Jack's affection and take him out for a nice night here at Wrigley's," Howerton said with one lazy eye looking at the man. "I have also come to accept the possibility that the two of you are homosexuals together. It sure is great to see two best friends become lovers."

"Piss off, Howerton."

"What? I am just sharing my honest feelings."

"Your honest feelings are about as useful as a cock in a nunnery," said Jack-John.

"Classy one, Jack. You know that I am toying with you. Just to get a rise, at any cost." He started to slouch over to one side of the booth. "So, when are you going on this half-brained journey of yours, Chris? I knew you were a flake out, saying you were going to stay here and start the revolution with us and all, and then you just up and leave. Just because your mom dies doesn't mean that you can just pick up your rat's nest and take off somewhere else. And for the Amazon? You've got to be nuts."

Chris shrugged him off. All that had needed to be discussed had already been. He did not need the approval of these two. "Tomorrow," he said. And that was all.

The stale odor of urine and yeast filled the air and made sitting there difficult to do for more than a short while, but they stayed and got lousy with drink despite it, the night creeping through time with them unaware. Howerton was of the ambition to pass out right there in the booth if his inebriation took him that far. Meanwhile, Jack-John and Christopher carried on a garrulous argument, unaware of their friend's heavy eyes advancing backward in their sockets.

It had grown cold outside by the time the men lugged Howerton's limp body out of Wrigley's. His head hung low below the V in his arms and he slowly started to slip with every step they took. Some dark figures roamed the night streets, leaving shadows on the buildings formed by flagrantly weathered brick in the light of the lampposts, and the two carriers chanted bar songs as Howerton drooled and silently gasped for breath all the way back to Jack-John's place.

A cobbled-stone path, paralleled by broken fragments of cinderblock, ran directly from Jack-John's gate to the first porch step. The man's house stood tall, spreading two stories high, and thin enough that it featured only a kitchen and living room downstairs with a single bedroom upstairs. It had long since been built and had withered to a shade of gray, balding from fallen morsels of paint. The abode's gutter rocked uneasily from a single screw fastened to the home's trellis. The rest of its metal body dangled downward, as it had started to curl into the thin steel from which it was corrugated like coiled paper shivering in the night.

The three men squeezed through the screen door. It snapped back and then recoiled with a sucking sound—the springs whining with an indication of rust. Jack-John turned the hall light on and it burned a dark yellow with several insects' bodies piled up and dead inside of the lens. Once they got him inside, Jack-John and Christopher dragged Howerton over to the couch. Christopher shook his head as he watched a small plume of dust gather from the arm of the couch. "I hope he doesn't choke from all the dust," he said. Howerton moved and flailed his arms to signal he did not like his treatment, but was powerless and rendered stupid by drink.

"Hey Chris, do you mind getting me the paper from over there on the kitchen counter?"

Christopher walked with a somnolent gait over to the kitchen where sat a large stack of newspapers on the linoleum counter top. He came back over to Jack-John, who now tugged at Howerton's limp body trying to roll him onto his back. Howerton's spine was positioned against the back of the couch and Jack-John motioned Christopher to throw the newspaper down where Howerton's crotch was and where his face would be. He then let go of the suspended hand and body of the limp man. Howerton crashed down face first onto the newspaper.

"That should keep him from pissing all over my couch. It wouldn't be the first time if he did."

"Yea. When he gets that drunk, you might as well lay newspaper on the floor and make him sleep down there and wallow in it like a hamster."

The two men left him there, turned off the light, rattled the springs of the front door once more, and sat outside on the top step of the porch. With the wind pounding against their skin, they sat in silence. Christopher rolled two cigarettes and lit them both. Two ember globes waned in the dark recesses of the porch while the stars flickered like little cellular astrocytes in the sky. What made looking at this sky different now from looking at it under the mystical canopy of some foreign rainforest he was so bound to? Maybe it would be the privation of dusty smog and sirens, or the absence of memory attached to the very sky presently across the horizon—a small half globe inundated with beady eyes from the watchers of the heavens. A distant planet mirrored them and faintly made an appearance in the sky, faintly even shone bright against the backdrop of all other celestial objects, faintly there now, but beautiful and extolling from another glance at another place far from there.

Carson

The heavy broad canoe came careening over the white-capped rapids and through the turbulent waters without pause. Waves spread out to the sides of the craft, following the spear point of the hull, and made imminent careers toward the oxbows and fish pools all along the bank. Water sprayed all the time as the crazed young man came rushing down the gut of the river, his body naked save for a torn pair of jeans and tackle vest. Jig lures and draglines hung from his vest and dangled about him like leeches drawn to fabric. The beautiful, green blaze of the stream frightfully jolted against the canoe and the man's seines bobbed behind and maelstroms of water corkscrewed into unknown depths below. The air smelled fresh and wild about the golden landscape as he jutted under towering firs and juniper needles outstretched on their last living limbs and the aspens hung low in the water, reaching out their pithy white arms into the river's torrents. Boulders lay stagnant in their craters along the bed of the stream. Screaming with wild ebullience, the man skirted around the rapids going straight toward the boulders. He had resorted to steering his craft with a single paddle. Water gushed all around making the boat a direct interstice between the man and the turbulent flow of nature below. Freezing northern water pooled up at his ankles, soaking his wrap-around sandals, and dead fish lay motionless and floating in the murky water at his feet. Nets and casts, empty cans of beans, corn, and beer started to fill the tiny cabin and clinked against the tin walls. He passed groups of campers sitting in lawn chairs watching him rush down the stream. Next, when the waves rose above the bow, he was knocked to the back of the boat and almost toppled over the curve of the stern. His arm pitched backward from the force of the water and became entangled in one of the nets seining behind. He could see a rock alcove jetting across his horizon as the river twisted and shot to the left. The boat went twirling, like a leaf on the water, out of control. From his tackle vest he pulled out a long fillet knife and started carving away at the thick mesh of lining that had wrapped around his arm. The boat neared closer to the large rock wall. No sand bank stretched between the curve and the wall directly to soften a collision and all he could see was the jet stream moiling into the wall. He watched as it curved away from the rock and diverted back out across the ravine. His arm loosened some when he hit a large piece of debris that had traversed downriver and wedged in between two rocks.

All went dark and cold about his body. He could see above him the opaque banana shape floating on the surface of the green water. The water began pushing him violently into large rocks, battering him with sediment and river riffraff. He could hear the water murmuring codswallop in his ears until he started to go numb. He finally freed his fingers from the tight coil of the seine and treaded the water, fighting to reach the surface. The canoe had traveled some distance from him when he leveled out his body and floated lightly through the current toward the overturned boat. He could feel the round, hard curve of rocks pummel into his stomach and knees while trying to float atop the surface of the stream. The water calmed at the bend in the river and the canoe spiraled slowly into a dry bed where it washed up and dug into the sand. Silt jumped the bow of the boat and anchored it to the bank. He could see it washed ashore as he fought to get out of the river's current. He made it riverside and after a good hike along the bank he met the canoe. He shook uncontrollably for a time until he warmed and managed to tip the boat back up on end. With the canoe in hand he waded through the still pool, gathering what had floated alongside the runaway craft. He found a few fish, some lines, the seine that had snagged him, a cooler still in place, and two beers stuck under the wedge of the middle seat on the inside of the canoe.

"Salvation!" he hollered aloud.

Carson tipped the canoe right side up and brought it to the embankment at the foot of a fresh spring spilling into the river from the mountainside above. He got completely naked and hung his clothes out to dry on a line he had fashioned from fishing supplies between two aspens. The sky was breaking through the canopy of the forest and the sun hit his skin and felt warm and inviting as he bounded the rock faces, finding his way to a flat rock to dry out on. The sun warmed him quickly and all of the numbness started to dissipate. Gnats and dragonflies buzzed overhead making humming sounds. He was a man not unlike other men, a man pining for adventure and chaos, serenity and singularity.

Sitting on the rock, he looked himself over. He could see the suntanned creases of his body and wiped the water from the brown freckles that covered his chest. He looked at the scar just below his rib cage. He remembered how he and his brothers used to take out with a bat, some broken in gloves, and a few busted up balls to the grassy lot behind their house. He remembered how the sands of the plains always quivered up in the air and spread out around them when the wind blew through the lot.

"Hold on to the bat!" He'd yelled at Michael.

He thought about Michael and how he had always been nervous and somewhat sinister from behind those big, wandering eyes. The boy was like a ghost behind the fleshy wall of his short stature. Even as a child, Michael was bound by some innate mysticism, always muttering something to himself under his breath, Christopher and Carson never quite knowing what was off with him, and it only got worse with time.

"Hold on to the bat this time, Michael. You can hit it. Right down the middle."

He sat up quickly, feeling the cold water from his hair rush down his back and onto the rock and little droplets of water followed and painted the warm earth below.

A pitch, a single pitch, and like every other time the small boy tried to hit the ball, he frightened and threw the bat. Carson could remember the rotations of the bat once it left the boy's hands. This time it came around quickly and sifted through the air like the blades of a fan, cutting tiny follicles of dander down and spreading pollen about the wayside. Small bits of oak stripped from the bat as it rotated after connecting with the ball. Carson remembered seeing the bat chip for a short second before he felt the unruly sting in his side. He could remember how disappointed he felt when he saw the bat go loose, and

23

then that great pain in his side. He could feel the warm blood starting to trickle and the pain turned into a great rage, one he had never felt before, and one he hoped he would never feel again.

He saw nothing and felt nothing when he came-to, breathing heavily over the scrawny little boy below him. Michael had curled up into a ball and was whimpering there on the ground with a tiny amount of blood below him where his nose had started to trickle. He shivered with fear from the pummeling and could not force himself to look up. He was genuinely scared and could do nothing but cry. Carson knew what he had done to the little boy. He sat down in the dust and pulled the chip of wood out of his side. He could feel the blood starting to bubble now from the puncture. He held his side where the gash surfaced and his body started to shake intensely and he felt the horror start to set in. His little brother cowering there on the bloody ground. He then felt the tightening squeeze of an arm around his neck. His airways started to constrict and the breath stopped at his throat and the blood redirected to the wound at his side. He fought with one hand to get the boy off of his back and used the other to put pressure on the open wound.

"Get the hell off of me, Chris!" He gargled, trying to shake free.

The two boys continued to wrestle until Carson finally broke free and pinned Christopher to the ground by the throat with one hand still at his side.

"You had enough yet, hero?"

He got up and pulled his brother up by the shirt and wiped the dirt from him. The two boys limped over to Michael who shivered there on the ground like a snail sheltered inside of its weak carapace awaiting attack. He squealed as they neared him and turned his head away, as if to block out anything else to come. The two older boys picked him up off of the ground and patted his dusty clothes until he was clean.

Carson remembered wetting his shirt and wiping the crusted blood from under his little nose and around his upper lip. He remembered holding him hand-in-hand as they walked home, the little boy looking up at him coruscating in the sunshine. He remembered how badly he felt for his brother and how he had humbled himself with such great regret so young.

There are times when boys not only feel like men, but also feel like babies all over again. A time when physical presence has matured past emotional sapience. Before God and before the universe there is a child's understanding of what the world has become. An understanding filled with doubt and eternal fires that blaze above all else, an esoteric creed. The fear of becoming venal, corrupt, harsh, evil, all at a young age. Where values lie like that of menhirs erect in some bog, something fleeting. A waste of life spent trying to reach it. He felt that way, and still did.

A cold and wet night came over the man. He burrowed down into the sand on an embankment and used his sediment bitten canoe as a lean-to, to shield himself from the rain. Rain fell on the boat and echoed the sound of the river as it licked the rocks further down along the bank. On his pants he stitched a patch that he cut from bandana cloth which smelled sweet and of perfume. Some initials were sown into the patch with white thread. Perched against the trunk of a tree with no food or fire for the night Carson went in and out of lucidity until he finally slept. Following his sleep there lurked around a miasma of dreams that came methodically until a new dawn arose.

He woke to the sun making its way across the horizon and sat on an uprooted log breathing heavily in the morning air. The sky had already gathered clouds and they too floated and rimpled with a pale hue that very few ever wake to see. Carson prepared his canoe to brave the last leg of his journey and paddled out into the flow of the river by the time the magpies started to call. The water carried a smoothness about it and the current had eased from the relaxed toil of the earth's pull. He rowed the canoe steadily around the bends in the river and waved as he saw young boys spanning their fishing nets and took his time, enjoying everything in its serenity, for the last twenty miles of his trip. It was nearing dusk by the time he made it to his pull out.

A speckle of light reflected off of the windshield of his car awaiting him under the shade of a willow tree just outside of Cody. Leaves tapped on the hood with their crenate hands anent the vehicle and the sun was just dim enough that it made the earth seem to slow. It was the time just before dark when the pulse of the sky, and that within everything, coincide and make the horizon fall flat and soft. A shrill hum could be heard from the outstretched highways further down the road where cars drove with their lights piercing the dim glow of dusk in little interpolating orbs of white. The grass warmed his feet as he pulled the canoe out of the water. The craft swelled about its starboard side and had taken a thrashing during its long journey. He tripped over a few broken saplings while bringing the metal craft along the bank and the sand felt good in his hands as he fell to the ground. He pulled himself back up, standing solidly with the boat in hand, and all of the residual liquid in the boat spooled out and softened the sand below. The boat desiccated from the inside and lightened on his shoulders. He walked it to the vehicle. Mounted onto the dent-ravished cruiser were two steel brackets boasting a couple of iron V's that looked like iron skeletons welded to the top of a metal horse. Some thick-grain worsted straps dangled from the appendages of the iron and had shiny buckles stitched onto them. The man slung the canoe off of his back and leaned it against the vehicle. He grabbed it from the bottom and hoisted it up into the groove of the first iron weld. Once he got the bow secured he heaved the back of the boat over the second weld and threw in the sculls and strapped the dinghy to the top of the car. A crisp coolness filled the air with the onset of the new night and his clothing still dripped with river water. Inside of his vehicle, as he drove down the dark highway, his breath fogged the windows and the landscape around him loomed with an uncertain vagueness. Earthen mounds rested where the ground had collided and left jagged cliffs overlooking the roads in the dark. He drove through the night without passing a single car and the wind was deafening as it battered the boat.

The slumped down cruiser pulled into the station coughing on fumes. A squat man with a humped back and thick neck hobbled out of the cashier's cabin and motioned over to Carson. Rusted Fords and Chevrolets sat on blocks owning the only ground between the highway and the road. Carson secured the straps faceted to the boat and then popped the back license plate and shoved the gas nozzle into the tank. The gas gulped slowly and smelt a little thin. Watered down perhaps.

"Carolina man?"

Carson heard the man's hoarse voice and looked up, over the back end of the car, to see him approaching.

"Yessir, haven't quite changed the plates over yet."

"You living around these parts then?"

The attendant took a look around the car, looking in it and on top of it where the canoe was suspended. His scrawny little hands fiddled about the windows and the big rim of his glasses gave him bottle-cap eyes.

"No, not rightly, I just don't live in the Carolinas any more. I figured I should get a license plate that fits a place out west, a place I may want to set foot in and stay a while," said Carson.

"That so? I don't think it really matters much about what your plates say, 'less someone comes around giving you grief, considering you a foreigner in their state and so forth. Being that everyone thinks they have ownership to a state and all. I guess except for you, and you not being a Carolina man no more."

Carson, easily disengaged with the conversation, gave another tug at the canoe to make sure that the oars were still in place. He dug through the cabin of the vehicle and pulled out piles of newspapers, pop bottles, and some empty packs of cigarettes. He brought the refuse over to the station trashcan, the rubber bin overfilling and attended greatly by flies, and managed to shove the trash in by packing all of the waste down as far as it would go.

"Where you headed?"

"North and some east. Not really where I want to go, but I have to see about a couple of things. Then, I suppose I will head south."

"Heading south? Carolina?"

Carson let the rickety springs of the license plate retract as he jerked the gas nozzle out of the tank and thrust it back into its slot. The cruiser had corroded with rust at the curves in the wheel wells and some of the areas he had bonded with plaster were starting to chip.

"Nossir, how much do I owe you?"

"What does it say on that dial there? Just above the little tank emblem. Should be a dollar sign right next to it."

He handed the man a bill and waved him off. The man turned back toward his post and started maladroitly for the station.

"Got any suggestions?" Carson requested of the man. The attendant turned around, slowly muddled by his own confusion. He thought for a moment and scratched at his belly. Black hair stretched out like dark cobwebs around his hidden navel.

"Any suggestions about what?"

"Where to get plates from?"

The man pulled down his comical eyeglasses and his eyes were opaque and glassy, crossed in two separate directions and void of congruency. He leaned down to the window, his thick neck heaving from the walk.

"Well, like I said … don't matter all that much to me where you get them from, or where you are living, long as people still travel and come by here. Gives me something to do."

Carson looked the man over graciously.

"Yea, I suppose you are right. When you look at it from someone else's point of view, it doesn't matter much where you are going. Always seems like you will return to the same place your plates say you came from."

"I can see how you'd get that," said the attendant apocryphally. "But I don't know why the hell you would ask me where you should live. I don't know the world out there from the last guy come in here, and the next one after you."

Carson laughed and offered out his hand for the attendant to shake. They grasped hands, the attendant's flaccid under Carson's puissant grip, and settled their acquaintance at that. He drove on through the countryside past maples and birch trees that sprawled languidly. He passed saw mills and dilapidated cabins that had once billowed smoke in the winters, and where children would play in the forests, shooting glass bottles and low flying birds—the ghosting memories of little trailing footsteps on the powdery white blanket of ground farther off over the hills on glowing knolls where clearings lie. The memories, locked in time, peered down through the corridors of the frost thickened forests where all trails are lost and there is no track to follow, where children of the past are lost in time, their remnants howling in the wind like a breeze. He drove east, the sounds of the cool coastal current ringing in his ears, and the stars flickered in and out. The moon was at his face.

Michael

The screaming echoed through the halls most mornings and usually went unnoticed. In his fortune he shared the second story with vacant rooms and wash closets, a few janitorial depositories, and an open studio once used for calisthenics. Hollow now. Something foul lingered in the room that he noticed when he awoke. He knew exactly what it was—*it* was him. He was stuck in a room with himself again.

He ate his breakfast in a hurry. Michael had never been one to allow his hunger to linger for very long, and as he ate, he thought of Christopher and then he thought of Carson. The man almost felt at ease, but the sun began to fill his room and he started to lose the ability to find joy in anything. The food had even started to make him sick, causing him to lose any ambition to be productive. A flock of birds came flapping and calling past his window, as if to entice something from him, and he watched as the sun flickered through their feathers. Several hours went by and he did not move.

Caroline knocked at his door, "I have your lunch," she said. He decided not take it. Today was not a day for dealing with others, he thought. He sat his chair and hardly moved as the hours passed with little interruption. Some thoughts of reading another letter interpolated from time to time, but the urge to move desisted with so much sunlight flooding the room. He stared down the afternoon with one twitching eye until his trepidation eased. The sun filtered out across the sky and the daylight faded and initiated the time of day that he could handle easiest. His time of vitality. Looking backward, he could not stand his own inactivity. It made him feel like less of a man. No one, not even in their weakest state, can face the realization that their existence is not worthwhile, even for the shortest portion of the day.

His strength had roused just enough with the setting sun for him to attempt to read another of his brother's letters. The next two in chronology were from Christopher. Michael retired to his chair. The day had gone and the sky shimmered with a star blown awe. The sound of whirring crickets called in the dusk, drowning the dull hoot of owls. He ripped into the first letter and set it on his lap. Next, he ripped the envelope of the second and put it neatly behind the first.

Michael,
You unbelievable little shit.

Michael put the letter down, already distraught with the first sentence, and did not know if he could keep his mental poise enough to read on after such a blatant affront. He decided to pick the letter back up and continued through.

I can't believe you found a way to live where people will feed you three solid meals a day and wipe your ass for you. It is like when we put Grandpa Jerry in the "folks" home, and every time we visited he said he should have been transferred there at birth. You pampered con artist. Do you plan on staying in this state of ribald self-indulgence forever? You didn't even bother to leave the nest to come visit me at school before all this happened, and now I only have a semester left. Even Loretta has come to my place, be it in one of her drunken maternal deficiency breakdowns, but at least she came. God knows why dad ever loved that woman. Doesn't matter now. And what is this bullshit I hear about you not allowing anyone to come and see you? I highly disagree with any logic you could have on that. Sure, you could exclude said other party, but not your brothers. And you didn't even come to dad's funeral. Why did I never come up with this clever rouse to act insane, and then fall apart when the terror got real? I sent a book to you. I don't know if you got it, or if you will get it, since you are blocking us out. I have the mind to march up there and throw a rock through your damn window. Not out of hate, but out of love. The book is Gravity's Rainbow. Read Entropy, if you can manage to get your brain focused on something other than the carpet. In lieu of all the banter, I honestly hope you start feeling up to life again. As soon as you do, we will get you laid, you hear? That may be a harder task than I can handle as wingman, but surely we can try to gather some of the girls from Rosedale Street to get that process started for you.

    Best,

    Chris

Michael set the letter aside with a simple grunt. A glimpse of a smile surfaced from the corners of his mouth. Even though the letter was vituperating, it was not abnormal from Christopher's usual style of writing. This made Michael feel good. He knew that he was not being treated any different, the way bank robbers must feel when they get away with their crimes. Michael picked up the second letter and read on.

    Michael,

    I thought about what I said in my last letter and realized that there is no way we will ever get you laid, but you should at least come out of there for a beer or something. Won't you let us come see you? I know Carson would find this an extraordinary delight, and I suppose, for myself, it would be nice as well. Not too much to ask, I don't think. Maybe we can bring you some cigarettes so you can barter with the others. Or is that not how your situation works? I'm not hip to the happenings of loonies and their counterparts, the incarcerated, and their particular way of life inside the confines of an institution. Write me back and let me know if things have changed.

    Chris

Michael set the letter down. It was hard to find a balance between Christopher's humor and the seriousness with which he handled situations. Maybe he had the right balance. Michael knew that he himself had found no balance at all. Maybe he had found some peace from reading the two letters. Yes, he had found peace in reading the letters. He leaned back in his chair and stared up at the tiles crawling on the ceiling. If he were to make it through another night, these letters would certainly help him to do so. He let his eyes drop and fell asleep.

He awoke abruptly in the middle of the night to the moon's glow orotund on the wall beside his bookshelf. He had dreamt of long tropical vines spiraling all around. He and his brothers had been in some lush and dense forest with thousands of strange noises coming from every direction. He could feel the mushy ground below as they walked and the vines were always wrapping around them, almost choking them, and his breath went tight. They stretched further and further out into the vast abyss of greenery, walking through some strange and incomprehensible landscape. Christopher led them out of the vines and a crushing drone of water surrounding the jungle overtook the strange sounds all around. It sounded like turbines churning. Its deafening hum growing louder. The three men came upon an opening in the jungle where the sound had been the loudest and Michael could not see any water. He watched as Christopher made his way out of the forest and into a white-blue horizon. The man left from sight, his entire body gone within a matter of seconds, and then nothing. The sound of the thunderous water hastened as he stepped forward to see where his brother had gone, and then it was there. It hit him like a beam of light when he saw the cloud-like plummet of water sucking down into a great canyon. Christopher floated down into it. His arms and legs flailed, as if by normal standards, but his body moved slowly, as did the terrified look on his face. So horrible was his look that it woke Michael from his nightmares and he sat up in his armchair whimpering, afraid to close his eyes again.

The first time he had been in the ward's yard neared close to a year prior. He had no real recollection of how long he had been at the institution. He could remember one other time that he had stepped outside on the fresh grass. It had been during a fire drill last fall. Autumn had been the season because the leaves, vibrant and assorted amongst the trees, had started to shuck.

Now, the soft grass felt very nice on his bare feet. A wind blew through the courtyard and reminded him of the summer breeze that came through the screened window in his bedroom back home. He kept thinking of his dream and it horrified him. He began to understand that cooping himself up in this place could not keep him safe from the very real possibility of his own mortality, and the mortality of the loved ones he had left behind. The fate of Christopher, Carson, and even Loretta, his mother, became a fear that started to boil within. A new fear. He had become so detached from his former life following the death of his father, as if everything had been suspended in time, or suspended in his own selfish neuroticism. A piece of him released. He started to forget the pale, lifeless eyes that looked back at him every time he closed his eyelids—the lifeless body slumped over on that soiled couch. The living members of his family were now his warrant, and he began to drift off under the pavilion just outside of the entrance to his ward.

"Oh my God! Mr. Corbin! Wake up! Wake up now!"

Outside in the courtyard a crowd had gathered. Several nurses herded disheveled patients around the scene taking place underneath the pavilion. Caroline shook the young man carefully. White-red spittle oozed from the sides of his mouth and he had a large bruise on his forehead that had already started to grow into a plum sized lump. His eyes rolled back lazily and started to flicker as he drew consciousness, feeling his jaw clench tightly. He could feel the pain searing down the left side of his tongue to the back of his throat and he could taste the iron curling in the back of his mouth. He came-to completely in Caroline's strong arms, her supple breasts rubbing against his limp body. Through the openings in her hair he could see the eaves slanting overhead and could make out his window directly above. His room looked bleak even from where he lay on the ground. With Caroline's help, he came to his feet and started to rub the large lump that now protruded from his forehead.

"What is going on, Caroline? Did you hit me with a brick or some other thing?"

"No, Mr. Corbin, I believe you have been having seizures through the night."

"I thought we were over this. Your neurologists don't know how to read a damn cat scan to save their lives," said the young man. He rubbed the back of his head.

"These things cannot always be definite. There is always the potential for an episode to occur, and your medication does not completely protect you from anxiety and stress, the ailments that catalyze these seizures. That is why they are called stress induced seizures."

She brought him inside the hot building. His discomfort grew with each step and he resisted as they made their way to the infirmary. He told her he felt fine.

"Can you clear out those mongrels and let me go and sit back down outside? I think it will make me feel better."

"I am glad you want to be outside. This is the only time I have seen you step foot outside of the hospital doors. I am all about change, but we cannot simply ask the other patients to go inside. It is therapeutic for them as well, and you do not have the right to rob them of their tranquility."

"Is there any place I can go where I won't have to see their leering, subhuman eyes?"

"You have a skewed vision of others, Mr. Corbin. I do not think that it is fair for you to place them below yourself. You are all in the same situation, and I haven't seen any of them having to be cradled in their nurse's arms like you just were."

"Erroneous, Caroline. I was unconscious."

"Only an extension of your sickness. You are not too dissimilar from the others roaming the grounds."

Michael squeezed the nurse's arm to indicate that she was going against his will, but she was a very strong women and pulled her arm from him and turned back to look out of the window on the north side of the building. The stairs ran just below it. She turned to the man and felt the lump on his forehead and made him open his mouth. She looked to see if any major damage had surfaced elsewhere.

"How do you feel?"

"Fine, just scrambled a bit. Nothing abnormal from how I usually feel when I have these things."

"Alright. You can come with me, but only if you calm yourself and approach the yard with open arms."

He said nothing, just followed her. She turned back around and headed outside. A thick cloud cover had spread across the sky and the wind blew, like a storm beckoned, but a storm would not follow. They went past the pavilion and headed north to a long row of trees. He could tell that these were the maples on the west side of the ward's entrance. He sometimes watched birds fly from one to the other from his window. The outside of the manor stretched, dimensions not unlike a rhombus, with a long rectangle in the middle of it. An archaic steel gate guarded the entrance of the place and a narrow driveway ran perpendicular to the gate with two rows of trees trailing along the sides. To the sides of these hedgerows ran various sitting tables and a shuffleboard foundation no longer painted. As they walked through the yard there were no patients on this side of the driveway. The fence that held ambit around the manor climbed with rusty pikes stabbing at the air in an attempt to discourage escape. He turned back to look at the ward, grand and beautiful in its seniority.

Caroline led Michael around to see where he might want to sit. He found a chinked cement bench resting under a pecan tree, which climbed over the fence from the other side. He sat and looked out at the gray sky. Caroline did not sit next to him. She stood and looked about the grounds, and then at him to see how much pleasure he derived from being outside. She noticed little. The young man squinted, as if to be the first view he had of the world, and it seemed a very bleak one.

"What made you decide to finally come outside?"

"You took me out here."

"I am talking about last night. I assume you got up on your own and came down. We left the door unlocked because you hadn't come out to use the restroom all day. I figured no one came and got you, as nothing of a break in could suggest otherwise, and I do not remember you ever having any problems with sleepwalking."

"I felt open, Caroline, like a book."

"I don't follow."

"Forget it."

"I am trying to understand, but I cannot rightly say I follow."

"Then you don't get it at all."

"I think that I do."

"You have no brain."

Michael continued to survey the sky without bothering to notice the immense hurt developing in the woman's eyes. She straightened up once she saw how shaky the young man's entire body became. He looked so pitiful, so harmless. His biting words unable to inflict irreversible pain. It was too easy to feel sorry for him.

"Then what do you mean? And I do not intend to continue caring for you if you cannot control your demeaning outbursts. This is not how we operate here at Stonebrook."

He turned and looked at her coldly. His eyes then softened, as if measured by the impact of his words on her face. The attachment to everything started to return. He had forgotten how to act. The world had owed him for the death of his father. Everyone owed him.

"I apologize. What I was trying to say is that I felt like an open book, or more so, the pages of a book when they sit inside. This is better than being the pages in a book when closed, of course, but when a page in an open book sits inside, with no circulation, it does not turn on its own. It could be the only page visible for centuries. But, when you take a book outside, it could sit for an hour on one page, or it could sit for a minute. Deciding on the weather, the pages can flip back and forth and never completely settle in the same place for the same amount of time. I finally felt like I woke up. Like I finally came to the sense that I am not the only one page in my family's book, and that there is not only one other page that will never move."

"Your father?"

Michael straightened up. The clouds started to move rapidly and neared the edge of the tree line. A hawk sailed overhead. He looked up at Caroline, whose face had softened. She came to sit by him. He waved her off.

"Never mind that. Caroline, could you please do something for me?"

"Sure."

"Before I lose my ability to think with relative serenity, will you go to my room and look for the next letter I have to read? I have to read it."

"A letter? I am not sure what letter you mean. Where do you keep them? How will I know which one is next?"

"Just do it! I must have one now if I am going to be able to stand reading it. It must be now!"

"I can't get what you want if you do not answer my questions."

Michael closed his eyes and started to shake uncontrollably. His anxiety had crept back in and it became torturous to watch as the severity of it grew. She had witnessed the extent of his tantrums and they could be quite awful at times.

"Okay, Michael. I am going right now. As I go, shout all you have to shout, but make sure that you shout to me where the letters are, and which one it is that you want."

She backed away from him slowly, like one would back away from a frothing dog, his face turning vermillion in tint. He grasped the cement bench as tight as his hands would allow, and without thinking, he yelled at the top of his voice.

"Typing table, bottom of stack! They are in order by date. Oldest date! Old oldest date! Unopened! Yes! Oldest date!"

She backed away from him. His voice started to calm and he began to mutter that same phrase underneath his breath. She knew that when his anxiety peaked he had to shout out some of his apprehension.

He heard his shouts from some place outside of his physical body and did not know why this happened so often. A very eventful night and day had ensued. New feelings rushed through him. Old feelings transduced from one period of his life to this very one. It was tedious to handle. He hoped that Caroline had not thought less of him. When he calmed, and his mind stopped its oral repetition, he opened his eyes and saw that the grass at his feet was of such a length that the wind had a great hold of it and it became an extraordinary sight to see. The life of the combined blades of grass jittered simultaneously and he could see the physical body of the wind through the grass, and to him, that was incredible. He then looked up toward the manor, the gables ebbing out from white to gray, the chipped brick laddering down and offset, the

mirroring of the seabird sky off of the crystalline windows. Through
the hedge of trees he could see a long black vehicle crawling through
the gravel in the direction of the gates. He followed the sound of it
until it rounded out of the ward and made its way off into the forested
land that surrounded the institute. He could not remember how far out
of civilization he had traveled when coming here. It did not matter. He
would always feel outside of civilization. There was no humanity that
he saw proper. He took his view back to the entrance of the West
Ward and saw Caroline coming from the pavilion. She looked so very
young and beautiful. He found himself looking more at the slit running
up her white skirt than the letter in her hand. He felt something
building inside of him. He thought of what his brother had said in his
letter, something about a lay. She came upon him and he straightened
up and once again became perched, timid and ungainly. Things were
always more pleasant when confronted internally. She handed him the
letter, which he took from her slowly, looking up into her marbled
green eyes.

"I am going to leave this to you. I have something to attend to, but
I will make sure to come get you before too long. That is, if you do not
feel you will have the strength to go back yourself."

"I will be fine. You tend to what you need to. This is just a job for
you. A solid paycheck." He heard himself talking, but did not know
why he said the things that he did. Caroline just looked at him blankly
and then smiled a fake, patronizing smile.

"Not much of one. My real pay is dealing with the patients that
treat me with respect."

Her smile faded and she looked up to the sky. A plane jetted
overhead. She covered her eyes with a broad salute over her forehead,
though there was no sun to visually impair. She looked back at Michael
again and then turned back to the ward. He followed the round bounce
of her backside as she walked, wishing that nothing covered what
swayed back and forth in front of him. He then turned his attention to
the letter he held in his shaky hands. It was on the sealed side, so he
could not see the addressor. When he turned it over he saw that it was
from his mother, Loretta. He immediately regretted ogling Caroline as

she walked away. He thought.

Jumping jacks and ticker tacks jittering vehemently past long-winding sidewalks where the laughter comes softly. On the backs of these small mutants the sweat pools and thins their cotton t-shirts. Dirt-filled fingernails snatching at the rubber balls and fumblingly dropping them over the star shaped plastic pieces, and the pigeons strut and cock looking for seedlings. The steam dripping free of gravity from the tar, and the children linger on the shadows of the buildings to save their bare feet from the pain of the asphalt. The loud cracking of the sky above following a jet stream resonation, the children look not up to the sky. Towering rows of brick heave forlorn into the gray sky, row toppling row, and cast down an eerie omnipotence on those infinitesimal creatures roving below.

Christopher

Christopher Corbin looked back at the fading city in his rearview mirror and could see the tops of the buildings and the gargoyles eyeing wildly with their mouths wide open as they lurched from their edificial entrapments. His pickup stalled down the open freeway, away from where human nature dug in its thick roots, and the trees grew tall and burst open with great foliage and all green save for the spindles burnt by the sun and hanging on tightly to the ends of their branches. On the side of the road walked a bag-strapped wonderer with wild beard and outstretched thumb. The old man wore high army boots, the laces of which danced about the freshly tarred asphalt. His denim jacket, worn unbuttoned and spread open, looked like transient wings flapping from behind. Christopher pulled over ahead and waited for the man to catch up to the truck. He could feel the weight of the pack push down on the bed and the man came around and yanked at the door. It would not budge. Christopher leaned over the shifter and the truck jeered, slipping out of neutral. He hit the clutch and brake and managed to get the machine settled before opening the door. The traveler hopped in, said thank you, and Christopher pulled back on to the highway and drove a great distance, fleeing the city without a word to the man.

They continued south past willows hunched over and furling with blue-gray moss and there stretched abandoned farmhouses where roamed paint horses with bellies bloated from rich alfalfa. The grumble of the six-cylinder knocked violently when he shifted and the gears cringed metallically from the stress of the pull.

"How many miles you got on'er?" said the man in the passenger seat.

Christopher could smell the seep of urine coming from the old man's booze filled pores. The haggardness of his appearance and apparel seemed not abnormal to any one drifter making their way across the country. The mottled red spots on his face, amidst the wrinkles, alluded to the life of drink he had been so prone to and his jaundicing skin and yellow teeth pardoned no assets to his appearance either. Christopher looked upon him with hidden malice. His stench, alone, was enough to inspire hate.

"One hundred and seventy thousand, give or take a few," answered Christopher.

"Surprising she gears like yat. Trannys usually don't go out that quick on shifters. Usually the bearings go out on them automatics before they do manuals."

"I guess you're right. She has been good to me though."

Christopher looked back over the road again and shifted, the metallic grind still present and something that would beleaguer him for a time to come. He could feel the old traveler's gaze upon him as he drove. When he turned to look over at the traveler, the man instantly looked away. The road stretched by with the yellow lines jetting quickly beneath them on the hot tar like spurts of electronic light. They were outside of the city now, past the presence of civilization, and the hills were always rolling and the sky was very clear.

"Where do you want to be let off?" said Christopher. "We've gone plenty south, and you haven't said anything about the direction."

"South is fine."

"I'll be headed west before too long."

Christopher turned over to see the man's face turn from a pleasant unawareness to a look of strange consternation. The hawk-slanted palate of his mouth, wide open with stalagmite teeth, started to column and then the mouth closed and his old cheeks puffed out.

"West is fine," he said.

"You have any idea of where you want me to take you? I can't rightly just keep you on with me the whole ride."

"This aint the kind of country you want to be alone in, boy."

"That so?" replied Christopher.

"Yap, I been all thew out here and I've heard some strange things going on. Real creep type stuff."

Before them, the trees climbed with high branches arching over the road. A shadowy tunnel of sunlight punched through the thickets of cedar and fell to the ground. The roadside houses quaintly stood, made of fine brick and birch, and there ran well-kept jack fences contorted in wooden rows along the road. Some women stood outside of their homes hanging clothes on wire-lines to dry in the sun and a group of dogs ran freely along the fence sides following small boys with Daisy guns. Picket fences stretched the perimeter of several Victorian style houses. The only thing that looked suspect was the presence of a few junked cars that could be seen at a distance from the road, but the grass had been mowed completely around them, leaving no weeds save for the occasional daisy that popped up triumphantly through the cut grass.

"I imagine that I will be able to keep myself in line," said Christopher.

"Yea, a well-off boy such as yehself will always do just fine in this world," said the hiker.

Christopher could see that the man eyed his small wad of cash in the cup holder. It was not much money, but the man seemed quite interested in it. Once the old man became aware that Christopher noticed his interest, he straightened up in his seat and stared down the road. The hiker then pulled the visor down and squinted innocently and yawned. Christopher could see the light where it hit the man in one of his filmy eyes. He proceeded to pull the visor out from its latch and tilted it down so that it completely shadowed the man's face.

"Thank yeh," said the hiker.

It was not until a few miles down the road that the traveler leaned up in his seat and looked for an opening in the willows. Once he found one he liked, he turned around to release the latch in the sliding door at the back window. He opened the window and tried to pull his pack into the cab through the opening. Christopher noticed what he was doing and turned with one arm still on the steering wheel and used the other to help him lug in the pack. Once they got it through, Christopher set the pack in the middle of the seat between them.

"Here," said the old man. "This meadow will be fine."

Christopher looked ahead and saw the clearing. A creek ran through that he could see through some willow branching. Beyond that a trail ran through a thicket that connected to the highway just above the gravel road they were on. The young man could now see the cars passing to the west through the great trees flourishing alongside the creek bed.

"You see that?" said Christopher. He slowed the truck.

Before Christopher had come to a complete stop, the man quickly released the door handle and thrust himself and his pack out of the truck. He waved off the young man and started at a dull canter, lugging his bag laboriously behind, and picked up speed going in the direction of the highway. Christopher yelled to see him off, but the man did not turn back. Before he shifted the truck out of neutral, Christopher looked down to find that the cup holder was empty. With very little thought or debate he kept the truck in neutral, jerked back on the parking brake, and took off after the old man through the marsh now separating them by a good distance. The thief ran with one gimp leg throbbing and Christopher followed in full sprint behind. Once Christopher had caught up to him, the old man tried to pick up his pace, but was almost brought to the ground by the weight of his pack.

It felt like rolling cement and icicles stinging him once he hit the creek bed with the old man's pack completely in his embrace and the entire weight of the old traveler helplessly on top of him. The old man squirmed like a toppled roach above Christopher, who could now feel the water start to rush over his head. Christopher could not breathe, sucking in water, the unnatural flow of the creek, the struggle that had ensued, the tiny waterfall pooling where Christopher tried to gather breath. After he could take no more drowning he let go of the pack. The old man rolled off of him and made it to his knees trying to flee up the small embankment and onto the highway. Semi-trucks and cars zipped by like locomotive guillotines built to sever any life that came upon them. Christopher came from the water coughing and choking on the phlegmatic bouts of fluid lurching inside of his chest. Again, he went after the old man, who now tried to scramble to the top of the embankment. His tiny arms and legs clawed at the hearth frantically as Christopher reeled him back down the bank and flipped him over on his pack. No struggle came from the man. The life had gone from him and he lie there with his wild blue eyes wide open and frightened. He curled up his old hands, clutching the money, and his legs followed upward to the middle of his stomach. He shook his head and whimpered. Christopher knew then that the length of the old man's crimes would not stretch beyond petty thievery. His eyes showed his desperation. They showed his grossly dissolved state of livelihood.

Christopher left from him and went back to his truck. His boots sloshed as he made his way around to the driver's side door and he took them off and wrung out his socks and set both his boots and socks in the back of the pickup to let them dry. He noticed in the back corner of the bed that there was something foreign, something that had not been there before. A tarpaulin with a slip cord sat rigidly on the hard bottom of the truck liner. He walked with bare feet over the sharp gravel, trying not to tread too heavily, and around to the back of the truck on the other side. He pulled up the object and felt the sides of the tarpaulin and felt the plastic poles on the inside and could feel the sharp stakes. He opened it and could see the worn tent frame on the inside with wrapped twine and tape around every inch of pole. It looked as though the tent had been used for centuries and, with enough repairs, would last a century more.

When he came upon the clearing and up the embankment to the highway with the tarpaulin in his hand, he could see no one walking the road for miles in either direction. The old man would have to go on without shelter now. Christopher went back to his truck. He sat in the driver's seat for a while, letting the truck idle, and listened to the clicking sound of his engine from under the clutches of its shuttering hood. What had he done, he thought. Did money have this effect on him?

Christopher continued south past the bayous and swamps and marshes until the roadsides became dense and sprawling with timber, far enough away from the ocean that he could no longer feel the salt on his skin, nor feel the sweat fall from his forehead and into his eyes.

Just before the lightning struck, the large oak lurched back and forth as the wind penetrated it violently. A large crack bottled in the sky and the darkness radiated with a silvery hue and the oak split completely in half. Christopher felt the rumble of the ground where he slept and the tree came down with such force that it jeered his sleeping body up like a solid thump from the sling of a ball bat. He settled back down inside of his sleeping bag and could hear the drops of rain linger slowly on the tent. Later, he awoke in his sleeping bag dripping sweat and thumbed down the zipper and reached with one estranged and blind hand for his headlamp. He pulled the headlamp down over his curling hair and clicked it on and scanned the outside of the tent to see the reflection from his car lights, the flashes of light scraping across the skyline. The rain was slowing to a drizzle now, but the rumbling in the sky did not desist by the time he came back to his sleeping bag. From his pack he retrieved a notepad and a pen and he began to scribble a letter into the notepad before falling back to sleep. The young man, forever calmed by the action of the storm, slept completely through the night.

On the road in the morning he could see the destruction left behind by the storm. Several deracinated trees had fallen across the road. Remnants of an old barn lay scattered along a hillside, completely demolished. County crews toiled about with flashing lights and chainsaws, cutting heavy branches into manageable pieces and dragging them off of the roads. Highway 20 stretched wide open now. He drove past the staggered trees through the Bienville and some trees had fallen into the arms of others and would remain there for years to come until they could no longer bear the dead weight. He watched the tarpaulin flap in the back of his pickup. Rivulets of greenish muck pooled near the man's pack as he moved slowly down the highway, arriving in Louisiana mid-day. He could smell the traces of sulphur in the air and the thick humidity that reveled in the moisture from the gulf. He pulled wayside some distance from the highway and undid the straps from the tarpaulin and gathered his camping gear and set up camp. The rain still fell. The tarpaulin, he used to cover his camp by attaching it to a worsted strap coiled around a large mesquite. He then spread out the cover at both ends and dug two tall walking rods directly into the ground. On those, he placed the copper holed openings over the pikes at the ends of the rods. The tarpaulin was of such a length that it gave him enough room to set out his tent, have a campfire, and make an adequate kitchen area where he could assemble his tote-around propane stove. He set the stakes at the corners of the tent sheet, outstretched underneath the tarpaulin, where rain could not enter. He assembled the tent rods and placed them upright and sheathed the slips of the tent over the rods and the tent came right to the top of where the tarpaulin stretched across. He made a small fire from dry mesquite. It would be enough to make coffee and cook some of the beans and maybe some of the bacon he had packed. It felt warm in the shelter and he watched all of the rain come down so pleasantly. The sound of crackling twigs from rain pattering on canvas. He unpacked the fly rod Carson had given him and pieced it together and let the line out and sharply flipped it, releasing slack, like some maestro directing an invisible orchestra. There was a box of imitation flies with his tackle that he put in his pocket and waited, coffee in hand, under the tarpaulin until the rain stopped. When the rain had gone the sun came resplendent between the retreating clouds. The man let the fire die down, finished his coffee, and assembled all of his fishing gear. Christopher made for the creek bank adjacent his campground and waded in the stream just off of the bank and the water was warm and moiling and he could see the froth of the creek shift like the edges of a recessed sea. After the rain, the trout and redfish flickered nicely in the stream's flow and deep pools sucked underneath the willows, and the fronds of waterweeds bent over fondling the line of stream along the banks. He threw out his line near the shadow of a deep pool and saw the silver flicker of a trout make an attempt. The trout zipped away from it last minute, as if it had seen the string flicker more than the fly, and Christopher pulled his line back and waded nearer the shadow of the trees and whipped the line across the upper run of the stream to hide the line in the shadows. His methodical swagger made him look like a water-bound cowboy lassoing boundless bovine in the sky. The redback came back, twisted, and then lunged out of the water at the fly. It was not long before he felt the satisfying hook of the fish pull down on the reel that the fish started downstream with Christopher in front. He reeled as the fish came at him. Barely able to pull it out of the stream. The line swung past the man and then struck out and straightened. He could now feel the full weight of the fish and reeled it in with all of his strength and the water speckled and jetted to the sides of the line and the fish was always jumping and fighting, struggling to survive, never getting the hook out of its mouth. When Christopher finally conquered the fish he netted it and secured the line around his waist.

Furrowing long and prominent with each movement, the water fanned out at the man's sides as he pulled himself through the stream with his catch fighting the net. Murky debris crept long past the two, the man and the struggling fish. Overhead, there hovered buzzards in their blackened suits with red throats gawking and waiting for death, their trajectory painting black coronets in the cloudless sky. He made his way back up the bank with rod in hand and the net tied around his waist. He could see the smoke coming out from under the tarpaulin where ashes still seethed in the fire pit. He took the cord wrapped around his waist and untied it and took it from the net and coiled it around his hand to keep it from tangling. The fish flopped inside of the net as Christopher picked it up, the mesh still wrapped around its silver belly, and wished it peace. He then dropped the fish back to the ground and took the opening of the net in his hands and closed it. He brought the entire net upward from the ground and swung it at a pine tree near the entrance of his camp. With the force from one swing he broke the fish's back, paralyzing it and allowing for death to come quickly and painlessly. His own assumption.

He had the fish opened wide over the grill by the time the sun had gone down and he stoked the fire with a peaceful admission of the events beforehand and the events that would follow. His pants, he hung from a rotisserie atop the small fire so they would be dry by morning and put his filthy socks atop the pants and he sat naked by the fire and ate the redback. It did not taste very good, but it would keep the pain from his stomach as he slept. He felt very happy, as he knew he'd be back on the road again tomorrow on his way to meet up with his brother, and they would have many things to talk about, and he would feel that wholesomeness that one strives for so very often when things go rogue and foreign, as they can so often do. The rain started over top of him again.

He crawled into his sleeping bag around midnight with the sky still bleak overhead, no moon showing, and embraced the feeling of warmth provided by the silk liner. All of the calm he had sequestered from the loll of the stream escaped him as the water kept coming, always tapping on the tarpaulin overhead. It was not until the rain stopped that he fell asleep and the sleep came on heavily and complete and the dreams came and never stopped. His dreams mirrored a vision of his future in which he waded through strange waters alongside strong men that marched through the forests of a foreign world with huge leaves for hats, gathering water to quench their thirst in the heat of the day.

Way out in that foreign wilderness, an eerie proclamation oncoming for all to exonerate. The ways of all collectively shameful. He seeks that one thought that men originated and evolved over time. The holistic truth that came from its original creation, alone, singular. Away from all others he sits and contemplates himself and no one else, for everything else is without his control. He thinks not of the things he cannot control. There would come the time of that great revelation and he would see what he so determinedly searched for. Through all of the death and the lives he had seen so mislead, he would find the truth.

Outside, the animals lurked in the new moon and all was lively and roaming in that great wilderness. Amidst Christopher's dreams the marching men walked with stiff legs and sharp machetes, cutting their way through the forest, always walking and cutting their way through to the end of the world where waterfalls keep their ends so very violent for those who dare them. And those wandering river dwellers meet their almighty, the only Gods on earth, stretching higher than manmade buildings and gaping down with great fury, the white rapids so very powerful and lingering so very slow right before they drop. Christopher Corbin slept comfortably in a wilderness so tame that he knew not of the wild that did lurk out there. He would come to know of it, and it would be much different than this.

Carson

Valencia Marie Mott lived alone in a small apartment in upstate New York. Nothing about her seemed very exciting to anyone she met, but her life was like a bubbling surge underneath a sea of calm. Her occupation as the sole writer of the local town paper afforded her no great opportunity, and in a town of fifteen hundred people, very little growth came from this position.

He would come and take her out of this world for what seemed like an eternity, and then she would have to return. Sickening it felt for her to have to live this subtle life without adventure. Sickening it felt to fall asleep to the sound of her own breath every night in his absence. His letters belonged among the short list of things that consoled her.

Valencia currently sat, staring out of the window at Morten's café, with a cup of coffee spiked with bourbon. The bourbon, a regular item in her purse, helped her writing. Her latest story focused on the building of a local canal. The city's response to high well costs. The problem with local irrigation had been that the pumps always went out during windstorms, and according to some of her research, powering back up cost a quarter of the year's fiscal budget for electricity. And that was the most important aspect of her story, nothing more, nothing less. She cared not for farming, nor dairy cattle. She was lactose intolerant.

Outside of the café the town square peaked in desolation. The only salient movement, the leaves on the maples. Not a soul to be seen. The young woman could see her reflection in the window, a bland and aging face she witnessed. It was not a face that she enjoyed looking at. Valencia turned to watch the counter boy pour coffee for two idle patrons, and expected him to notice her. The boy turned and nodded at her and it made her feel once more restored, for her life was of such a nature that she needed acknowledgement to survive. Before the burning sensation in her face subsided she heard the screech of tires and the sucking whir of gravel skitter across the pavement outside. She turned to see the old cruiser pull into a parking space across the street. A thick-bearded man crawled from the driver's seat and slammed the door. He took a sharp look around the town and then turned to adjust the straps of the canoe strapped to the roof of the vehicle. Once he secured the craft he proceeded to walk away from the car toward the city park on the purlieus of town. She watched him take his shoes off and shove them in his back pocket. As he walked, he plucked at some of the tree leaves that stretched over the pathway running through the park. He then pulled a book from his other pocket and took a seat on the grass and folded his legs. The sun punched through the maple leaves and speckled his face. Valencia paid the counter boy five dollars and left the café with noticeable haste.

She crossed the street and walked toward him with a half-drunken gait, knowing for certain that it was Carson. When she came upon him he looked up at her with blue eyes unblinking. His furrowed face and strained retinas made him look both stern and sincere at the same time. He smiled at her with pearling white teeth and came from his position directly off of his shins without using his arms to stand.

"Carson!"

"Val, girl. I have been away from you for too long."

He held her close to his chest. She could smell the musky stench of his body. Carson had not bathed in weeks. She was all too used to the smell. It hardly bothered her anymore. She even had begun to like it.

"How are you making it? I heard about Loretta."

"Much better than after father. You know how my relationship with Loretta was."

The two of them stood there in the finely cut grass, the cool blades of wild earth softly padding the man's bare feet. She took his book from him, looked over the cover, shook her head, and gave it back.

"You have to stop reading westerns. It is a lot of junk. You used to love the greats," she said. "I remember in school when you would always be reading something thick and Russian. Always an un-borrowable book that no one else would want to tackle."

"Come off it. I now have new greats. Greats you would know nothing about."

"However you see it. Come, let's get you showered."

She lifted the man's arm and wafted the invisible plume of stench that radiated from underneath that cavernous lot of armpit so foully lingering there. She plugged her nose in a cartoonish fashion and took him by the hand and they walked through the park past the marigolds and all of the sweet smelling flora.

"You have to get used to this smell, honey. It is one of the only kinds that I can make."

"You disgust me sometimes."

"It is true."

She gave him a shove as they continued to walk to her apartment. The place was only a few blocks from downtown and they arrived at the building within a matter of minutes. The ground was forever getting harsh on the man's feet, but he kept his shoes off, fighting through it with a strange determination. She could see the struggle in his eyes when he transitioned from grass to pavement, and then to loose gravel. He squeezed her hand tightly, as if to relive a lost moment, but she knew it was just his way of fighting the pain he felt in his feet.

"Why don't you just put your damn shoes back on?"

"We are almost there. It isn't so bad. I just miss holding you."

"Coward," she said playfully.

"Come on now. You know what they say about river folk and the need for hoofed feet. Good river feet take years to cultivate."

Valencia laughed and let Carson lead the way onto the sidewalk and up to the door to her apartment. She wrestled with her keys and then the door until she finally separated the door from its jamb. At the top of some carpeted stairs lingered a sole door, half painted and bloated, the numerical imprints no longer legible. They went up and entered the room. Inside sat dozens of stacks of papers, none of which seemed in any tangible order, and they were filed in equidistant lines from one to the next. Carson took to skimming the headlines that appeared on the faces of the mounds.

"How many issues have you put out here?"

"More than I care to keep track of."

"It seems like you are doing a fairly good job at it. You know, if your place ever catches fire, then all of this junk will do nothing but help the fire spread, spread faster than you can react to, and trap you inside here with all of these useless articles."

"That is a refreshing insight. I never thought of that." She threw her purse down on one of the stacks and ambled with tight knees over to the kitchen.

The kitchen itself looked like a remnant of some campy disaster. Traces of yeast clutched to the refrigerator door and morsels of indistinguishable meats and other detritus had piled up under the stove burner. Carson inspected the stovetop with disgust. He pulled the iron grid from the stovetop and tried with his knife to scrape some of the gruel from the open orifice of the gas burner, but could barely remove a gram of charred particle pasted to it.

"I am actually concerned now, after looking at the condition of this stove. You're bound to run into some incendiary dilemma before too long with all of this shit caked on here."

He continued to try and scratch away at the stove as she riffled through the refrigerator. She offered Carson something to eat, but he declined and shook his knife at her to indicate that he was busy. She bobbed, dancing with a carrot in her hand, over to her purse and removed the flask still decanting there. She took a long pull from it and then offered it to Carson. He declined that as well, giving her a foul look.

"Beer?"

"Check the fridge. I don't drink it much, but I'm sure some has been left in there," she replied.

He wrapped his hand around the refrigerator handle and some dough cracked off and fell to the floor. There would be some small rodent to come and abscond with it at a later time, he was certain of that. Inside he found a bottle wedged in between some leftover dishes wrapped in wax paper. He wiggled it out and cracked it open on the counter top. It was pleasant going down, gulp for gulp, and he found himself wanting another beer before it was even finished, but there were no more to be had. Valencia capped her flask and came upon him directly after he set down his bottle. It was not long before they both toppled over one of the stacks of papers and everything went wild and scattered and the commotion that could be heard from below sounded like the rustling of varmints in the walls. There was little to be said during such a state of ravenous flesh binding. When they had finished she handed him a fresh towel and sent him to the bathroom for a shower.

The sun had gone when she came to him at the window. He stood with his hands sucked into his pant pockets and looked upon the small city. The town's lights flickered in their waning shutters and it was hard to make out any solid figures, excepting a man sitting under a lamppost at the foot of a gazebo in the center of the park.

"What do you suppose he is doing?" Carson pointed out the diminutive figure perched upon his vagrant haunches.

Valencia pressed her crimpled nose to the glass and then turned back and took a hold of Carson's arm. "That's Marty. Only homeless man we have ever had here."

"That so?"

"Yes."

"If he is the only one in the entire town, then why can't enough people come together and help him? Or at least let him crash on a couch, here and there, and get him a warm meal?" he said with his eyes fixed on the figure in the dark.

"We have tried. He will steal anything he gets around, if you don't keep an eye on him. He doesn't try anymore from the stores, but he's tried to take from almost everybody here."

"And you all haven't run him out of town?"

"He won't go. He acts like he has never done a bad thing to anybody. Like he is the victim of some great tragedy. It is damn sad if you let it get to you. I wrote an article about him one time. Don't suppose he ever read it, but he got a fair amount of sympathy for a few weeks after it came out."

"I guess you did your part, then. He was probably able to wipe his ass with it." Carson laughed. He turned from the window and took her thin wrists in his hands and put her palms against his chest. She felt the broadness of him and came to a seat on one of the stacks. He came and sat next to her.

"Are you leaving tonight?" she asked.

"Yes."

"When are you coming back?"

"You need to leave here. This place is a wreck. You can't be thriving here."

"I make a living here."

"Come with me. Write on the road. Journal your travels," he said as though he ultimately knew what was best for her. Carson got up from his seat and knelt down in front of her and snatched up some of the articles in one balled fist. She looked at them, and then at the rest of her apartment, and noticed that her stacks had never been so out of place. It made her feel uneasy, as if the entire equipoise of her sanity had been shifted.

"You can't relish in these materials. They are not real. They are not visceral. I am proud of you for your writing accomplishments, but there is only so much you can do here. I bet you, even Marty would tell you that."

The sadness in her eyes softened. She laughed and then the sadness returned once more. Carson set the papers on the ground and made it from his knees and took her hand and placed it to his right knee. She could feel the break in the denim of his jeans and could feel the softness of the cloth sewn there. He ran her fingers across the initials and she knew they were hers.

"You know I keep you with me."

"And I bet you don't change your jeans often."

"That is so."

She smiled and came to him in the darkness of her apartment. He held her there for a time until he had to leave. As he went for the door she followed him. When he pulled the door from its jamb it almost fell off of its hinges.

"Make a living ... hardly."

"It is all that I can do."

"Well, you ask your editor if you can take some time to road journal. See if they can send you material to work on from the road."

"Where will I receive it?"

"The pony express always finds a way."

He rubbed the side of her cheek with the back of his hand once more before heading down the stairs. She followed him and watched as he walked under the post lights stretching down Park Street. He turned to look back up at her.

"Gather your things, and fireproof your apartment. I will be back when I am done."

"Where are you going?"

"South. I am meeting up with Chris. He's got a journey of his own and I want to send him off right."

"When will you be back this way?"

"Not long. I will send you word when I am heading back. Don't forget to prepare."

"I will. Carson … "

She watched his silhouette fade into eminent darkness, and nothing else of him reappeared. Valencia Mott returned to her apartment and sat by the window. She waited there for a time until she saw the cutting red glow of the cruiser's tail flicker on and then float away into the lightless atmosphere of that inconceivable beyond he was so bound to.

He was no more gone from there than he was present in any direction that he traveled, but he had to meet his brother. That kept him moving—the road incarnate of some inconceivable journey set out before him. The fury of destiny quickly became apparent. All the time going, it felt as if his car wanted to let off of the ground and assume flight, far away from the rolling hills he climbed.

Carson Corbin arrived in Nashville mid-morning and spent a great deal of time standing riverside the Cumberland. Across the river he could see the great arches of the steel crossways in singular and triangular rows, the water foamy in the morning dew. A few boats puttered by. The time of the year had come when all of the trees were on fire and the crinkled brown bodies of leaves meandered lifelessly in the wake of boat streams. He lugged the canoe from the top of his cruiser and brought it into a small alcove and stood on a smooth rock barrier and eased the craft into the water, pulling at the sculls and slipping them carefully into the draw of the stream. He propelled effortlessly out into the heart of the river and rowed until his arms grew tired. The skyline slowly became a fading remnant of something manmade amidst the aura of everything existing naturally in this world.

A few young boys paddled by the begrimed dinghy some time in the afternoon and saw nothing but a pair of battered shoes propped up on the starboard side of the craft with nothing attached to them. They reeled back on their oars and swung their paddleboards around to inspect the lifeless craft bobbing independently in the stream. Once they came upon it they could see the grizzly-faced man cross-armed on his back atop a pile of clothing and filthy blankets. He looked to be a homeless vagrant coiled up in the transient abode of some floating bombshell. One of the boys took his oar and poked at the man's limp body. Before he could reel back in the oar, the boy felt the pull on his grasp. He instantly plunged into the cool water, his paddle following. The boy flopped wildly in that black darkness, barely able to swim, and resorted to such a state of panic that he could not think to float until he felt the pressure around his neck, where the collar of his shirt tightened on his Adam's apple, and was freed from the forever-leaguing murk below. Within moments, the boy went from drowning, to facing the burly captain of, what would later be known to the boys as, the Cumberland canoe. Carson looked upon the boy with wild eyes and outstretched hands.

"Damn, kid." said the man. "You need to get off the water if you can't swim any better than that. I didn't know I'd wake up to the churning poorness of something as inept in the water as you."

The kid tried to catch his breath, but still sputtered water from the back of his throat. Carson patted him on the back and tried to calm him. Carson leaned over the canoe and used the paddle to pull the paddleboard closer. The other boy floated near, half wary of the grizzly man handling the board.

"You know how to swim?"

The other boy nodded his head, "yes suh."

"You watch out for this one. That was about as pitiful of a swim as I have ever seen from a teenager. Hell, I've seen infants paddle better than that. You okay?"

He took the boy by the shoulders and gazed into his wide pupils. The boy said yes and came from his seat on the bow bar, nearly tipping the canoe over. Carson settled the craft and brought the paddleboard close to where the boy stood and guided him back onto it and handed him his paddle.

"What were you doing, sneaking up on me while I was sleeping like that?"

The boy could not gather enough breath to speak with coherency. He shrugged

"We thought you was dead, suh. We was just poking at you to make sure. You looked dead enough," said the friend.

"Well, I'm not," replied Carson. "Where did you boys take in?"

"Down thataway, suh," said the boy. He pointed at the small quay across the river which housed a few berths. "We should head back." The boy looked at his friend, who quickly agreed. The two boys turned their paddleboards and started across the river.

"Take care, then." Carson waved them off. He yelled back over at them from the craft. "Don't be sneaking up on anybody else sleeping, you hear?" He did not receive a response, only did he return back to his cot piled up in the gut of the canoe.

After he had rested, Carson Corbin drew up his paddles and made back for the Nashville skyline. By the time he had arrived back at his cruiser the lights of the city danced on the water aberrantly out of form. No structure to the reflections now. Just glistening draws of ambulant dusk playing on the water. He strapped the craft to the iron guides and drove on toward the lights of the city like a moth dedicated to a flame. Before he would continue on for the latter half of his drive he would need alcohol in his system, enough to continue on at ease, succulent minded, open.

He found a dark lit pub once lined into the brick of a corner store. On a few bar stools sat some louse men and whorish looking women that he eyed not. He grabbed a schooner, paid the few bucks, and went to sit at the back of the pub. He drew a book from his pocket and read over the back and introduction, never quite continuing on where he had left off. It was not the place to get into it. He mainly used the book as a way to keep from meeting eyes with these hillbilly dragoons drooling over their pint-filled lives now sweating in glasses before them. After his first twenty ounces of hoppy beer he felt warm in the face and soft in the body. He almost felt like talking to those staring him over from the bar, but kept his equilibrium and left the pub without saying a word. When he got to his car he felt good about ignoring them. They would have kept him there later than he had wanted. Carson knew that they would have kept him drinking. And he would have continued to drink so that he could stand conversing with them.

He had traveled far from the city by the time the alcohol started to wear down on him, but he drove on through the night. The territorial embrace of the great American south turned to clay and the rock crags arched so ferociously out of the ground that one might think that the sky had opened up and shat directly on the earth, leaving strange mounds for all to ponder—celestial detritus attracted to the very spot in which he drove. The sun hovered over the straight plains of Oklahoma. The sprite awakening of a newborn day. Dust littered his windshield and all but eased his eyes on those long highway roads stretching forever into a familiar existence. It was quite a struggle to make the last push through the greener parts of Oklahoma and on into Texas by early morning.

The wings outstretched and translucent, they went softly and free from peril. The old maid, now gliding in the sky, looked glorious over all that lurked throughout her aerial kingdom. He could see, through the glades in her silver wings, the glow of the waking sun. The rest of the sun's light glistened, transparent on the back of her broad shoulders and wingspan, and all of the fish below in the cool water dipped wildly down to great depths to stray from her infallible claws. He could see her sailing there, mid-atmosphere, and saw her for her greatness and she eyed not those mechanical locomotives below, for they were not beneficial to the nourishment of her family. Those accipitrine eyes ticking wildly, searching out all potential kills.

Christopher

The houses running down the side of the hill, and connected at their balustrades, were all a decrepit cedar and greening from their bark facades—the same material used to erect crosses in some nearby cemetery. In the valley the sun came shooting off of the lake and the surrounding clouds bubbled with a dark velvet tinge in the dawn's horizon, smoothing the water like glass against the faceless sky. When he turned down Mabery Street and stretched the great hill below, a few fowl scattered from the road and some aquatic amphibians groped in the grass, gulping loudly and showing their bloated bellies in the newborn sunrise. The old cabin stood, connected to two other identical houses, and separated by lattice. Rogue vines grew along the archway of the cabin. A railroad tie buried in the ground at the front of the building. He could see that the house on the hill above had construction work done on the sewage lines and the ground snaked openly from the entrance of the house to the gravel driveway. A pipeline had been dug and filthy water sprang from the open orifice of the clay, protruding over into the yard of the cabin. The ground carried a dank fecundity when he came from his truck and retrieved his pack. Christopher traversed a stone path that lead from the drive to a great fleet of stairs descending down to the cabin's porch. On the porch sat two wooden rockers and a small end table with a flower vase atop it. He picked up the vase and a thick, white film of spider webbing came with it. Its elasticity kept it anchored to the table on the other end of the vase. There on the table sat a small golden key covered with plant soil and dead moths. A spider had established its dark abode underneath the vase over the years and its hoarding had become quite abundant. Christopher took the key and wiped off the dirt onto his pants and proceeded to unlock the door to the cabin.

Inside it was stale smelling and very hot. The dark corridor of the entry way ran past the bedroom where, in an empty room save for a queen bed with no covers, several pictures hung on the wall directly facing him. The pictures made for a haunting memorial there in the darkness of the room. The faces hard to make out. He could see his mother and his father—pictures of Christopher and his two brothers when they were young. All of which were in a linear procession of the family tree, forever trapped in this dank sarcophagus. He shut the door to the room and continued to walk down the corridor and into the large living room that let out to wide bay windows. From his view he could see the calm beauty of the lake directly. Sailboats puttered around on the glassy waterfront taking in the morning breeze. The cabin overlooked the valley from a grand escarpment that sloped straight down above the curl of a water-flooded alcove. He could see from his omnipotence the small boat docks bobbing softly in the water like horses on iron carousels and their steel purlins creaked and groaned in the flow of waves that kept coming in all of the time. A crane came from its throne atop a tin roof and swooped down across the plane of the water and swiftly snatched up a bass in its great gullet and took it to a dry bank and pecked at it as it squirmed and tried to flop back to the water. Christopher turned from the window and paced around the small living room, thumbing the dust from the table stands and checking to see if any electricity still ran to the place. The cabin no longer had juice. He came into the kitchen and opened the refrigerator door, but there was nothing inside save for a rancid stick of butter suffocating in the warm cooler in which it had been left. He took the door at the other end of the kitchen that led to a curved balcony, which wrapped around to the back of the house and out to a broad porch overlooking the lake. The table and chair set chained to the floorboards of the porch looked as though it had always been there and would continue to be there even when all of the humans on the planet died off—the furniture's existence being something integral to the stability of the cabin itself. He could see the barren porches of neighboring cabins now sheathed with leaves. Christopher sat down at the table and looked out over the rolling water and felt the fall's cool breeze. He watched as the leaves spiraled upward, dancing in the shimmering dawn of a newborn day.

Carson

Puttering down that familiar road, he came upon the dent-riddled pickup supported entirely by spare tires and parked dopily in the driveway. "Hell," he said to himself as the cruiser rolled in beside the pickup. The man got out and looked over the junk heap that his old pickup had become. Carson looked at all of the gear piled in the bed of the truck covered by the tarp; a few reels, a ripped seine, a camera bag, some walking poles and other loose refuse.

The front door of the cabin stood slightly ajar when he came upon it and some of the heat slowly leaked out. Flies and other insects followed him into the house as he entered. He opened the door to the old room with the gallery of pictures and then quickly closed it and went into the living room. Walking directly upon the window, Carson saw the man's limp body lying in one of the foldout chairs at the end of the balcony facing the water's edge. His feathery hair danced in the breeze and the sun groped the top of his head. Carson knocked at the window with his fist, but no response came from the man. He knocked louder and louder, but still no movement, not even a twitch of the head. When he came around behind the young man he noticed that his face and neck had filled out some, and lying there with eyes closed and body completely motionless, he resembled their father as he lay in his casket—the oak box reeling slowly down into the open abyss of his final beyond.

Carson shook him by the shoulders. The man quickly came-to, gasping, and then a fury developed in his eyes. Carson looked down at Christopher, who had come out of his sleep with such great abjuration, and watched his eyes soften and go completely serene, the calm he had always known in his brother. He smiled widely at him. They sat in silence and looked out as the water rolled in on the banks and the cranes were out and always hunting, swooping off of the wing and pulling out great fish, taking them to their nests to feed their young.

Eugene

In the brief eulogy that Jack Holt gave, it was said that Mr. Corbin, a man survived by his estranged wife and three boys, was a man of few words. That he was gentle and calm, reclusive but worldly. Stern, but affectionate. The boys saw the man in a different light, though, as children are insecure creatures with the weight of sensitivity always heavy on their shoulders. Their image of Eugene may have developed in response to his inability to appreciate their flaws—for fathers can be patient with their children, but rarely yield to the imperfections that offspring exhibit—the flaws not inherited directly from their loins. But his goodness and fairness did not go unnoticed and he did treat them with respect. Jack Holt, Eugene's best friend, had not strayed far from the truth in his posthumous praise of the man. Jack had the authority to give such words, as he often witnessed the struggles between man and woman, the love between father and sons. Yes, Eugene Corbin had been a fair man.

Eugene had a way of talking through his past by way of story or anecdote. Much of his deep-seated depression came from the women in his life. His wife or mother. Eugene talked of his mother often, and with great sadness. He had even recounted the time that he watched the doctors as they administered electro-shock therapy to her when he was a child. He hoped that he would not have to see any of his boys fall into a similar mental debilitation. He said the treatment had not changed her much. She had always been an unfit mother—how she would sit and stare out of the kitchen window for hours, unaware of any commotion in the house. He had matured at a young age because of this. Eugene related with the boys in this sense. The failures of a mother understood, as something to be accepted, not nurtured. Regardless, Eugene acted as a sentimental man would and was very much in love with Loretta. The boys loved him for his attempts at salvaging the marriage, though any attempt was proven unsuccessful.

They loved him for encouraging them to pursue an optimistic view of life. He used examples from his own childhood to illustrate this, and that made his stories much more cutting and worthy of consideration. He died on a Tuesday in the ninety-second year of his life.

Eugene Hank Corbin died in his living room, alone, while his youngest son was at the market. When Michael returned to the house and heard the television, he assumed his father to be asleep. The young man went into the living room and sat on the couch next to the man's recliner and watched the television for a time until he fell asleep. When he awoke late in the afternoon he went into the kitchen and made a pot of beans. The leftovers, he brought in to the living room and placed on the television stand next to the old man and then went back to sleep on the couch. He awoke past midnight, as he always did when the terrors of his sleep jarred him from his slumber, and went into the bathroom and vomited what was in his stomach and then came back to find the cup of beans stale and untouched. After taking the bowl back to the kitchen and rinsing it out in the sink, Michael came to his father's side and said goodnight and went to his bedroom to try and sleep. The window to his bedroom was open and he listened to the whistle of the wind come in; he felt like a child again on nights like those. He could not sleep, but he felt at peace. He felt uncorrupt. Early spring always gave him a break from his usual panicked state, though it would not last long. He knew that very well.

In the morning on Wednesday, Michael came from his room after little sleep and went to make breakfast for the both of them. A horrible smell came from the living room that made him redirect his track from the kitchen. He noticed that the old man's face had remained in the same position as the day before. The smell was intolerable and his first thought was that his father had lost control of his bowels while sleeping. He opened the door to the carport and went over to his father and tried to wake him. The man fell limp at his side and the lights were completely out of his eyes. The blood no longer traveled through his body and Michael could feel where it lingered there in his veins—lifeless, liquid weight. He noticed the blue lining under the man's eyelids. The eyelids now looked like whitening slugs desiccating upon the edge of a dry leaf.

He had Eugene completely undressed, holding him under the scalding water at the foot of the shower bed, by mid-afternoon. He scrubbed the old man from head to toe, using a wash pad that had been overused and that now peeled from its core like some spongy furuncle, and knelt with his clothes completely doused, the old man in his arms, and the water came down mixing with his tears and the waste from the old, dead man.

When the paramedics came they found the old man lying in his bed with his best suit on and his arms were crossed. They found Michael in his room with the lights off and his back was to the doorway. He was staring out of the window, rocking on his heels, and was unresponsive when they questioned him. They had to have the police take him in until the coroner's report came back to say that the man had died from natural causes. By that time, they had already mandated that Michael stay in a mental institute for a month-long evaluation. Michael Corbin rather liked his stay, as it had been an escape from the horrors of real life, and did not leave when his mandate was up. Eugene Corbin died alone, but not by himself in the end. It could have been worse for the old man. It could have been better. It is always this way in death. It is always this way in life.

Christopher

The rain drops had been sizeable that day, he remembered. Clear bodies of water like ice cubes melting on some hot and terrible afternoon. Gigi swaddled Michael with towels so he would not scratch at the fiery red dots all over his body. Carson peddled cards in a clean stack across from Christopher and slapped the face cards when they came and took the piles, starting anew. A near howl racked the china plates now shuttering from a crack in the sky. When Eugene came in he talked to Gigi. She handed the baby to the man —who almost did not accept him because he had not had the pox yet. Eugene rocked the little boy at his waist. The baby now bawled terminally in his father's arms. The two older boys waved to their father. He dripped black rain from his suit. The company had let him go for the day. Gigi gathered the boys from where they played in the corner of her apartment and asked them if they would like to stay, or go with their father to see the woman. Carson went with his father, holding his hand as they left the apartment in the rain. Christopher stayed with Gigi and baby Michael. He did not wish to see the woman. The thought of where she was scared him. He would have rather been near the fireplace at the back of the apartment, where the open window yawned, than where his father and Carson were going. He was quite positive of that, even at the age of seven.

They were a long time coming out of the stream when they got into the larger body of the river at Harrison's crossing. Carson straightened the craft at the stern and his brother netted the port side from the bow of the canoe. Water leapt from the sculls arching on either side of the boat.

"What's your return plan?" said Carson.

"I haven't thought too much of it."

"Better to start planning, if you aim on taking my canoe with you."

"You'll get it back."

"I have to hold you to that. I have no intention of going with you just to make sure she gets taken care of."

Carson pulled back on his portside oar and let the stream shudder past to the left. The water rolled and sliced in the sun's sharp gaze. A boulder reared its bald head on one side of the canoe and almost struck Christopher's dangling legs. "Pull those damn legs up or pay attention. One or the other," said Carson, skidding the canoe easily across the plane of the Brazos.

"You've got it. Someone's got to net, and someone's got to steer and let the netter carry on."

"And what if you break your legs when I can't see a rock?"

Christopher turned back to look at his brother paddling. He adjusted in his seat and pulled his legs up into the trap of the bow.

"I feel like I'm sitting in a damn kindergartener's desk, all squished up like this. I fear a loss of circulation to the legs."

"Don't listen to me, then." Carson pulled the skiff back around where the stream ran closer to the bank. Scraggly oaks stretched out past the riverbed and came down on them like coarse fingers dandling at the men's shirtless bodies. The air held humidity well, even in late fall, but the coolness of the shade disguised the heat still abundant in the open.

"What are you going to do? You can't go out and be river-bound without your canoe," said Christopher. "I know that you are likely to die without it."

"Go to Washington maybe. It will be cold enough by then, and all the water will be frozen anyhow. I know a guy who owns his own rental cabins. I could probably get a job splitting wood or slipping some articles out from the road."

"How are you going to do that? I've read your shit," he looked at his disapproving brother. "What?"

"Only to you. Just 'cause you hold yourself in such high esteem for what you consider as your ever-gracious contributions to writing."

"I have no contributions. Your letters just show nothing of you."

"At least they are written."

"That is so."

"Plus, I may take Val with me. She can earn us some scratch."

"Ol' Valencia? I'll be. You've got scratch, though. Why do you need to pimp yourself out to her? Just for her to make a few dimes with her small-town magazine jargon?"

"She is a good journalist, Chris."

Carson eyed down a translucent cobweb dangling from the oak scrub. A fat spider reveled in the spate of suffocated Lepidoptera. Christopher leaned back on his seat and slacked his net to attempt at the fish feeding in the deep alcoves where roots lie.

"Headline: The mayoral staff of the Chinook tribe is signing a petition against the bears for shitting on their welcome mats," said Christopher holding his digits up, as if mimicking a scrolling marquee. "They cannot, however, understand the English language well enough to know the difference between the word bear and human."

"You don't make any sense, brother," replied Carson.

"Only in my mind."

"Where it all resides, except for maturity."

Christopher leaned over the side of the boat, past the net, and flung up a spit of water into his brother's face. Carson clenched the oar in his left hand, put it up under his armpit, and reeled the other up and out of the water. Before he could bring the paddle round, and into his brother's chest, the wall of sand they struck jarred them both out of their seats. The river spanned no deeper than a few inches where they struck the archipelago strangely lingering there mid-river, and no vegetation came from the abrupt isthmus conjured from sand—a non-eroding delta encapsulated in the dark vastness of the Brazos, forever waiting. Christopher watched the net trying to escape in the water's low pull, the mesh still trolling as if autonomous from the fisherman's hands. "Shit fire," said the man. He looked like a helpless baby for a minute, wiggling and trying to roll his bare belly up from his seat in the boat. As soon as he got one foot out of the boat and onto the sandbank, an army of sediment mechanized and went directly into his shoe. His sock no longer held at his ankles, only did it linger in a wad at the front of his shoe. Christopher pulled the boat onto the small island. His brother sat and watched from the stern.

"Good enough of a place as any for lunch," said Carson. He waddled his way out of the boat with Christopher anchoring it with his one dry foot. "What did we bring? I haven't had any nutrition, other than what they put in beer."

"I believe that's alcohol."

"There's more to it than just that. There are hops and barley and some malt and what have you," replied Carson. He brought the canoe around to its side.

"Not with that Pabst. It is piss water and alceeehal," asserted Christopher. "I made us a couple of sandwiches. Had to put them in my fish cooler … figuring I wouldn't catch anything."

Carson pulled a beer from the cooler tied to the back of the canoe. "At least they won't taste like fish."

"They're tuna sandwiches."

"Different fish taste. It is in the nose anyhow." Carson plopped himself down on the sand and dug his bare feet in. He gulped the beer quickly, crushing the can before finishing, and the yellow liquid ran down his cheeks. "Hand me another of them will you, champ? Get yourself one, if you want."

"I'd rather have a beer that has some weight to it. I'm not like you or dad. Dad would just about drink anything, if you told him it would get him drunk." Christopher popped the lid to the floating chest, grabbed one, and chucked the white can at Carson. He missed the toss and the can rolled down the sand bank, almost making its way back to the water. "Really?" said Christopher. He went over and picked the can back up from the bank.

"Weak toss, give it here."

He caught it this time and popped it open and commenced to gulping it down. Christopher slugged his way through the sand to a rotten log overturned and hollowing out atop an escarpment on the edge of the small isthmus. It protruded just enough for him to straddle. The rock face holding it also held imprints of trilobites and shell markings from some ancient aquatic inhabitance. "You going to be alright to get us to the weir?"

Carson looked over at his brother, the can upturned in his hand, with a look of bemusement. "Well hell yes. I have been through a lot more of these," he shook the can, "and managed my way around class rapids without a scratch. I think I can handle the mighty Brazos." He laughed into the oval mouth of his aluminum appendage.

"Good enough. Do you want your sandwich?"

"Nah. Liquid lunch. I figure that this is a time for celebration."

"Why's that?" asked Christopher.

"Us getting to spend some time together … being in Texas … me taking you to Bourlan so you can head south … the final rest of our mother … you pick."

"These are things considered for celebration?"

"I couldn't see much else warranting a celebration."

"I suppose. Not really an uplifting celebration."

"It is how we allow ourselves to reveal our true emotions in a time of what most would assume disparaging. I am not exactly ecstatic about the situation we have been put in, but it is all the same for everyone in this world. It is just our time. You deal with things the way you do, and I will do the same." Carson rolled back on the bank and half buried the can in the sand. "Say you spend a large majority of your life striving to be more successful, or to have accomplished more…"

"Yea?" replied Christopher. He watched a blue jay jounce on a far bank, searching for water worms and pecking at a slug that inched along from under its aged carapace.

"And what do you appreciate? When do you celebrate? Are there only small victories, or do you wait for the time when you feel completely satisfied? I would hope it possible to see everything as a great celebration; one of life, death, warm pants drying in the sun," said Carson

"And you celebrate it all the more with those Pabsts?"

"Just a consolation prize, my boy."

"Carson?"

"Yea?"

"Do you think I will regret leaving Michael alone?"

"What do you mean? Neither of us has been able to even as much as visit him. Your presence anywhere is just about the same as nowhere to him. I would like to imagine he will be better by the time you get back, but my hopes for him, and his own convalescence, aren't exactly linear."

"Think he'll ever let us visit?"

"It is possible. He didn't take too well to dad. Wonder how he will take to mom. I can bet you he still doesn't even know."

"He has to. They wouldn't pass on giving personal information like that to him."

"They would if they thought it would stunt his rehabilitation."

"Damn, that is some kind of harsh karma that boy got. Watching over dad like that, and then smack! Stuck in a hospital, no opposition."

"I am sure he fought a little," replied Carson.

Christopher watched two dragonflies skim over the top of the river and then over his brother's head, locked in their aerial nuptials, and Carson batted at them with the free hand not clutching the beer can. The Brazos must have stretched thirty yards from bank to bank in width, one of the largest sections in the area. Verdant hills stretched beyond the river's curve like earthen breasts, hazy and grand. Anvil-shaped ridges of limestone peaked through the cottonwoods where cedars grew to the heights of small children. Loose vines dangled from the forested canopy overhead and cadged the water all along the banks where the river drafted and spooled bubbling. The fields on either side of the river sprawled, flat and unmanned. Some livestock roamed and birds followed and pecked through the patties they had shat. Barbed wire ran uniformly all along the field's edges and some of the lines had been battered so that the anchor poles lay flat on the ground, extirpated, and the rest of the wire languidly followed. The river divided the fields and kept livestock from crossing laterally. Cedar was most certainly abundant on the backside of these prairie lands, but some hardwoods managed to stand ground riverside. These provided the most shade because of their height. Christopher watched Carson get up from his sandy bed and chuck the empty can into the canoe. The cooler bobbed beside the canoe where the stream still pulled at it softly. He grabbed another Pabst and sat at his command in the back of the canoe looking over the paddles at the front. The craft sank an inch more into the embankment under the man's weight. "Come on," he shouted.

Christopher came from his perch on the log and shoved the sandwich bag in his pant pocket with the water still thick in his shoe. He watched his steps on the hard sand sink and then expand with water perforating underneath. The isthmus rested atop an impenetrable reservoir where ancient amphibians may have rested to wait out another million years. The man handed the oars back to Carson, who took them, resting one in the cabin of the craft, and stabbed the other into the dry bank to help push the canoe from the sand wall. Christopher took the craft by the bow, lending one dry foot to the inside, and used his other foot to stretch the boat back out into the stream. A buoyant momentum started to materialize. They slowly retreated from the bank. Animals groped and searched for anything left behind, hoping to find scraps of food, but there was nothing to be found.

"Hartsel's tonight?" said Carson as they crept through the dilatory body of the river. So much to be said for what happens underneath, where the murk clouds what is transpiring below, very much hidden from man's omnipotent eye. "Might as well get some culture while we are here. No telling when we will be back around these parts."

"The culture prominent in these parts is just about as prominent as the culture developing in a Petri dish," Christopher responded. "Is Hartsel's even still standing? I figured it would have fallen into the Brazo by now. Those damn stilts its on are just about as ridiculous as anything I have ever seen. The damn river doesn't even come but about twenty yards from the very base of those wooden legs. And that is at the river's highest."

"It does have quite a charm to it, don't it, Chris. I can see it now. Jay-Bug and Dubb sitting back in their rockers, feet up on the banister, drinking shine and pissing off of the porch."

Christopher listened to his brother's rant as it trailed from behind. "Dad never did like you tagging along with them. Said they were trash all along, and you hadn't the mind to listen."

"I knew damn well what they were, and what they still are. But being a boy in an area like this one, you don't rightly get to choose all your friends. And if you could, you still wouldn't be getting any scholars out here."

"I did fine," said Christopher.

"Because you tagged along behind me when those other boys weren't around to pick on you. And if I wasn't around, you'd be off in the river or craw-dadding, or whatever the hell you did without me."

"Yea, and I didn't need the Kuds boys to keep me company, wasting my life away night after night."

"Whether you like it or not, Chris, you and I turned out just about the same, regardless of what I did when I was younger. We both got educated and look at us now. Living off of what we were left from Eugene. How does that make you feel about how much better than me you think you are?"

"I'm not squandering it all away. There isn't enough there to make last, especially if you waste it. You will find that carrying on and celebrating every day will wear a little thin quicker than you think."

Carson pulled back on the paddle and sent the canoe into a lofty calm. The boat twirled lifelessly in the open halcyon of the river and Christopher turned to look at the man in the back seat of the boat. "I am not getting on you any, just don't compare us so closely," he said.

Carson let up on the paddle as they advanced. "Good," he said. "There's no reason to start some sort of morality contest here."

"Okay," Christopher replied.

"No reason to get high and mighty because you are avoiding the Pabst as of present. Once we hit 'ol Hartsel's, I'm sure you'll get on the juice, same as me."

It was nearing sundown by the time the two boys slowed their boat in the stillness of the river where the stream halted. A weir stretched from bank to bank holding half a dozen culverts that ran through the concrete to the other side and fed out below the acclivity of the dam. A walking path, lit heavily, lined one side of the river, and on the other, children climbed gigantic boulders resting in dry sand. It was evident that the boulders now stood as archaic monuments recalling the antediluvian success that the river had once enjoyed.

Beyond the boulders on a flattened plateau where gravel inundated the saddle of adjacent hills, the old cruiser sat amongst some other gray matter. The likes of automobiles static in industry. A path ran on the east side of the river and stretched past the weir to a dry bed, past the archaic rubble thwart the shore. Christopher was the first out of the canoe. Blackened tiers of water rippled against the weir and the canoe came round and clinked against the cement, bringing the craft flush up against its impenetrable façade. The cooler whipped round also, snapping like a bungee on its twine strap, and clanked against the cement wall. The two brothers made their way for the cruiser with water still slugging from the upturned canoe resting on their shoulders. They looked like a unified metallic unit now crafted by the gods of technology—like a newly formed minotaur.

Hartsel's was built in the year nineteen and fifty and had been named after Gerald Hartsel, a neighboring boy shot dead while on campaign in France. Some war relics plastered the walls. Shell casings. Clips of the Wehrmacht lines being bombarded. A picture of Heinz Gudarian with stenciled genitalia near mouth. Some other pro-American propaganda that could easily be bought today. Those frequenting the joint appeared to be of the lowest forms of life that could be found in any one place, and at any given time. This was not entirely of moral conviction, but of the fact that any such part of their brain, salvaged from what the fetal alcohol syndrome had not taken, had now turned to liquid from nothing but drink. These were the types living off of the epicurean drive that their minds encouraged, and by living, this meant letting their bills go directly to Hartsel's every hour their breaths did not hold that sleepy, alcoholic vomit. When the two men entered, stomping the gravel from their boots, they could see several vaguely familiar faces. The lecherous inhabitants of this dank sepulcher held onto their mugs as tight as one would hold a newborn infant. It had been more than two years since Carson had been in sight of anyone from these parts, and his brother, a year more. It became evident that those already drunk and soporific would not recognize them. That was a placation outright. Carson ordered a Pabst. "A pint for a dollar," he said to his brother.

Christopher asked if they had any reds, they did not. He asked about their ale selection. "Listen, buddy," the bar tender said, "all we got here's Pabstees fer a dollar, Bud a dollar more, Michelob fer the ladies, and Momma Kuds got the good stuff outside." The bar tender pulled a Bud from a pig trough filled with ice and gave it to Christopher.

"You buy that beer at Tommy's?" he asked the man.

"Nah, got er flown in from Milwaukee, sure as shit."

"How much a case cost there at Tommy's?"

The bartender started to anger with the young man and Carson could see it. "Come on now, bud, leave this fine gentleman alone. He is just doing his job. Leave it be."

Carson did not know the man, because Carson was ahead of Christopher in school, but the man now playing bartender had "gotten at" one of Christopher's high school girlfriends. It was no matter now. Christopher could see the metaphorical division provided by the bar island. He could not even remember which girl it had been.

The two of them made their way through a long corridor leading to the back porch where Mamma Kuds sold her soup. They passed the open face of the outhouses nestled into a rear wall. Curtains stretched across the orifices of the two openings with the appropriate labeling of: *nuts and sluts*, and using one of these makeshift latrines could easily be compared to pissing off of the balcony, excepting that the women would have no wooden box to sit on.

Sure enough, Jay-Bug and Dubb reclined in their chairs with feet outstretched on the balcony and a lingering stench of skunk came from the white O's seeping up from their silhouettes. Mamma Kuds' stuff sat on a tote-around at Dubb's side. They appeared to be the keepers of the trade. The old porch creaked under the men's steps when they came upon the Kuds brothers lounging. Neither of the brothers turned around to greet them.

"Came for juice?" said Dubb.

The night had cooled enough so that the Kuds brothers both wore tattered Carharts, the only jackets they had probably ever owned, and hats that slouched sideways on both of their shaved scalps. They could have been twin brothers if not for Jay-Bug's extra three inches on his brother, and his glasses. Another plume of white smoke manifested from where they sat and then receded into the darkness beyond where the porch opened up to the river. They could see the slicing whiteness of the half-moon dancing on the water in its lunar orb, the smell of river and skunk amalgamating.

"How much you selling it for these days?" said Carson.

"How much yeh wanting?" said Jay-Bug, coming out of his rocker. He towered over the two men standing in the opening of the building. "We sell the croker stuff at twenny a jug and the pinejuice a few bucks less, give er take some, pendin on the batch."

"No deals for old friends?" said Carson.

Dubb got up from his rocker to turn around and check the specious statement. Both of the Kuds brothers looked over the Corbins and seemed reluctant to accept the acquaintance at first glance. Carson came closer to Jay-Bug to see him better in the light. "How much of that shit have you been smoking? It's me Carson."

"Carson?" said Jay-Bug, looking puzzled and slightly agitated.

"Hell, Jay. It's those hoity-toity Corbin boys. Member ol' Car. He used to be hell on wheels, member that! Boy, shit, you boys all went on up to college dint yehs." Dubb was much paunchier than he had been in school, but was just as fast-talking. Most likely, a manmade stimulant fueled his joviality and colloquial yammer—the same stimulant that could change his demeanor in a second. "I heard bout both you two from the paper when they name those goin yon and off to college. Must think yall's some hot shit now."

"No better than you boys," said Carson.

"Look at em right now. Near schoolteachers now with them breachers, check em out, Dubb. What's them, slacks?" said Jay-Bug, now alert.

"They are jeans, same as what you are wearing," said Christopher.

"When I want yeh to open that mouth, I'll tell yeh when it's time," said Dubb crudely.

"Is this how you treat all old friends, fellas?" said Carson.

"Fellas, huh … Hey, look here at this old boy caller'n us fellas.

Hear that pitch in his voice, like he got something stuck in there, don't let him drawl none. You forget where yeh from, boy?"

"I can see how this is going to go." Carson took a long pull from his Pabst and set the can on the table where resided the murky brown liquid in jugs. "How bout I take one of the jugs of pinejuice off your hands and we call it at that." Carson opened his wallet and pulled a twenty out, some other notes peaked out of the brown pocketbook.

"We don't sell none to fags, they bad fer business. Where'd you geet all that scratch, been foolin' fer it?"

"Isn't any of your goddamn business, Dubb!" hollered Christopher, already tightening his grasp on the unopened beer bottle in his hand.

"I aint talking to you, shithead," replied Dubb. "I's talking to yer faggy brother, now I done told you I'd get to you when I wanted yer mouth open."

"Hell, I member you boys now. Little Chris there used to come along with us when we went dragging out in the river, and you, Carson, hell you were a pistol out there on the ball field," said Jay-Bug.

"Nice to see a fond memory found its way up there in one of your heads," said Carson.

"Fuck yeh anyways," said Dubb.

"Believe it or not, but we came here to see you old boys while we were in town, and it isn't turning out quite the way I wanted."

"Why would you want to come see us?" said Jay-Bug. "They aint nothing here fer boys like you twos. You aughta be out there chasing that foreign tail. Damn …you look at these girls round here, like getting yehself thown in a cat trap."

"They aint worried about nothing like that, a coupla queers like these here," said Dubb with a vile repugnance.

Carson turned his attention from Dubb, "So how you been, Jay? How is Momma Kuds?"

"She's been better, caint get out the house much, sick as a skunked dog. Still makes the juice, keeps it all in the tub."

"Hate to hear that. Send your best for us." Carson elbowed his brother softly.

"Yea, send your best."

77

"We heard bout your momma," said Dubb with a smile. "Heard the 'ol coot went down to hell's prison. Now she can rob the devil, aint that just bout right, Jay-booger?"

"Don't know, don't remember 'er much," replied Jay-Bug with a lachrymose sleepiness in his eyes. He had transformed, mercurially, into a lifeless droid by some foul drug currently present in his veins and brain.

"I know I don't have to tell you to stop before you go too far. You don't intend on stopping until you have pissed everyone off, do you Dubb?" said Carson.

Before Carson could peel his way out of his jacket, a short stump of fist went into his cheek. It felt to be the diameter of a child's hand and the intensity with which it was thrown was commensurate. Carson shoved off the languid punch and pulled his jacket off, wrapping the right arm of the sleeve around one hand and stretching the other sleeve tightly in his other hand. He fell upon Dubb with hell, choking him against the balcony, the man's drum-like belly keeping Carson from getting a good strangle on him.

Without knowing exactly what to do, Christopher proceeded to throw a punch of his own into Jay-Bug's big, dull face. As hard as the hit connected, Jay-Bug did not feel the punch quite like it was intended. Jay-Bug Kuds instantly snapped out of his lethargic placidity and came at Christopher, swinging his arms in a frightful flurry and connecting with the man several times before knocking him down.

All went black for Christopher until he woke up, the wheels churning over loose gravel in the night. He could feel the low rumble of the cruiser panting its way through the countryside. Cement domes bobbed in the distance radioactively and the roughnecks would be carrying lunch pails and thermoses to the plant before too long. Carson slammed the gearshift and eased up on the clutch with concomitant zeal and mewled terribly over the rev of the engine when Christopher became aware of their speed. "What in all..." he said, watching the lines of the road go by without break.

"Damn, that Jay-bug sure knows how to punch up on you. Hell, you didn't get in but one hit. Here, take this." Carson handed his brother a jug of Momma Kuds' stuff, to which he ejected the cork with a stiff thumb and began to imbibe. The liquid was sweet, but took a fierce turn as it hit his esophagus. He couldn't tell now which pain was more unpleasant, the one in his throat, or the lumps growing from his cheeks. "Guess that is the last we'll see of those Kuds boys."

"What'd you ... you kill them?"

"Hell no. I just about got that Dubb strangled out of his wits before I got Jay-Bug off of you and took to him some. He capitulated as soon as I threw down a punch or two on him. They let us off with a jug of the croker stuff to settle us all even. Said Dubb hasn't been taking too well to Momma Kuds being sick. Said he just about starts a fight every night."

"They ever turn out like he wants them to?"

"Hell. Dubb's about as weak as they come, and about as yappy as a tiny pup. Fights just about the same."

"Well, old Jay-Bug put one over on me," said Christopher rubbing his jaw.

"You should have let him be. He is definitely the fighter of the two, but he's got to be on something that makes him near as docile as a broke-leg cow. I've never seen him so calm until he started wailing on you, but he broke some once I got a hold of him."

"Glad you did."

"Let this be a lesson that those piss beers can still keep a fight in you, make you sharp and what not," said Carson as he hit the gearshift again. A deer crossed with a natural impunity. The glow of the high beams skittered off of its belly and then resumed coarse on the road ahead. A truck entered the road from behind, trailed, and then let off down another side street. "You remember that I'm not going to be there when you head off. You can't get yourself caught up in anything like this here when you hit the south. That is no place for a guy to get in a jam like that. You'll most likely end up on the sharp end of a spear with all of the kooks down there."

"I doubt there's going to be inbreeds the likes of the Kuds down in that part of the world. At least not with those sort of drugs in their system," Christopher said.

"You sure are looking at the world through a child's eyes. They are everywhere, and they don't stop breeding, nor get any better. No different down there, just speak a different language. They may seem more cordial because they look to benefit from you, but you keep your personals tight. If Dubb was any less of a puss, we could have been out our money, and you would have no way to get to the Amazon."

A rift in the asphalt sent the cruiser off of its wheels by a toe's length before it planed out and grounded back on all fours. They could see the four-way ahead with a sole red light clicking from top to bottom in its steel sockets. A police vehicle was escorting another motorist to the side of the road and both vehicles settled in the dust and the sirens wailed going wild in the night. As they passed, they could see the man stumble from his vehicle and fall into the arms of the officer, who quickly went about fettering him in cuffs without the man's cooperation. The unlucky are always quick to admit it the day they come out of the tank with disheveled hair and booze still pursed on their lips. The drunks stood no chance against the militant highway patrol. Their warrant, a car close to the lines or a taillight waning slowly in their periphery.

They made it home sputtering on fumes that night to the sound of the lake lapping and the moon was freshly painted on the water. Carson brought his brother in by the arm and put him on the couch in the living room. He found himself telling him goodbye. He would see him once more in the morning, and hopefully he would not stay away too long. The absence of his brother had made an ineffable impression on his well-being. Daylight was a long time coming as he sat on the back porch, listening to the docks creep, with jug in hand. He was most certainly going to miss Christopher. It had been a long time for this reunion, and he felt it would be even longer for the next to come.

Michael

Michael,

It is without a doubt that I am embarrassed for you. Nevertheless, I am sure you have been just as embarrassed on my account, so the odds have been evened. Do you think your father would have approved of this behavior? Here I am asking questions, those you will never answer. I tried to come and see you, but that little redheaded bitch did not allow me. The nerve...

I have the right to see you, son. It is my prerogative. I had to carry you around for nine months, and you were the heaviest of the boys. Did you know that? Why don't you tell that to your nurse!

You cannot possibly think that you will get away with this forever, Michael. These are children's games you are playing. Lord knows I have played them myself to get out of trouble. What could you possibly be running from that makes you want to dump your inheritance into a place like that? It is awfully appalling. I am sure your brothers will have something to say of it. I can't get a word from either of them, not since the funeral, and even then they wouldn't look at me. Such ungrateful little savages you all are.

But I want you to know that I love you the most. Out of the three, you are my sweetest little boy. Don't forget that, little Mikey. You would not remember, but it was just the two of us for the first year after you were born, before they first took me away. We went to Kansas and I had you and kept you there and you were the sweetest little baby. You just got so sick all the time and had croup. A very pitiful little baby. Your Gigi came and found us and said you needed doctoring, but I knew what was best for you, and you just got stronger and better on your own, and were strong again in no time. She never thought I was a good mother to you, but I think you know that I was. Don't you?

Well, now it does not matter, I suppose. I have no control over where you are, or what you are doing. I can't have that with your brothers either. It surely is horrible how children can treat their parents when they get the notion in their head that their parents aren't any good. You would have made some of the sacrifices I did, though. I promise you that. For the well-being of the both of us, I did what I had to do for us to survive, Michael. And that is something I will never be embarrassed of. So you find out what it is inside of you that makes you too weak to live on the outside. You find that, and you justify it. You justify what it is that makes you who you are, or you will never be able to live yourself down. I know that much.

I just love you three so damned much that I can't stand it. Your father never loved you like I did, and it is his fault that you are in there, not mine, you just remember that. I don't mean that. I can't say that. However, I don't want you to make any of this about your dear mother, do you understand? I have some of my own issues to work out in the advent of his death. Your Gigi would be proud of you, though. I think. She would usually tolerate weakness.

I think I am dancing around my own weaknesses here. Children do pick up things from their parents, and I was surely afraid that one of you would be more like me than I would have wanted. Maybe that is why I love you the most. It is hard not to love those things you see so close to your own, even if it is out of pity. Let me at least have that. I am not sure what it is that makes you who you are, but I do know what makes me who I am, and by now I feel my skin is tough enough to handle it all. What I can say to you is that you need to take this time to try and toughen up the best you can. This world does not give out any favors to people like us, son. You just remember that. This is the best way I can operate in putting together my thoughts for you.

What I may blurt out in anger will stand as-is on page, because that is how it needs to stay. I will not take the time to deliberate my speeches. They come out the best this way, as I am sure you deliver your messages with a similar approach. You remember that you are like me my sweet Michael. You remember that you are my favorite, and I can handle the embarrassment for now. You just get to work on rehabilitating. I do not know if you will get the same encouragement

from others, so you take this for what it is worth.
  -L.C.

Built to overlook the grounds, the ward's northern entrance held a balcony on each story. Though the patients were not allowed access to these balconies, the nurses, doctors, and staff used the balconies on their smoke breaks. Currently, the balconies appeared to be unoccupied from where Michael stood. The long columns that sided and supported these platforms climbed with heavy drainage piping attached to them. Each drain scaled the building, bracketed tightly on welded hinges every five feet, and slithered along like a metal baton decorous of some militant, erect and awaiting orders to kill.

Michael Corbin started at one of the drains with a peculiar urgency and began climbing, using each bracket as one would the rung of a ladder. He took his time, taking the drain story by story, to the top balcony. He did not realize it at first, but he had gotten four stories up within a matter of minutes. He considered the emotions that had mechanized this climbing endeavor. He thought he could do anything—if the activity had the possibility of being his last. At the top balcony of the ward he stopped to feel the surface lacerations now weeping from his hands. Blood trickled out of the cuts procured from the sharp metal. It was without thought that he found himself with this strange kinetic mobility. Conversely, it was with too much thought that he found himself plagued by inaction almost every day of his life.

A long eave shot straight up at a curve in the building shingled with what looked like the broken sides of a clay pot. This would allow him access to the slope of the roof. He crawled up the slope on hands and knees gripping the clay. A few of the shingles cracked and slid down the roof as he traversed, but that neither fazed nor decelerated him. Michael clenched to the letter in his one bloodied fist as he climbed, the thoughts swarming pettishly, and watched his movement from some ulterior space overhead. His actions appeared not his own. The composure of his figure now demonic looking. His eyes blackened and completely empty. He could feel that he had no control of his body as it moved up the roof to the very top of the building. On the ridge of the ward, grand and Gaelic where nothing taller stood, Michael could see the trees bowing under the stature of the building's shadow. He let go of his mother's letter and watched as it floundered to reach the ground in the wind's circuitous waves. Looking at the green finale below, he could see his own shadow atop that of the building. He knew that he now reigned as the supreme being of these estates, and no others could take that from him. He stood, his arms outstretched, with mottled scrubs flapping in the wind. Each turn of the wind pushed him, as if pursuing a taunt, and challenged his equipoise as he hovered over the grounds like some sad molding of Christ awaiting ultimate doom. An eagle scouted above and hovered momentarily over the man, coasting on the wind's high draft. Its yellow eyes shifted and turned to a mouse starting to burrow in the sod. The diurnal being took leave from the man and made for its kill just beyond the ward's barriers. Michael watched himself from above, knowing that the likelihood of survival from the drop would be unlikely, if at all possible. He neither knew nor cared.

What is a day worth when there is no measurable change in the way one feels? When the way one feels is like that of being in a game that replays over and over, while knowing that there is no end. A game unyielding to forfeit. The controls not one's own. When the opening to the soul is the mind, but the mind will not let itself, or anything else, be free. Free to feel, free to think, be ravenous in its delights, and delight in so many things. Yes, these are the things that keep humans occupied from the reality of their constraints. And if it were so for Michael Corbin, he would not mind continuing to live in this world. But that was most certainly not the case. What about the rest of them? Do not think about the rest of them. Never think about the rest of them. That is what gets us into trouble.

Riding high and above the waves on extemporaneous notions of an afterlife, Michael brought one foot forward and let it dangle over the roof's edge. He knew that he did not have much time before the other would follow. Some patients below could see the figure atop the building from the courtyard. They started to rile with anticipation, their irate murmurings incomprehensible. A groundskeeper looked up to see what justified the commotion. Michael could hear the shouts from below. He almost toppled when the wind picked up again, but recovered and kept one foot dangling with the other anchored to the roof. The hoots came louder now, almost calling him toward them like sirens guiding ships in the night. From below it was impossible to make out the face of the balancing figurine now poised in suspended descent. Another gust came. He closed his eyes, felt the levity manifesting, and felt the complete freedom inside. He could feel himself gliding down like the sail of a weightless craft, forever plunging into the great beyond, below where mermaids sing and summon their lovers home, further down into the depths of some complacent serenity, further down where thoughts float away and never return and the lightness is so grand that there is no other worldly place imaginable, for there is no world left to be considered. There is only the soul, free from the prison of the body, and it is released to travel another millennium through time, carrying with it the progress and industry gathered from the mind previously occupied. The time it spans inconceivable. He let his other foot go from the roof and felt himself completely let go.

Before he could even feel his gut lurch, the arms that grasped tightly around his chest forced his eyes open. He could see below, the trees bending and showing streaks of white in the wind, a single leaf floating upward toward him. The calls from the other patients quieted with an anticipating calmness interjecting. He looked at the hands that grasped tightly across his chest. They were a male's hands, puissant and hairy. A golden wedding band stretched across his left ring finger, a medical school ring across the right. Michael could hear the man's loud panting from behind him. He had not moved but an inch from where he had stood on the roof previously. He felt so light in the doctor's arms that the doctor held him suspended for a time. The doctor pulled him back with little restraint down to the balcony. Michael did not feel like fighting him off—only another failed attempt. Perhaps this was for the best.

"That was a ways up there, Mr. Corbin," said the doctor, still panting. "You did a hell of a job at cracking those dreadful old shingles up there. I think it is time to give the insurance company a call. Just brilliant"

The doctor called for a nurse. She came to the balcony quickly, wearing a dazed look on her face—like this could potentially be the most terrifying event she had witnessed at the ward. He motioned for her to tend to Michael's cuts and give him a sedative. She did so, barely touching him as if his suicidal ambition would inflict her like a contagion. "Some of you damn cases keep us quick on our feet. Did you know that, Mr. Corbin? I can't remember the last time I had one incident-free day. You make three for the day. All safe of course. Do you still feel special?" He looked into Michael's eyes, which had now been filled with a deserved lassitude. "I didn't imagine it would. Nothing you can do here will separate you from anybody else in this world. There are no great minds, the way I see it. It is all a matter of strength. Either you understand that you cannot continue to do this, or you will perish and leave nothing behind. I know there is something in you that won't let that happen. Is that so? Anyhow, Caroline will tend to you in your room later. I will send her in, and she will have to see to this mess. I am far too busy." The doctor checked the man's hand to approve the wrap. He then grabbed him by the head and checked both sides of his lobes to make sure no swelling surfaced. He could see none. "Get him on, Lucy. He has no need to be out here. He has had enough."

The woman took him by the hand and brought him into the room attached to the balcony. The sedative had nearly rendered him senseless. He could hear the doctor's voice once more, but the speech focused elsewhere.

"All of you down there. Yes, you … attention up here. Put your damn shirt back on, Gawdry! I will have no more outbursts from any of you. This is not a parade. I said put your shirt on, Gawdry! I won't say it again … good … And if any of you get an idea like Mr. Corbin's, we will see to it that you are not allowed any outside visitors, indefinitely … That understood? Gawdry! I'm coming down there, you insolent bastard!"

Michael,

Another year has passed without a response. What are you doing up there? All-the-more, I have graduated, but did not take the stage. Why would I want to join that lot of lingering bugs feasting on that last morsel of collegiate freedom? You missed nothing by not going to school. Though, when you are in college, you have complete freedom. Four years to feel as if you are making use of your life. It is like time is suspended there, for the future should inevitably hold some greater truth. Not so ... children of thought. Maybe you are smarter than we all suspected. You are on your own sabbatical. Life is now a search for something, and I hate to say that I am not sure exactly what it is. I have always been able to take to the road for a time of solace, but it is just not as refreshing as before. It is funny how we lose our youthful enjoyment of things. I can imagine what geared your actions. I found an add asking for a boat crewmember in Jersey. Should be worth a shot. I always wanted to take out in the mornings with the steam rolling off of the shored rocks and see the sunset coming back in and warm up next to a wood stove in the winter. Could you imagine a seagull floating, following you home at the ship's stern? These are all my aspirations for a better life. If it is not one thing, then it is another that fuels my hope for the future. I am never looking at the present. It will be so even when I get there. Looking to the season's change, only reveling for short periods in what there is of present. That is what you need. Hope. Looking forward to something. Even if it is cursory in nature. Hell, that is what keeps me going. Do you ever remember having moments of serenity when you were young? Like sitting outside when fall first came, or remembering the smell of a gym in the winter. Those were mine. And now it is the presence of an uncertain, but intriguing and idealistic future that awaits me somewhere else. Red slanted roofs with rocks catching in the tide. The gloat of a striped lighthouse forever churning and calling men home, and men coming home cold and ready for a drink and ready to get warm. You have to have some things you would wish to enjoy. And it can't be sitting in a dark room. You are wasting good time and imagination. Trust me on that. Not a one of us has been tied to anything yet at this age, and we are certainly lucky in that. Come set the riggers with me. We will watch the gulls swoop, and we can play cards in the hull every night until we get all the fish we can stand. Make a few bucks. Look down a few warm beers. Maybe even pool our money together and go across the ocean. Go to Madrid, Paris, Kiev. You name it.

Look here, I am already scheming for something different somewhere else. Where is your imagination? Your hope. Come on boy-o, we could go to Ireland, see the kin folk, wait for Godot. Anything striking you? Well, let us hope that you are doing much better. I tried to come that way a few months back, but I got stuck in the city doing something or the other. I think I will take the Jersey job, now that you got me all worked up about it. Now that Dad isn't around to tell me that I am a waste of potential, working a job meant for an 1850's vagrant. I will be closer to you in any case. I will look for other jobs and keep you in mind. Well enough then, that is it for me. Have some decency and write me back.

Chris

Michael Corbin woke to Christopher's letter resting on his chest. He read it without anxiety. The sedatives still had the advantage. They kept the anxiety, the remorse, and the pity at bay. He too, saw the ocean rolling and sucking back into the larger body of the Atlantic, where seabirds circle in the hazy sky forever stretching beyond the coast. That was certainly a peaceful thought.

Caroline must have set it there. Did she not see the letter that mechanized his previous actions? Was she trying to destroy him? Certainly not. He told her to get the letters before. She thought there was a breakthrough, yes. Certainly she thought there was a breakthrough. And then this. He had gone back several steps. She would not be happy with him. She would pity him and that would be worse than death. It would only last for a short while, once he explained. Yes, he would explain that he could not take the words any more. The words, the actions, the false authority he struggled so much to fight. He just needed someone to soothe him. Yes, he would tell her that, and she would believe him and all would be resolved.

His self-devised universe seemed inescapable. On an insular, self-destructive, quandary of life no longer imaginable, he sat in bed. He wondered to himself what the next day would hold for him. He surely could not keep at this if failure continued to triumph over him. Loretta had gained too much power over him, allowing the letter to throw him into such an uncontrollable tantrum. He could control it now. He would not be destroyed by her words any longer. He could escape the torture. Could he escape the formless power she held over him, though, from pity to love? What a vile thing to hold over a child's head. Yes, he could be stronger than all of the memories, the strange wander.

It was a long time into the night when his thoughts eased and he slept. The sleep came on without terror, and a very soothing rift of lucidity followed, a sleep that rejuvenated his waking moments, the ones so desperate and terminal. Michael Corbin dreamt that he lay on a large boulder. Water kept coming from overhead, the source not visible. It was very pleasant. It seemed as though the water held no weight. The water's structure, a visual mass coming down and spreading about him, never touching him, was like a hologram projected from above. Michael liked to think that the water would eventually drown him, but never did a single drop enter his mouth. Through all of the water plummeting down he could see the denouement finally. He could see villages, where men carried in long slates of cooked meats, and women had varieties of herbs and vegetables strung around their necks. Children ran through the translucent villages popping each other with grape guns and makeshift slingshots. He could see himself stoking a fire and wearing nothing but an aggrandized evergreen leaf on his head. The children came by and circled him and seemed to know him very well. The villagers offered him foods, and he ate, and had the fire going, and they danced until he saw a canoe roll by in the far off distance. He could hear singing through the woods where the children followed and went toward the canoe. The water kept coming over him until he could no longer see the traveler. But the man had worn armor. He could have sworn it. He looked back to find the village burning and the men and women trampled over one another to escape the small cottages, even the children were being trampled. It became too much for him to watch and the water began to overpower the waning image in its trajectory. The white kept coming through the green, and the burning village, until there was nothing left of it but the waterfall, and it was soothing once more and Michael Corbin slept in peace for the remainder of the night. Nothing of the afternoon's activities filtered in through his sleep. It was best that way. Those issues were best left for the waking hours. There would be another day for him to assume responsibility for, and he would have to abide that soon enough.

Carson

The young man could see that his brother had almost finished the entire bottle of Kuds' stuff when he went to wake him on the back porch. Christopher kicked Carson in the shin to jar him from his sleep and he awoke coughing with the sun now something so foul that he could not face it directly.

"It is that time," said Christopher.

Carson nodded and looked out across the lake, his hair matted and ruffled out on the back of his head. In the breaking light of day, the oldest Corbin boy looked similar to a dried out old man with physical features comparable to that of a hound—the skin around the eyes and neck slouching. He offered the bottle to his brother. Christopher declined. Carson uncorked it once again and took a swig. It seemed a very painful process, but it would soon inspire his existence. Christopher turned to look out at the lake, the balcony now covered in brown leaves. Carson came from his seat and unzipped his trousers and pissed off of the porch. Steam lingered below where cobbled stone coalesced. A copse of cedars rigid in the distance. He looked at his brother's silhouette coruscating in the morning light. A slick of dew peppered his shoulders and his old breaches were torn and ready for travel. There is no time quite like the one before a long journey. A time when memories somehow seem to escape the wanderer.

"Think we will hit the train?" Carson zipped up his pants and pulled a toboggan from his back pocket to conceal his disheveled hair. "I don't think I have ever gone through Crescent without getting held up."

"It's possible, but Bourlan isn't but a couple of miles from there."

"True. You sure you want to go, little brother? We could have one hell of a time together. We can get rafting jobs in Yellowstone, or ranger jobs in Yosemite."

"We will save it for when I come back."

"Fair enough."

Carson went around the porch and back to the door at the entrance of the kitchen. Christopher could see him cross through the window. He disappeared and went to the back room and then returned with Christopher's bag.

Christopher continued to watch him through the window. He held up the bag and motioned for Christopher to come along. It was time to leave. Christopher turned to look at the lake once more, took in the cool Texas air, and then went into the kitchen. Carson mumbled something from the front porch, but it was just a habitual morning yammer. Christopher locked the door behind him, set the key under the rug, and followed as his brother took his bag up the steps toward the cruiser. "Are you going to see to it that the old girl gets taken care of?" asked Christopher. He went to his truck and grabbed some of his gear out of the bed and went around, locking both doors.

"Yep, she will sit right here. I will talk to Jerry next door. Let him know to keep a look after her. I aim to pick up a cheap cover at the store on the way home, maybe a twelver while I am at it," replied Carson. He chucked the bag in the back seat of the cruiser. The canoe was fastened on top and he checked the slack in the rope and nodded. "Damn, I do a good job at that. Boy scouts paid off."

"You weren't a boy scout, were you?"

"Nah, but I just about could whoop any of them at anything they got patches for. Rowing, sewing, fishing, knotting, you name it."

Christopher came to the passenger's side of the cruiser with his gear in hand. He opened the door to the back seat and threw the gear in. "You will make a good wife someday," he said chuckling. "You a good baker too?"

"Yea. I am. Women like a well-rounded man. You wouldn't know one iota about it."

"Maybe not. I guess I will just have to rely on my looks, instead of having to try to impress folks with all of my little talents and extra-curriculars."

They both got into the cruiser and Carson knocked the gearshift into reverse and the car puttered slowly out of the gravel. A thin trail of oil followed. Tacked to the vinyl ceiling of the cruiser, a myriad of pictures. Mountains roved in the backgrounds above marbled ponds where ospreys sailed. Long rivers snaked and curtailed behind gray boulders where mists billowed. Several of the pictures contained strange travelers. Christopher found himself looking through the large scrapbook printed above his head while they drove to the Bourlan airstrip. A cassette player had been bolted up under the dashboard with electrical chords running through the hull of the vehicle and into the engine compartment where they connected to the battery. In the cassette player a Banjo lick played out with a grungy reverberation. They climbed a back road on the other side of the lake where cedars ran in pinetums and the slates of limestone made the ground look ashy and white. The dust looked like snow. The skulls of downed bovine rested there as well, their ranks tantamount that of the dead trees still climbing. Christopher read something written on a burned piece of paper tacked up next to a picture of the three boys. Carson could not have even been a teenager in the picture.

I see little ones with mouth open and bone peeking through
Those with mouse-sized hands and gunk in eyes
Nothing but the light, the taste,
Some touch, picking up scraps on the floor
I see cracks in the dash, a ripple in a pond
A house is burning from haze in sky, but from where the spark
    starts
It is never known, it is to never know
Thin strands turning from white to brown to gray
I see those around, those they see not
That they cannot clench fist
For once it tightens it is meant for brawling
I see outstretched indexes scolding and jabbing
Thumbs inside moist palates, sucking raw bone
Tit to thumb to rubber to glass
To glass to mind to sleep
To glass to mind to sleep

Christopher took his attention from the poem overhead. He watched the road stretch by. The flora around the lake looked much different than the scrub brush often found in Texas prairies. He watched his brother's eyes droop as he struggled to stay awake. Today had already been eventful enough for him.

"Someone must think of you as a drunk," said Christopher.

"Why do you think that?" he replied.

"Your little poem seems to indicate that." Christopher pulled down the note from the vinyl and read it aloud to him.

"If so, then I must think of myself as one," said Carson.

"You wrote that?"

"I believe so. You should be able to tell by the hand writing."

"It is more chicken scratch than I am accustomed to, but I guess I can see it. The O-s are a little weak, like you tend to do. And you never quite knew how to cross your T-s all the way," said Christopher.

"Good deductive skills." Carson took the note and put it against the glass by the odometer. He smiled over at his brother and shifted into fourth.

The road was long and winding yet, the lake to their left. Some houses came into view at a break in the cedars. Trailers on jacks stood erect on corrugated steel that held sewage tanks underneath. Some old Mavericks and Novas sat abandoned, encircled in a chain-linked scrap yard, and several chickens ran freely, pecking and gawking with bobbled gizzards bright red. A couple of old men sat on porch rockers awaiting a passing car to heckle with coffee still seeping in their makeshift presses. The Corbins came to a crossing where train tracks ran adjacent the road. No traffic could be seen for miles.

"This will make a first," said Carson.

"I guess the road is paved ahead for me to get out of here as soon as possible," replied Christopher.

"I wish you weren't going yet, old boy." Carson's eyes looked placid from staring at the road so early in the morning. "You got the fee to pay the boat master at the river Styx?"

"I have the fee, but this is no Hades I will be heading to. Feels like I am leaving it, though."

"Come on now, old man. It isn't that bad," said Carson sincerely. "I think we could make a good go at it. Start a family business." The man eased the car at the stop sign and jiggled the gearshift methodically. He hit the clutch again and put it in second and cruised through the intersection, leaving the lake behind.

"You will do anything to keep from going back north to the unknown," replied Christopher. He stared down the long stretch of road from the passenger's window. A plane leveled out in the sky with wing flaps undulating. "You try your hardest to get me to go about with you as soon as one of us gets to leaving. I would be damn surprised to see you ever follow through. I would bet anything that we would end up getting drunk every night. We would just cut up until we had nothing left to do but go to work at the plant, living out of the lake house."

"That's no way to talk. You know we have more drive than that," said Carson. They climbed another hill and the airstrip came into view. Some planes were being hauled out of the bays. "I just think it is a nice thought, us being together and all."

"Yes. But I don't see us ever getting anything done."

"We would if we had trades."

"And what would yours be? Sewing and fishing?" said Christopher as he scratched at the patch on Carson's knee. "Well maybe not sewing. That is mangled as hell, Car."

"Let it alone." Carson smacked at the man's hand.

"We aren't getting any younger. We might as well see the world while we can."

"Do you have Loretta with you?" asked Carson with a rejuvenated sense of awareness.

"Got her in the urn, kettle black and all."

"Well hold on to her until you are ready to let go, because you know how she gets to taking off." Carson laughed.

"I figure I owe it to her to take her off somewhere she can't be found."

"Won't anybody be looking."

"I am sure there are still some tax men on the bounds, lurking in the bush," said Christopher smugly.

"Even after it all, Pops would have thrown a hissy about seeing her put to rest."

"He was a traditionalist. One man, one woman."

"I don't think she saw it that way."

"Doesn't matter," said Christopher softly.

Bourlan field, a small airstrip on the outskirts of town, rarely saw boys like the Corbins. Only people who knew those who had planes could hitch a ride, for a good sum, and luckily Eugene Corbin had some connections with wealthy men from his firm. Those men knew other wealthy men, and those men had planes.

Carson left his brother, after the laborious task of securing the canoe inside of the large passenger plane, and watched as the craft skated across the pavement and above the tree line within a matter of seconds. His brother would now be off with his gear, tackle, and the remnants of his mother. On to greater rivers, where humanity rarely traverses, he went without fear or remorse. It was not a wanton matter. When Carson took back to his cruiser, his mangled shoes licked the pavement with deliberation. The sky cracked. He watched as the avionic mass overhead flattened out and started to careen. He took a drink from the bottle stashed under his driver's seat and sat and watched the sky for a time.

On the way to Johnny's Corner the cruiser held an able build, even in her seniority, and Carson hugged the corners rounding farm buildings and fields of green where yellow daisies bloomed. A cement plant billowed thick white smoke from the top of its reactor. Trees, sky, and smoke followed. Johnny's corner sat on one side of a two-way crossing. Outside sat two men on a slide-bench and one of them currently packed a tin of snuff. Carson pulled in, parked, and went toward the store. He flicked a hand at the two of them and the one packing his snuff bent his bill in recognition. Inside, a thin, homely girl was stocking the front rack with gas cans, oil tins, and some fuel system treatment. The girl had the build and slimness of face reminiscent of vermin and Carson watched her as she bent over and shuffled on bent knee to stock the shelves. He searched for a line where her back might have shone, but found none. He assumed she wore a few tattoos to compensate for such a lack of attraction. Various boat supplies hung from nets stapled to the walls like some relic of a seaside attraction. A few cookers, parked in the back of the store, roasted slabs of meat on big iron racks. To the side of the cookers sat the coolers, those housing pops and alcohol. He followed the lines of cans sitting in their fluorescent abodes and went directly to the beer. He looked over his choices briefly and then decided. Carson came to the cashier's table with the twelve pack of beer and waited for the girl to scurry back behind the counter.

"That all, honey?"

"That will do it."

"Five-fifty. Say, I haven't seen you around here in a long time."

"That so?"

The girl took his bill and divvied the change. She looked at him for a time and then stood back, crossing her arms, and pointed at herself. Her index almost the dimensions of a pencil. "You know who I am?"

Carson looked at her speculatively, as if trying to recall a memory. "Yea, you've worked here a long time. I used to come in here before. I only live a mile away."

She shook her head at him. An irascible snarl stretched from underneath her pointy nose. The kind of snarl a dog gets toward something biting its hind. "Carson Corbin, right?"

"Yes ma'm," he smiled. He still could not place her anywhere in his memory.

"Berta Albright," she said loudly, as if it would capture his memory. "I started two weeks back, so that aint how you know me." She shook her head again and looked out of the store window. "You only live a mile from here?"

"We have a house off of the lake. I came in to see my brother for a few days. I don't know you from here?"

"I got fired from the Lake Tavern in town. You ever been there?"

"Once or twice," replied Carson.

"More'n twice."

"What does that mean?"

The girl looked him over and rolled her eyes. She could have been attractive without the corner–store smock around her thin neck … and if she gained some weight. Her eyes implied the astonishment typical of a small child. "That's where I know you from. You would come in with your buddies some nights, and leave with me."

Carson smiled nervously and put a hand around the handle of the beer box so that he had what he needed in case things got worse. "Oh yea, Berta. You must have lost weight since then. Time has been good to you."

She blushed some. "Of course you remember me. Probably was the best lay you ever got."

"Damn good," said Carson as he started away from the counter. "It has been good running into you."

"You want some company tonight over there at that house of yours?" She started to take off the apron to show her freedom from the unflattering job. "I don't mind catching you up on what you've been missing."

Carson raised the box of beer at her and smiled as he headed for the door. "Let me get some work done, and I'll come by later to see what you are doing. That okay?"

"Sure thing, honey, but don't drink too many of those. We don't want you having any problems now."

He smiled once more and turned to head for the door. *Who the hell …* he thought for a long time, trying to remember ever picking her up, but he could not recall her even the slightest bit.

He emptied the twelve-pack of three beers by the time he opened the door to the house. Carson shook the box and knew he would be doomed to go back for more before the night's end. He would then have to deal with her again, and that would be something foul indeed. On the back porch he watched the birds call and cross the lake. A sole boatman jetted across the glassy water with the sun reflecting off of the boat's windshield like some celestial orb now speeding across the open terrestrial dawn. While he sat there and squinted down the sun, his mind started to fill with panic and dread. It was a feeling he was accustomed to. He watched planes secrete clouds in long lines overhead until he felt the need to combat that creeping dread with an arduous activity.

As a boy, he had built a storage shed into the side of the hill underneath the porch. He stumbled down to it with a beer in hand. The light bulb flickered for a moment and then burned out when he pulled the light string at the entrance of the shed. He opened the door completely and propped it back with a cinderblock. Enough light now leaked into the room for him to find his way around. He could see the tool shelf propped against the wall with its metal panels reflecting the sun. Some yard tools shadowed, propped against the back wall, and a haul of wood sat faceless and covered in webbing. An unknown creature scurried rampantly from a hole in the shed to the shelf. He jumped and then kicked some gravel at it, but it had gone. The young man walked deeper into the shack to inspect the unfinished project sitting in the center of the building. Carson felt the edges of his first canoe. The woodwork was fine and salvageable, but the wood had not been cured, nor would it hold up to water–warp. A few stacks of wood lay inside of the hull. From under the slits in the banister Carson slid the contents of the canoe onto the porch. He pulled out the craft and checked it for spiders and other creatures and set it on end and pushed it up over the banister. Two sawhorses sat abandoned in the tall grass across the front yard where the neighbors had let their weeds grow wild. Those, he tugged from the grass and set on the back porch, distancing them accordingly. He went back into the shed and prodded through the dark silhouettes sitting on the tool bench until he felt the sharp teeth of his saw. He found a few buckets of varnish and lacquer that he brought up along with the saw and set them on the porch.

He ended up staying at the house off of the lake for the next four days to build his canoe. By the time it had been sanded and painted completely, he felt that it was the best thing he had ever created. When he ran out of beer or food he jogged the mile down to the corner store and got what he needed. Berta held up her offer to him whenever he would enter, but he always told her he had work to do, and within those four days he had managed to build a canoe. He decided that it would be Washington he would travel to, and that he wanted Valencia to go with him. He was sure of these things, and by the end of the week, he left the lake, the house, the Kuds brothers, Berta, the Brazos, and all else behind.

While cruising the interstate he looked over at the passenger's seat where his brother had sat and felt the seat where an impression still drooped. He knew his brother's path was one meant for harvesting. A harvest of all events leading up to that journey alone; the childhood, the death of the father and mother, and all of the things that plagued his mind. Carson knew he would eventually have to come to terms with his own harvest, and that would be a reaping indeed.

The wind blew through the passenger's window and he could see something transparent flapping from the tuck of the seat cushion. He tugged at the bag. It started to give from the seat and finally surfaced. He held it up to the sun to see what was inside. There was a note in a small baggie, along with a silvery powder. The feel of the powder was soft and ashy from inside of the cellophane and he knew what it was. In the parking lot of a rest area off of the highway, he brought the car to a stop. The note inside of the bag was signed by Christopher.

With his brother's words going through his mind, he tied the bag again, set it in the glove box, and continued north for the east coast. Valencia would be waiting for him where he left her, and her company would calm the moments of dread for certain. Women always had a way of doing that in one way or another. Of course, they could always cause dread as well, but he was not concerned with that directly.

The prairies of Texas lay flat in the brown stillness beyond the highway. Oak trees stood erect in sparse thickets where water sources once sprang. He could see the drivers of the cars he passed and they all looked straight ahead on the path in front of them, never once looking around to see if anything had changed in the fields. For these were matters not for the travelers of this great world. Like ants trampling ass-to-ass in single file line, the drivers continued on with their symmetrical lives. His mission was to make it to upstate New York with very few moments of feeling the dread creep in. It was always the dread of the unknown that would combat the excitement of that same unknown he feared, but he would make it, and his life would be satisfying, though fighting the dread would be the greatest challenge.

·

II.

Loretta

Loretta Corbin disappeared for the first time her junior year of high school. Her boyfriend, a man four years her senior, had convinced her to run away with him. He was rebellious, volatile, and he fueled her wild energy. He wore a leather jacket, rode a Harley Davidson motorcycle, and smoked two packs of Marlboros a day. He was a walking American effigy, a personification of the red-white-and-blue. Perhaps she picked up her life-long habit of smoking from him—the gambling and drinking as well. But these were small matters, as those around her would later find out, and a darkness had grown within her during her time away.

When Loretta finally came home she told her mother of the motorcycle accident that had killed her man. She told Gigi that his body had been charred beyond recognition from the explosion. The gas tank had been turned out completely, as if shot open, and the only recognizable parts of him that remained had been his boots, the pant legs burned through, and the fleshy slicks of raw meat and bone still connected to the feet inside of the boots. Loretta gave the description of the scene with terror ripping its way through her trembling larynx and it quickly became evident that she would be changed forever.

Loretta had returned with a callous demeanor. Her entire being had changed in every twitch and nuance. She had become vindictive and sneaky. A newly conceived child of vanity. Gigi soon realized that little could be done do to help her daughter and it broke her heart, but fed her resolve to find purity in a world so plagued by deceit. An aspect of Gigi's character that would later mold the Corbin brothers into young men of similar resolve.

Loretta disappeared again after her nineteenth birthday. Several years later, a private investigator would come to talk to Gigi about the whereabouts of her daughter. Gigi did not know where to start, her heart breaking more and more with the persistence of her maternal instinct galvanizing. All the while, Loretta's conning was starting to make her a very rich woman. She was molding the art of thievery into perfection, her trail remaining cleverly thin, and Gigi never knew the true face of these cons.

Later in life Gigi would tell the boys of these things. Eugene as well. She did so in order to comfort them. The old woman speaking of the dishonor of her own daughter, a chronology of a woman's defection. It was unspoken, but their mother's life had become somewhat of an attractive thought to the three Corbin brothers, the mystery and guile of it all, the heist-like excitement of a person's life. To be free, capable, fearless, a renegade.

As for motherhood, Loretta was scarcely in attendance, but the boys put up with the chaos. They knew no other way to perceive a mother's duties. For children, this will always be such. Simply, there was no question that she had provided the womb that had conceived them. The reason Eugene sat by and took all of her abuse seems simple. She had a spell on him. She made that her business—the business of capturing men and holding them in a weakened state. The very thing that became the torture of Eugene Corbin until the day he died in his ninety-second year.

When the boys first learned of their mother's deception Carson had been no older than ten. He, being the oldest at the time, understood it the most. He fought it the most as well. There develops within a child a great moment of clarity when it is learned that parents are not flawless, and what follows is a realization that there are no heroes or idles, no firm affirmations of morality, no exactness to the process of raising a child. Despite these things, he tried his best to make sure his younger brothers were protected, and that he set a good example for them. He was good for that.

Loretta seemed to love her boys very much, when present, and found herself to be a very smothering woman, as if the duality of her personality tried to hold on to them as long as she could before she inevitably pushed them away. She proved to be the best mother when the boys were old enough to want alcohol and cigarettes. Providing such substances for needy teens was much easier than being a responsible mother. Michael never seemed swooned by any of it, though. He always reacted slowly to her bribes and his reaction to his mother became very strange over time. Loretta soon came to realize that her son had developed into a very strange child. She even began to worry about HIS sanity. The possibility that he had received the consequences of her prodigal life became a consideration of hers. In seeing him, she always regretted what she had done with her life, but it was never enough to make her change.

As far as the boys were concerned, Loretta would always be an equivocal parental figure in their lives. Fortunately, Gigi leapt at the chance to pick up the slack. And as they got older, and more conscientious of pecuniary matters, the boys feared Loretta's cons, learning that all men and women should be cautious of those who are inherently given trust without earning it, such as a parent. It gives clarity to the uncertainties of this world by thinking in this manner. The boys knew they were living blindly to her actions and they knew some devious reality would soon surface. And with this, the boys built the basis for their social interactions on the assumption that they had to keep an eye on their own matters. For in this world, with those of immoral conviction scattered about, nothing is certain, and all beings should be inventoried thusly before trusted.

Loretta died alone in route to Florida; a stolen rental car found in the parking lot of a Casino on the border of Mississippi and Louisiana, along with her body, stiff and condemned to the rim of a trashcan in her hotel room—the same trashcan that had cut off her air supply when she had not the faculty about her to get up—they found twenty-seven dollars, a bottle of vodka, and a journal in her purse. No identification. The car had been reported stolen for months. The rental company, given an alias. The local police could not identify her, but the men from the bureau of investigation eventually did. They had been looking for her for some time. They had years of larceny charges to collect on, but nothing would come of it now.

It was not long after they found her body that they sent her to the crematory and sent the ashes to Christopher. He had been the one to request them. He felt that some things in this world needed settling more than others, and his disdain for his mother became one of those things that could now be resolved. The cleansing of her physical remains an indication of closure. That is the way of those still living, if only to alleviate the pain that accompanies loss. Loretta was meant for more than the life that she had created for herself. Her children's lives would transcend the life she had wasted, the memory of her existence only supportive of the speculative caution with which they would conduct themselves. That is the way it went with Loretta Corbin, and no belief exists that it could have been any different.

Christopher

When the plane entered the harbor a few Brazilian boys gathered around the shore to watch the men unload the craft. Christopher could see, from across the bay, a few large carrier ships and boys loading them with large sacks and oak barrels. The boys presently on his shore came and helped Christopher and the captain pull the canoe from the plane, securing the craft with their long sticks. A few young girls were sitting on the docks peeling nuts and watching the shirtless boys. Christopher paid the captain half of his due. An assurance of the man's return. The captain shook his hand and motioned for the boys on the bay to fetch him the gas. Christopher took a canoe end from one of the boys and handed him a dollar. The boy took away with it and the other boys followed, trying to get him to share. They did not know the loss of a dollar's value when split in pieces.

The river was glassy and very wide when Christopher took into it from the bay. He could barely see across to the north how the other side stretched. He would head west, deeper into the draw of the country. He checked his food rations. Stocked to last for close to a month. Rice, beans, and corn being the bulk of the diet. He also had a jerky, tortillas, and quinoa. He drew out from the bay, turning his canoe into the body of the river, and watched as several ancient-looking locomotives puttered past in the middle of the river. He saw an old steamboat and what looked like a Trojan fleet-ship row past with men, midsections the girth of oak trunks, heaving and turning long oars over in the wooden tholes of their domain. A battalion of indigents paddled in a line on standing boards and eyed him with heavy brows and no emotion. Christopher was foreign to these people. His pallid skin. The quality of fabric from which his clothing was sewn. He followed the line of paddle boarders for some time until they split off to the north. He followed the river where it turned to the west and thinned.

The flora all around was vascular, almost plastic looking, and very green, and the density of the forest seemed infinite. It was thin and open and always stretching out into the empty country and everything seemed to creep within this extraterrestrial domain. A few shacks stood erect, set on stilts, and the water came up to the porches and he could see the barrels on the inside of the buildings where ships would load products and leave commerce in small lock boxes bolted to the shacks. He wondered how such a system could work. It seemed easy enough for this trade to be depreciated by any person willing to steal. There were no guardians of the trade, no regulators of the craft. He passed women soaking their clothes on the bank. Some scrubbing their little children in washtubs filled with river water, unafraid of the dangers lying within the depths of the Amazon.

He came upon a small village near sundown. The lights that hung from the swampy trees mirrored on the water such that the shore looked much closer as he drew toward it. He could see several obfuscated figures moving slowly through the trees and heard the sound of a bongo or skin drum lightly rapping. Christopher found a cutback delta with a sand bank inlayed against the shore. He used one of his oars as a gondola as he got into the shallower water and pushed his canoe onto the bank. Once he had an opening of sand at the bow of the boat he unloaded the craft and brought the canoe onto the bank. He unloaded his pack and took everything out of the canoe. There skimmed saurian creatures through the fat blades of grass on the bank and he could hear their squeaking. He dragged the canoe to the bank and rambled through the bushes until he found a dugout underneath an uprooted tree. The plant life all around seemed bountiful enough to cover the canoe with. Once he had it concealed he marked the tree with his knife and tied a piece of fabric to an adjacent tree on his way to the village. In what visible light existed he mapped out where he had taken out of the river and marked his trajectory so that he could return for the canoe.

It was not long before he came upon the village. It consisted of several wooden shacks aligned in a circle with a communal meeting place directly in the center. Presently no villagers could be seen on any of the porches and a bonfire blazed behind the shacks. Christopher walked to the end of a grouping of buildings and could now make out the villagers sitting quietly around the bonfire. A broad-chested man walked the ring of the fire addressing all of the villagers and his voice bellowed deeply and clicked as he talked, as if he gave a secret Morse code. Christopher crept along the side of one of the houses and watched from the darkness. He remained unnoticed for some time listening until he felt a small hand wrap around his. He moved quickly from the small figure at his side until he could see the boy's face by the light of the fire. The boy could not have been older than ten and he wore a bandage on his head now souring with crust. The little boy looked at him blankly and took him by the hand again. Christopher complied and followed as the boy led him to the fire.

The leader did not acknowledge Christopher's arrival directly and continued on with his address. A woman with a long nose and a baby nestled against her bosom leaned over to kiss the little boy on the top of his head and nodded at Christopher. He nodded back. The leader spoke in what Christopher knew to be rooted in Spanish, but most of the words he did not know. The man's audience sat mute while he spoke, unmoving, as if they were put in some trance that his words alone conjured. When the man had given his speech, he pointed out to the American. The entire clan turned to look at Christopher. The leader addressed him in English.

"We have with us a new figure tonight. A visitor on his way down river, yes?"

Christopher sat still and nodded, but the man could not see him clearly in the dark. "Yes, a traveler," he responded.

"A traveler. A friend, yes?"

Those sitting around the fire greeted him in unison and some villagers sitting close to him outstretched their hands.

"Good now," said the leader. "And what is your name, traveler?"

"Chris," said the man with a break in his voice. He heard the villagers repeat the name and could hear some women whispering in the group.

"Chris is strange name, no?" The leader turned to address his group.

Christopher tried to translate what the man was saying, but could not. The little boy kept looking at him. After a while the boy started to probe the man's bag to see what he carried. The boy's mother grabbed him by the neck and demanded that he stop. The boy smiled back at Christopher and shrugged his shoulders. Christopher began to dig through his pack, the boy watching him with inchoate fascination, and pulled out a small carabiner and handed it to the boy. The boy looked at it with a mystic scrutiny and began to tinker with the latch, opening and closing it, spinning the safety clamp. Christopher showed him how rope slid through the carabiner easily. The little boy smiled widely and showed it to the woman and she nodded at Christopher in appreciation.

After the fire had died down Christopher followed the woman and the little boy to their cabin. The leader had left from the group without saying another word to Christopher, and the young American did not see the leader again for the rest of the night. The little boy made a cot for Christopher in the back of the shack where the animals slept and showed him where to draw water and where the animals relieved themselves.

"Let's have a look at that," Christopher said to the boy, pointing at the patch on his head.

The boy pulled at the bandage, trying to get it to come off, but the adhesive tore at his skin. The boy whimpered and Christopher sat him on the cot and brought over a pot of water. He soaked the wrap until it softened and then peeled it off quickly. The wound that festered there had become infected, the skin around it bloated and dark red. The inner part of the wound oozed out a yellowish discharge. Christopher scrubbed at it tenderly.

"Damn, this thing hasn't been looked at in a while, no?"

The boy did not answer. His eyes had grown wide and soft. He whined when Christopher scrubbed at the wound, but remained resilient to the care and did not move. Christopher had packed a medical kit from which he brandished a bottle of iodine and gauze. Once he had the boy's cut scrubbed out he swabbed it with the iodine and wrapped the clean gauze tightly around his head. "Better?" he said. "Mejor?"

The boy nodded and looked up from the cot at his mother standing in the doorway. She smiled back at him and then at Christopher. "This is very nice of you," she said. "We have little supplies for wounds in our village. We must hold on to what little we have." She had a look of shame in her eyes.

"It is no problem," he replied. "The boy needs better health. It will be hard for children to survive with such a lack of care."

"We are a tough people. It will be uncomfortable, but we will survive."

"You'd know better than I would."

The little boy came from the cot and went to hug his mother before going into their living quarters. Christopher looked through his supplies and handed her a small vile of iodine and another pack of gauze. "This is what I can spare, to pay you for taking me in for the night."

"You bring what is most needed," the woman said, accepting the supplies, and went after the boy.

Christopher packed his medical supplies back into his bag and set the bag next to the cot. That night he could hear the residual embers of the bonfire crackling in the night and the calls of strange animals. He could hear the little boy whimpering and the woman's moaning. It was very different here, but it was exhilarating and it kept his mind from wandering. He could hear the pigs snorting and the chickens clucking until he eventually drifted off to sleep.

In the morning he woke to the sounds of the woman mashing corn on the back porch. He went through his pack thoroughly to find that everything had remained untouched. He came out to tell her good morning. She continued to grind the corn into a powdery residue. "Where's the boy?"

"Sacristo?"

"Is that is his name?"

"Yes. He is in woods, either hunting or fishing. You will find him near water." The woman brushed one of the piles into a wooden crate and took it to the side of the house. "You leave today?"

"Yes. I was going to tell him goodbye first, and tell him to take care."

"He will not understand. But if you would like, you may find him."

"I want to thank you for letting me stay."

"No need. It is how we live, if only to help," she responded.

"That is good," said Christopher.

"Yes, it is. And you have safe travels."

Christopher nodded. He turned, gathered his bag, and took off in the direction of the river. On the bank he found the leader of the group and a few other men. They had pulled his canoe from its hiding spot and were applying a thin coat of syrupy liquid to the hull. They had already attached a thick stranded seine to the rear of the canoe and built in some fish traps out of wood and fabric by the time he arrived on the shore.

"What are you doing?"

The leader motioned for the men to keep working and walked toward Christopher with his hand outstretched. "We wanted to find your boat and make it better for your journey." He took Christopher by the shoulder and brought him over to where the men worked. "It was very smart of you to hide it, but you are in a different country."

Christopher felt the hull with one barren and unsure hand. The liquid that was on it felt like a resin used to cover wood. "It is a hard thing to know first hand," he responded. "What is all of this?"

"A gum we get from the trees. They say that the piranhas do not like the smell when the boat is in the water. Keeps the monsters away."

Christopher smelled his hand. It was similar to the smell of a strong alcohol. "Smells like it could get them drunk."

"That may be," commented the leader with a hint of humor in his voice. "We also set you one of our fine nets. Men fish these rivers for centuries with these nets with great success. Understand?"

"Certainly. And what can I give you in return?"

"We want nothing, though we need much. Nothing you have can save our village," said the leader with his attention wandering. "If you come across any people of your origin crossing the river, you tell them that we are a good people. You tell them we do good for ourselves. You tell them they have no need to try and harm us. Can you do that?" The leader took the man's pack from his hands and placed it in the canoe and had his men take the canoe out to the water's edge.

"I would like to think of myself as a rarity in these parts. You are saying that I may come across people of my origin, as in America, here?"

"Very much. They take boats all up and down these waters. The white man is very industrious in this land, understand?"

"Yes, I understand. I will do what I can. What of the boy? Where has he gone?"

"Sacristo?" replied the leader.

"Yes, I wanted to tell him goodbye."

"He does not like to see men come and go. Many travelers on these waters. He is very much young and lacking strength. I am sure you will see him when you pass through the woods. You can see him off then."

"Sure. Thank you, again. I will remember your village."

The leader nodded his head and followed Christopher out to the canoe and helped him into it. The other men gathered at the sides, handing him his oars, and guided him into the river. He traveled in the opposite direction of the river's flow and the current of the Amazon was such that it did not bother his rowing. It was always a slow start at first, but he managed to pick up enough mobility to float it with ease. As he paddled along the bank, under the great canopy of the rainforest, he looked for Sacristo, but could find him nowhere. He imagined the boy running through the woods following the trail of some great animal and hoping that Christopher would still be there when he returned. But it would not be so.

He passed several sights he had not expected to see the next week rowing along the river. Riverside gas stations with fuel pumps newly erect came across his bow at random intersections. He even found men that spoke good English working the pumps. He saw a sign dangling from a steel frame that had holes punched through it like those found on many American back roads. The colonialism remained similarly evident, and he was forever coming upon things he knew to be foreign to this country.

He came across a landslide where a sifting line had been set up to gather what gold could be cached from the amalgamated soil. A cavalcade of indigent workers walked the stairs of the great structure with large basins in their hands and others stood on the shores with rifles, urging the rower to carry on. He rowed past, watching the men work. The gears always grinding against the big metal cog under the washbasin. Younger workers sifted their pans in the piranha filled waters with little fear and it seemed, to Christopher, that two work bosses hovered over the operation at the top of the landslide in slick brown suits. Whatever trade came from the small shacks he saw earlier must have been innocuous commodities in comparison to gold, oil or gas. These products, contents of a much broader nation, dealt elsewhere.

Christopher came upon a small trade station a mile up the river from where the gold mine produced. Two Johnboats tied to the cleats of the small trade shack bobbed in the water with their Mercury engines clicking and a few thin-looking men lingered on the porch. The river violently lapped and gulped underneath the porch and Christopher could see what looked like chips of styrofoam skimming atop the water all along the shore and under the dock. The men pulled their hats up to size him as he rowed up to the dock. One of them left the porch and went into the shack and then came back out with a rope in his hand. He chucked the rope at Christopher as he neared the dock. Christopher caught the rope with one hand still on his oar and looped it around the seat in front of him and then pulled back on the rope. The other two men continued to stand there talking, not offering a hand. The man at the other end of the rope cleated it off and bent down to help the boy pull himself in.

"Will build big arms rowing out the days, no?" said the man as he pulled Christopher in.

"That is the hope," he replied. "What's all that going on with the people panning back down the way?"

The man looked at him with bewilderment, an unknowing of the man's words glaringly clear. Christopher pointed back down the river and made a panning motion with his hands. Then he rubbed his fingers together, as if sifting through dirt or counting money, both gestures indicative of what he tried to communicate.

"That is for gold. The soil is turned, very easy to count." The man looked over at the others who continued to stand and watch. He said a word to one of them in his native tongue and the man said the word "sift." The man then turned back to Christopher. "Yes, the soil is very easy to sift."

Christopher looked up at the man standing on the porch. He had a thick gray moustache running down to the edges of his chin. The other man standing next to him had not been following a word of the conversation. Only did he sip his coffee and look off down the river in the other direction.

"I take it you know better English, sir," he said to the man with the moustache.

The man came up to the side of the dock where the canoe was cleated. "Yessir. Let me first be polite. I am Horatio Cornish. You are an American, I see. I am one of the fortunate, also. I come from Helena."

"Montana? Quite a different climate down here, isn't it?"

"You would be surprised at the things that can annoy you equally in both places. It is the river's game here. You trade cold for hot and humid, but you have a hell of a time surviving the critters here. Damn bugs are about as prevalent as they are on the Yellowstone River ... but more dangers lurk out here."

Mr. Cornish reached his hand out to help Christopher from the canoe. The other man tied it off behind him.

"What brings you out here?" said Christopher.

"My mother was from these parts before she had me in the Americas. I promised to visit her motherland some time in my life. And with me being in the oil business, I figured now was better than ever."

"How is the oil business going here?" Christopher followed Cornish to the west side of the porch and the two of them looked out on the open field behind the shack where ran a small gravel road; a late model Ford parked at a distance of twenty yards from the shack. The other two men had gone into the shack. Clunking noises followed in broken rhythms void of cadence.

"Quiet in there!" Mr. Cornish yelled at the men. The noises calmed. "Not very good, son. Pardon…" he stuck out his hand. "Your name?"

"Christopher Corbin." He shook his hand.

"Hell of an American name."

"Yea, but we are all mutts of the same country," said Christopher. He looked downriver and watched a small ferryboat troll across the stream.

"The American bull-dog had to come from somewhere," replied Mr. Cornish.

"So … what is the trouble with finding oil here?"

"It isn't finding it that is the problem. It is the transport. The cost of transporting materials from any place we can dig is paramount that of what we make off the damn stuff. You saw those locals fetching gold. All primitive equipment, and they work on land grants they get from traditional rights. All of those damn savages get free transport and contract out before any of us can get in there and do anything. You'll see them sucking oil out where it is thick, but it takes them ten times what'd take us just to come in there and drill. We could suck it all dry and be out of their hair in just a few months, leave them with a hefty tip too." The man spat into the river and watched it run under the boards of the shack like a thin, brown tapeworm. He pointed out to the ferry on the horizon that had now been puttering on for some time. "You see them right there?"

"Yes," replied Christopher.

"Jonas' Ferry Company. They take tourists out fishing in these waters. Damn folks come into some big local port and get these ferries to take them down a whole stretch of the river like they are some damn bushwhackers. Nothing like what you are doing."

"Well, I would hope not. I was expecting to not see any one from the states. Seems I have been wronged thusly."

"You have a weird way about you," said Cornish. He looked over

Christopher. His canoe and pack. He looked back down the river where the stream carried some current. "How far do you plan on making it in that little thing?"

"As far as I feel like taking myself. I am not trying to kill myself any, or even strain too much, for that matter."

"You good on supplies?" the man asked speculatively.

"I have only been out on the river a short while, from my count, and all my rations have been leveled and calculated almost spot on for what I intended."

"And how long are your rations to last comfortably?"

"A month or so."

"You won't see many more shops like this on up the way you are traveling. I can guarantee you that," Mr. Cornish took a pouch of tobacco from his back pocket and pinched out a plug. He offered the man a plug mutely, but Christopher denied. "This may be the last you see of those ferries, too."

"In that case, you may be the man to pass a word to."

"What's that?"

"There's a tribe down the way ... about a four day's row at a good pace. They are in some need of medical supplies. Just the basics would go a long way."

"Down that way?" the man pointed back in the direction from where the young American had traveled. It was an ignorant question, but by the tone of his voice, he may have meant to sound that way. Perhaps he knew exactly what the man was talking about.

"They seem to have what they need in the way of food, but there wasn't a pound of medical supplies between the whole group. No alcohol, iodine, gauze—one. Their leader seemed intent on making their docility known."

"How long do you think those folks have lived out there in the bushes?" said Cornish.

"Centuries, from looking at the basic structure of their village."

The man smiled and spat some of his tobacco juice out into the stream. One of the men had come from the shack lugging a burlap sack of metal tools and headed for the other end of the porch. Mr. Cornish patted him on the back as he walked past. "Bueno, amigo." He took Christopher back around to the entrance of the shack. "And how long do you think they will live on like they done thus far?"

"I would hope a while, Mr. Cornish, but that doesn't mean folks can't help make life easier on them." Christopher followed the man into the shack to see what wears he could acquire from the small riverside shop. "Even if it means letting up some on their rivers, or dropping off some supplies when there is extra around."

The store was comprised of a majority of digging tools, pans for the gold miners, and some dried foodstuffs. A single tank of gasoline was anchored at the back of the shack where the reservoir must have been dug out underground. There was no telling how much gasoline could have been stored there. "Well ... I would be more inclined to help them, and their kind, if they would give a little on some of my inquisitions about what they are sitting on."

"They have oil under their land?" said Christopher as he thumbed through some of the packets of seeds alphabetized in a metal catalogue box. He took some exotically named seeds and a sack of dried maze.

"You bet. They are all up and down this river, the natives. Have *owned* the land since they inhabited it. I have got to go more than fifty miles inside the country before I can get to any open land. Then, there is the trouble of getting it back out to the river." Christopher held up the goods to the man to indicate what he would like to buy. "Take them. Don't mean a thing to me. The reason I set up shop here aint to sell none of this piddly–shit."

"You aim to keep an eye on the river?" said Christopher inquisitively.

"Yessir. That is a mighty fine wit you have, son. You come on back if you want work. We could always use an English speaking driller further up the river. I give my workers fine living quarters." Mr. Cornish went through some drawers at the back of the shack and pulled out a pint–sized bottle of murky liquid. "Take this, too. I prefer to drink it, but it can kill infection if you get arrowed by one of them savages out there."

Christopher took the bottle from him and held it up against the failing light in the shack. It looked dirtier than the river water, but he kept it anyway. "Well, I was just trying to relay the words I received from the camp. I am sure some one will be willing to help downriver."

"Good luck on that one. You beware of them that follow you along the riverbanks. They don't mean no good."

"I appreciate the supplies, Mr. Cornish. Perhaps I will see you again on my way back."

"Take care of yourself. We'll count on it."

Christopher met the other man back out on the dock. He had started to unwrap the rope from the cleat and held the canoe as Christopher eased back into it. Christopher untied the rope from the seat and tossed it to the dock. Mr. Cornish came out of the door carrying a padlock and locked the shack behind him. They both waved Christopher off as he drifted out into the stream and started to paddle against the current's slow pull. Christopher watched the two men wrap around the porch where they turned out and headed for the Ford pick-up. The vehicle started with a grumble in the stale afternoon. Mr. Cornish got in the truck on the passenger's side and the other man hopped into the back alongside an upturned wheelbarrow and other digging materials. Christopher rowed away from the shack and the ferry continued to putter on the horizon behind him. He watched the truck bounce down the gravel road, through the clearing, and then it disappeared behind a verdant knoll now protruding from the clearing. He thought some about what the man had said and became suspicious of the man's opinion more so than he was of the natives. That was a calming thought, only on the assumption that it was true. He did not want to think about it conversely. That would get him no further downriver. Fearful thoughts of uncertainties are no good for any man. These are destructive matters that Christopher had spent a lifetime trying to avoid. And what of this Cornish's words to have had any legitimacy? The man cared not for these people, or their inheritance. If things were going to happen in South America the way they did in the American West, misery would soon follow.

He steered his craft, skimming the waters with heavy oar and weak arm by night, the moon's round body as clear on the water as in the sky, the light lapping of water on the shores and the amphibious symphony following in blade or bush, a foreign serenity settling inside of the man. He paddled several miles more without seeing any other living creature, nor did he hear the steps of man or animal in the wilderness. He wiped his neck with the cool water and swatted at gnats and mosquitoes. One certainty grew within him; the insects felt much larger here. They had much more to feed on, and he feared some illness developing. He found himself too tired to row by the light of the moon and brought the canoe to a bank for the night. He did not make fire, or erect a shelter, and he lay, coverless, watching as the constellations flickered conspicuously in that vast blackness overhead.

The next morning he went through his pack and found an ample supply of dried food left. He had yet attempted to trap a rodent with the trap he brought, nor had he released any of his mother's matter. He believed that today would be a fine day for spending some time in the rainforest trapping. He made sure to hide the canoe and travel bag off of the shore and brought his bowie knife with him, tying it to his side. This he would use for cutting rope or skinning animals, or, at the height of desperation, defending himself. The first thing he did before entering the forest was tuck his pants deep into his boots, as well as tuck his long-sleeved shirt into the gloves he wore.

Foreign places that have been romanticized in the American mind hold certain nostalgia once immersed in them for the first time. This forest had been presented to him in various different forms since his youth, and now it had crept out of the realm of fantasy into a tangible reality, bringing with it the realization of man's capacity to appreciate certain existential elements by sight and sound, by complete awareness, a feeling of belonging. He felt the elements of the earth that sprouted from the ground like strands of extraterrestrial hair, the geological structures surreptitious in their marshy cloaks. Black rocks, bare and volcanic, looked down from overhead where he could see them on the hillsides through the forest canopy. The birds illuminated the forest unlike anything he had ever seen and when he heard their wings flapping, he looked and could see every spectral tint by the flight of a single flock.

He walked further into the forest notching his path from tree to tree and looked upon the grand colors and creatures inhabiting this strange land. Nearing noon, he finally decided to test his trap. The wooden box fit nicely in a carrier bag he wore and, along with the trap, he also carried a matchbox, a raw lunch, the urn, and his medical kit. He had seen a sundry of rodent life already. Trapping would be undemanding. He remembered how he had made the trap in his lonely apartment in the states. How he had split his finger wide open and how it had just now started to scab over in time to surpass infection, the serendipitous realizations of life. Christopher thought of Howerton and Jack-John and imagined them working their book collective in the days and drinking at Wrigley's at night, their lives passing them by without care or notice. It had always been that way for them, and would continue to be until they existed no longer.

He set the trap in a hollowed out tree and baited it with a hunk of cornmeal. The animal life in the forest was so plentiful that he might have been able to spear hunt with little trouble, but he decided to trap instead. The trap was his way of establishing a territorial advantage—a higher intellectual acumen over the animals made evident by his industry. His thirst, he could not quench from the salt of his hands, so he left the trap and headed for a spring calling from the north.

The fall sounded very great, and as he continued toward it, the forest harbored a darkness within its depths that he had not expected. Looking upward all the time, upon the mammoth-like height of the trees, the sun's scarcity at the forest floor made his footing unsure. Worsening with the darkness, there sprang a humidity unlike anything he had ever experienced and he instantly feared being among the lowest forms of life on this base tier of the rainforest.

When he came to the waterfall his gaze fell upon the largest clearing he had seen inside of the forest. An immense pool lapped directly in the middle of the opening and the sun came upon him there with no trees to fight for energy. His stomach dropped at the sight of the waterfall etched into the hillside beyond the pool and standing as large as the barrigonas. The face of the hillside from which the waterfall cascaded was so grand and bare that it would have been impossible to climb without gear.

He got completely naked and climbed into the great pool by the time the sun had started to fade behind the forest canopy. This was the cleanest water he had seen since his arrival. He had been on the river all of this time without once getting in. Creatures of foul intent could have lurked in either body of water, but this one was so clear that he could see his feet; thusly, he could also see anything that might try and attack. He heard a raptor's gawk overhead and watched a few tamarins' acrobatic movements in the understory of the great forest all around. Christopher swam up to an opening in the waterfall and climbed up on the slick rock and entered a shallow cave just on the other side of the water's drapery. An abundance of etchings marked the inner walls of the cave. He could make out the etching of a man with a bow, the sign of a jaguar, and a long snake that encircled the man and beast. He could see where a fire had blackened the sides of the cave. Potash from a residual fire. The natives were on the bounds in this great land, either hunting or scavenging. He walked in their footprints and become part of their land, their culture, the weight of their survival. He felt the age and the history embedded in the stone, the plight of those drudging before.

When he swam back to his clothing thousands of ants had formed, carrying leaves in a long line from the bank to their mound. Their organized highway system seemed much more efficient than anything humans could construct. Humans spend too much time worrying about themselves to act in such a manner as an ant—the creatures devotion bound to the central figure of their civilization, a tangible being. Christopher Corbin dressed himself and pulled the urn out of the bag. There is nothing ceremonial about the dispersion of ash and bone, the residual elements left of those no longer in existence. It is a much different feeling than the burial of a body. Something less concrete. The spreading of ashes remains a much more individualistic endeavor, for Christopher was faced with spreading the ashes of the woman who had birthed him, and from whom he had become so estranged and truculent toward. And he was now faced with making amends with the dead.

Christopher climbed out to a ledge that hung over the pool, urn in hand, and could see below where the water bubbled. The sun had completely revolted from the opening in the great canopy and the air had cooled. The breeze from the cascade filled the clearing and an uncertain bleakness quickly overcame this tiny oasis he had found. He unscrewed the cap of the urn and looked down into the container at the white ash and fragments of bone and tried to gather an image of her in his mind, but could not. He was certain that there had to be some fond memory residing somewhere in his body. Though he had been fond of his mother at times, he could not conjure a single thought. He did not owe her anything. With an unmotivated mumble, he uttered "to march to the beat of death's lonely drum now" to the speckle of symbolic ash and dumped a small amount into the pool and watched as it amalgamated with the shore foam and dispersed into the water. He looked back into the urn to measure the amount of matter left in the container. A third of her remains had been released. More to be released at a later time. At a later recognition. At a time when something spiritual may inspire his being. Soon, he would return to his trap to find that he had caught a baby Paca, and he would make his first right of passage in this forest, for he knew that he could now be self-reliant when it came to providing food. And this was a thought much more satisfying than trying to recall a memory of his deceased mother.

Michael

"How do you feel today, Mr. Corbin?" said Caroline as she entered Michael's room. He did not answer. "We have seen some great improvement in you, haven't we?"

"What answer would you like to draw out of me in response to that?" replied Michael.

Michael sat his chair in a blue button up shirt with slacks on that had the pant legs rolled to his ankles. He had started making his bed in the mornings and dressed himself immediately after waking. He felt that his robe only made him more anxious the longer he wore it in the mornings. He had also forced himself to read a few letters a week. As far as he could tell, there would be no more from Loretta. He read of Christopher and Carson's adventures, and was given some perspective on how operations went on the other side of the desk. He was not completely different from them. Michael now had hopes of changing.

"I am interested in your perception of your own rehabilitation."

"Is that not the problem, the way I perceive my own reality?"

"That, in itself, is very perceptive of you. I have many different patients, none as intelligent as you, and they all have different ways of rehabilitating. Some of them never do. I would hate to see that happen to you."

"And what would make me more intelligent than any one else in this ward?" said Michael, fishing for her to expound upon the compliment. He responded very well to compliments. Every person enjoys hearing others commend them for their attributes and Caroline was not ignorant of that. In fact, this happened to be one of the most successful of her rehabilitation techniques.

"You know that you form cogent thoughts on almost any subject ... when you feel like talking. The only destructive force I see in you is your advanced anxiety. This can lead to anger and desperation. These are the things that ruin you, Mr. Corbin, not your intellect."

"Would you say that there is any connection between the two?"

"I would say that it is very possible that you over examine things because of the immensity of your intellect."

Caroline could not see it because she stood behind him, but Michael smiled quite widely at this, and he felt of himself a superiority that he rarely felt.

"That is a nice thought," he said.

"On the contrary. This means that we have to work on both parts before you can be rehabilitated, and this can be a difficult process."

"But possible, nonetheless."

In a polite, but evident way Caroline pandered to him as one would a small child. Though she herself could not have been much older than he was, her actions toward him were very maternal. To many patients her actions could have been misconstrued as advances of affection. Michael was intelligent enough to know that she was good at playing other's needs, but that did not keep him from fantasy. If materialized, a relationship with her could help pass the time. Any sort of physical connection with her would likely reduce stress. Lately she had been showing him more affection because of his small successes. He saw it as a reward program that he had entered into with her. Currently, she rested her hand on his collar to smooth out where he had knotted it in the back. She pressed it out slowly and he could feel the hair stiffen erectly on the back of his neck.

"Yes, it is possible. That is what we hope for all of our patients here, and you are still a very young man. You are here by your own conviction. You have not been committed, nor have you committed any violent acts against another patient while here." Caroline came from behind him and walked over to where his typing table sat. She pulled out the small chair propped underneath the desk and turned it out to face Michael. She sat down, crossing her legs with nubile elegance, and Michael tried to keep his eyes from wandering as she did so. "What we are most concerned about is the harm that you could inflict upon yourself. You understand that, do you not?"

"Yes." His voice broke and started to shake. In his new confidence with himself he could not help but think about sexual acts with her.

"My seizures are also of great concern. I feel like I may worry about them so much at times that I am capable of causing them." Michael crossed his legs, mirroring her actions in an ungainly show of affection. He looked out of the window and could sense the burgeoning procreation of a new spring—a fresh new birth of all living things, the flowers blooming with their damp petals bowing and ready to burst. "And that is a horrible thought."

"The good thing about these seizures is that you have the power to obviate them from returning. It is completely dependent on your mental stability. If you keep with your routines, then you can steady yourself and feel at peace. And with that peace will come a stress-free synapse transaction, giving you the ability to fire on all cylinders."

Caroline looked at him with sincerity and concern. She turned to some of the envelopes that now sat on top of the typewriter and thumbed through them, as if familiar with each one. A blank sheet of paper, unused but folding at the top, rested inside of the typewriter's spool. She tugged at it to coax the action of the spool.

"This is a pretty nice Underwood you have here. My daddy had one like this that he used to type on when I was growing up," she said. Her eyes grew in recollection of some haunting memory, a hint of sorrow. "Of course, by the time he was done with it, it was in terrible shape. Not like this one."

"Do you want it?" asked Michael.

"Oh, certainly not. I believe that this typewriter could save your life, if you would ever make yourself use it."

"Can I ask you what your father did for a living?"

Michael crossed his legs again and tried to sit in an urbane fashion, if only to appear interested in their conversation, while enacting a peculiar reverse psychology unknowingly.

"He was a writer. He wrote mystery novels for forty years, or so." Caroline thumbed over the keys on the typewriter. "He used to work all morning, and then we would walk together down to the pier near our house. It must have been a four mile walk round-trip, but that was all the exercise and fresh air he said he ever needed." Caroline pecked at the keys. Michael could tell she was slowly typing something. "He used to get so worked up about producing that he never thought he did good enough. It turned him into an anxiety-ridden man, not unlike someone else I know. I always thought he'd done well enough for our family, but it was always in his writing that he was concerned."

"How could it save my life, if it produced more anxiety in your father? I believe that I want to stay away from stressors if I am going to do any better." Michael leaned up in his chair to try and see what she had started to write, but could not get a good look. He also tried to scan the seam of her dress down to where she had crossed her legs once more, but kept enough control of himself to look back up at her when she spoke.

"I believe that the anxiety had always been there, but writing was a way of harnessing some of that resting anxiety. Eventually, the stress transmuted from the stresses of life to just the writing. He made it to the age of sixty-five before he could stand it no longer. It is never forgivable for a person to give into depression, but I feel that his life would have been much shorter without the writing."

"Do you think that you do this work to save people like your father?" Michael still ogled her somewhat.

"I haven't known anything else. My mother was a nurse at this institution, and I followed in her footsteps. It is just in my nature to help people. To try and better their quality of life. I am satisfied enough with my own reality that I can lend my time to helping others become satisfied with theirs. I know, in my heart, that some people are born to help others. A chemical in our brains pushes all other selfish tendencies aside, and we gather our tranquility from the lives we touch. I do wish that I could have helped my father, but I feel like our walks may have been rehabilitative enough in their own right."

Michael came from his chair to console Caroline, for her eyes had started to well some with soft tears. Clumsily, he came to his knees and rested his hands on hers and then put a hand on her shoulder. "That is a hell of an optimistic outlook. I would guess that, if we cut you up into pieces, and split up your optimistic attitude between all of the patients, we would all be cured."

Caroline smiled at him and then wiped her eyes. She rested her head against his arm and then straightened up. Her hands fidgeted with his collar again.

"Thank you. Though slightly morbid, I appreciate your consolation." She came from her seat at the typing table and took his hand. "What do you say we get you outside some for the day?"

He could feel the warmth of her hand within his. It became evident that she was switching gears on him and her maternal affection had returned. Michael felt as though he had been succinct with his consolation and that he had not started to ramble verbally with his thoughts, as he was often accustomed to doing. She became more attractive to him with every conversation they had. Even if it had been one that ended badly. He knew that his levity was not everlasting and that the chore of any person that dealt with him was dealing with his erratic bouts of anger. Though Caroline was skilled in dealing with abnormal emotional tendencies, it seemed to hurt her the most when he scolded her. It could have been that she was confused by his capricious shift out of coherence. It seemed as though something lived inside of him that held such a begrudging enragement with everything earthly and human. However, he had proven himself to be of good counsel. At least presently.

He looked her over once more, trying not to be too apparent in his ravenous aspirations. "That would be fine. It seems like spring is on the bounds and the sun does not seem to be too brilliant."

She let go of his hand and went for the door.

"Get yourself a good pair of walking shoes on. I will see you down there."

She turned and went out of the room. He watched her all the way until the door was completely closed. A pair of his loafers sat at the foot of his bed, and as he put them on, he looked outside to see the clouds move across the sky with great ambition. He watched sparrows bounce from tree to tree pecking at the wet sod and grubbing for worms. Several other patients were out in the courtyard doing stretches with Dr. Smothers. He had them doing side stretches and had them flailing their arms in strange aerobic convulsions and they all looked out of sequence. Michael could hear the doctor yelling.

"Gawdry! You look like a damned goon. Get your arms together in sequence with mine. You see how I do it. Briggs! You look worse than Gawdry, and he has less of a brain than you do! Come on folks, this isn't neuroscience. Gawdry! How many times do I have to tell you to not eat the damn grass!"

Michael looked across the yard to see Caroline at the main entrance of the building. She had changed into a pair of sneakers, but still wore the tight nurse's dress that he enjoyed seeing her in. She walked out and looked up at his window and waved at him to come down. He waved back and stepped away from the window and tied his shoes. When he looked back out, she was standing by Dr. Smothers. Michael could see that he had his hand on her hip. Then he watched him slide his hand lower onto her backside. Then he slid it even lower to the inside of her leg where the meat of her backside met her upper leg. Caroline brushed off his hand and smiled playfully and walked back over to the entrance of Michael's ward. Michael felt the jealousy and anger boiling within him, but it was a calm anger. No definitive proof existed that Caroline had fucked Dr. Smothers. He knew he must go down to meet her. No other choice existed. He was more of a man than that. He could not sit and pout. His rehabilitation needed withstanding.

Outside, the air was warm and crisp feeling. Spring's ephemeral warmth had arrived in New England and a breath of new life blew through the ward's courtyards. When Michael came to her outside she was sitting down on the front step of the building's stoop, overlooking the patients as they exercised. Smothers continued to yell at them violently. Everything about the man now made Michael's blood boil. He hated him for saving his life, for yelling at the other patients, for touching his girl like that. Michael could have seen him struck dead right there with no remorse. Even if nothing had transpired between the two, the man was married, and had been way too handsy with Caroline. The man's wife would certainly agree if she had seen. If Michael could inflict pain on him, he would, given the chance.

"Nice day for staring at mutants?"

She turned around and came from her seat on the steps. "That is not a very nice thing to say. I have talked to you about that. Are you not going to be well out here?"

"I will be just fine. I will be fucking fantastic. And I will skip and throw my hair around and be a flighty little bitch." He looked at her with that possessed smile he held so many times when his mind went rogue.

"Okay, Mr. Corbin. Maybe we need to get you back into your room," said Caroline, trying to usher him back into the building.

He pushed her hands off of him in such a violent way that he almost knocked her down. He could tell that somewhere in his mind a voice was telling him to calm down, but it was impossible at this point. He had spent the entire walk from his room trying to calm down, but had only become more enraged. She turned to holler for Dr. Smothers, but before she could utter a single word, he grabbed her by the neck and put his hand over her mouth. She struggled, trying to break free from his grasp, but it was to no avail. He found himself dragging her back into the building. She tried to wiggle free and struck him about the face, and anywhere that her fists could land, but it was of no use. He was quite strong when he got to a certain point. Michael could feel the remorse starting to grow within him as he watched her struggle. No longer was he a victim of her transgressions. No longer was she the woman who looked at him with such acceptance. He had become the monster he feared so much. No longer did he feel like he wanted to fight for anything, much less her. He let her go and sat down against the wall and began to sob uncontrollably. She came from his grasp and took off toward the door. Before she reached out to flee the building she turned back and looked at the sad shell of a man sobbing against the wall with his head in his hands, his collar pushed up against the wall. She had to lean over to catch her breath. Caroline looked out of the window to make certain that no one had noticed the attack and decided to address him before she pursued a call for help.

"What is all of this about? What were you planning on doing to me?"

She could hear a muffled answer come from behind his crying.

"What?"

"Are you fucking him?"

"Who?"

"That asshole doctor."

"Smothers?"

"Yes."

"Well, of course we make love."

Michael looked up from the wall where he stooped with his head in his hands.

"He is my husband," she said.

"Husband?"

"Yes. We have been married for close to five years now. What were you planning on doing to me? I need to know what my next move is here."

"I just didn't want you to yell out to him. I did not mean to harm you any. I just thought you were sleeping with a married man."

"I am. But I am the woman that he has chosen to spend his life with."

"How could I have not known until now? I have never seen him touch you like he did today. And you don't have a wedding ring of your own."

"It is not professional to act on your marital urges while at work." She straightened out her uniform and fixed her hair. "My line of work is not very conducive to wearing a ring. I work with my hands regularly."

Michael started to tap his head against the wall in recognition of his stupidity. "And your last name is Smothers?"

"Of course. Perhaps you should find out more about the women you obsess over before you attack them." She smirked at him with a strange acknowledgment of his actions and went out of the building.

Michael sat there in his own pity for a time until he managed to get up. He went to the door and watched her walk across the courtyard. She waved at the doctor and went back through the doors of the main entrance. He was glad that she did not mention anything to the man.

That would save him some embarrassment. He collected his dignity and made for the door. Some fresh air would calm his nerves. Perhaps they could recover their friendship, even after this. He did not know what would come next for him, but he did know that he never intended to be a violent man. With an optimistic view of his previous actions, he knew that he was a passionate man, and that was better than being a lifeless man.

Carson

"This here's Sinclair country," he said as they passed the truck stop at an industrious pace. The sun was setting slowly over the mountains of western Montana. A curling blue, faceless blur had become of the sky. Valencia leaned back in the passenger seat of the cruiser with her feet up on the dash. She shifted upward to look out of the window for a moment. An emblem of a dinosaur with a Sinclair sign tight in its jowls stood next to a single-pump gas station with lights flickering, possibly buzzing.

"Looks like we are in Dinosaur country," she replied.

"Nope. Where I come from is dinosaur country. This American west is Sinclair country. That is when all the gas stations turn from your normal Shell or Valero, to Sinclair. You will see an abundance of DQ's as well." Carson shifted into fifth gear. He put his hand on her knee.

The low planking sound of the tires on asphalt came whirring in through the side windows of the cruiser. The back seat had been filled with Valencia's belongings—clothing mostly, and some stacks of paper—a few kitchen appliances. The speedometer read sixty-five and the tachometer dropped back down, almost parallel with the dash.

"DQ's?" asked Valencia.

"Dairy Queens. They are just about in every town out here," he replied.

"Glad to be with such an aged gas station and fast-food enthusiast." Valencia leaned her chair forward and took one of the pictures down from the ceiling of the cruiser.

"I used to be enthusiastic about the DQ. That was before they stopped the dollar burger. Everyone inflates their prices now."

"I just can't believe we will be in Washington tomorrow. You are certain that you will get work there?"

"Yes'm. I called Jim and he already has us a cabin ready, and some work for me to start as soon as we get there. He also said that we get our own work vehicle." Carson squeezed her leg and smiled. "It is getting to be the most tolerable time of year from what he says. What do you say?"

"I came along. Not much else I need to say. I just want you to stay busy. I have my own work to do, so I can't keep an eye on you the whole time we are there. And you know that you will start to get miserable if you can't find something to do." Valencia pushed his hand away from her leg and looked out of the window. Light rain speckled the glass. "I won't be able to stand it if you get bored out there, assuming you have not changed much."

"I will be fine. There'll be fences to build and paths to clear. I may start trying to build and sell canoes."

"That is a thought."

"Indeed. I think you worry about me and my idleness the way I worry about Mikey."

"That is because you are an adequate brother."

"Strange compliment, but I will take it. I am not to be worried about. I am a grown man who can make his own decisions. I intend to treat you with respect. You know that, don't you?"

"Yes. But that doesn't mean that I will not worry about the possibility of you having one of your dark days. That thought, alone, made me hesitant to come."

"You have your days as well," replied Carson. He now drove with one hand on the wheel and the other picking at his beard.

"Very true. We will be just fine. We are grownups, and can address issues as they come."

"Good enough," said Carson.

"I am glad you decided to come for me," Valencia said.

"As am I," he replied.

"Please don't make me regret it."

"I won't."

When they pulled into the ranch it was late afternoon. The cruiser had struggled upon entering the mountains and Carson's relief followed as they passed a sign hanging between two tall pines that carried the emblem of Jim McNally's ranch. Further down the road a tail of smoke spiraled from a chimney atop a small cabin. They could hear elks bugling. Some bits of snow still sat against the hills with pine roots breaking through, the copses of pines and aspens forever deepening in that white mist beyond. The smell of this great nature was effervescent and profound, a beauty never appreciated from picture or story alone. A figure at the window of the cabin moved, standing up, and left from sight. They watched as the side door opened and a tall, lurking figure clambered out into the snow. Carson pulled in after the man. He came around to the passenger's window and tapped loudly on the glass until Valencia rolled it down.

"Whatcha say, neighbors." The man's voice was hoarse, but cheerful. "Near ready to turn in, I imagine. Look at this pretty little number here. What is your name, sweetie?" He leaned in and extended his greeting to the girl.

"Valencia Marie Mott," she answered and exchanged pleasantries. "Jim?"

"That is right ma'lady. Damn, are you a pretty little thing. Why didn't you tell me you were bringing this New England breeze with you, Carson? My lord, you are one hell of a beauty."

Jim McNally had almost climbed inside of the cab by this point. Carson reached out his hand to shake the man by the shoulder. "I appreciate the hell out of you for helping us," he said.

"Not a problem at all. I need help, and you guys are a godsend. I know how hard of a worker you are, Carson. Shit, girl. You ever seen this man work?"

"I have seen him try to figure out how to open up a bottle with his teeth when he couldn't find an opener," she replied.

"Only a testament to his determination," said Jim. "That man next to you is just about the hardest, most industrious son of a buck I have ever seen. He would damn near kill himself with effort before he ever gave up on a job, from what I have seen him do. Probably the same way he does with his ladies, by looking at you."

Valencia smiled at the man.

"Come on now," he said. "Pull on in and come inside. I will give you the particulars."

Jim McNally slid back out of the window and turned toward the cabin. He motioned with one arm for them to park behind an old Dodge that sat collecting drifts of snow. A shepherd came to the door and looked out, but would not dare the cold. It nudged the man's knee with its wet snout and followed him back inside.

"He is enthusiastic," said Valencia.

"Just about the craziest person I know, except for Michael of course," replied Carson.

"That isn't a nice thing to say."

"It is the truth. Doesn't make any difference whether or not it's a nice thing to say."

"I guess so," she said.

They pulled up behind the Dodge. The cruiser slid into the slicks of snow when he hit the brakes, almost striking the truck, but regained traction before they reached the bumper. Carson got out and went around, opening the door for Valencia, and she followed him, leaving their bags in the back seat along with their large winter coats. The two of them shuffled through the snow, underdressed, and Valencia almost slipped trying to make it to the entrance of the shack. Inside, the cabin was warm and smelt heavily of pine and spray foam. Jim stoked the fire with an iron rod, orange at the tip. His shepherd sat on a rug, now inundated with gray hair, with an authoritative acknowledgement of its own territory. About the cabin hung several silver pots and the taxidermy of big game. A moose, some elk, a bear flattened out with its jowls straightened by the wooden floor. They could hear the ululation of a wolf lost somewhere in the wilderness over the crackling of embers. Carson took Valencia in his arms to warm her. Jim turned from the fire to see the two of them standing in the hallway shivering.

"Come on by the fire. No sense in being cold if you don't have to," said Jim.

They walked through the hallway stepping over the animal pelts on the floor and stood in front of the fireplace with hands outstretched like vagrants around a trash barrel. The dog looked up briefly and then put his wispy, old head back down on the rug. The cabin's design was such that it consisted of only one room with no partitions and a kitchen with a curtain dividing the washtub and toilet. Jim's bed, or small cot, sat in the back corner of the cabin. Bookcases lined the walls, separated by the kitchen and bathroom, and it truly seemed to be an isolated existence that Jim McNally lived. His purpose in life assumed this simple form, and no other purpose did he assume.

"You sure are living the high life," said Carson. "You aren't out here building bombs, are you?"

"I could be," replied Jim. He set the prod against the fireplace and walked over to the kitchen. Jim shuffled through some of his cabinets and called for them to go ahead and sit down. A love seat and rocking chair sat by the fire, as well as a coffee table and a couch end, but no couch. "You still take whiskey stout?" he asked Carson.

Carson let Valencia sit on the love seat. He took the couch end. "Whatever you have would be fine," he replied. "Valencia likes the hard stuff. I wouldn't mind a beer if you have one."

"I have a couple out in the snow if you want to go grab one. They are just sitting in a little pile near the front door. Might as well drink them before I forget about them and they end up sitting there flat when the snow thaws out," said Jim. He poured three glasses of whiskey—two full, and one shot for Carson. "Just my kind of girl. Valencia, you are a hard liquor drinker, no?"

He brought the glasses over to the coffee table and handed Valencia her drink and set Carson's down on the table. He sat back in the rocking chair and waited for Carson to come back in before he would drink. Valencia smiled at him and nodded, smelling the dark liquid as it rocked in the glass. Carson came back with the ring of beers in his hand. Much to Carson's dismay, only three cans remained in the plastic six-pack ring. He popped one out and raised it. "Cheers."

They raised their glasses in unison and began to imbibe. Carson shot his whiskey quickly and proceeded to gulp the beer. "Where is the closest store?" he said, letting the beer and whiskey settle in his stomach.

"You ready to leave this soon?" replied Jim.

"No. Just wanted to know, for when we need provisions." He

shook his beer can to signify what he was mostly concerned with.

"Well, you won't have to worry about that tonight. I have enough booze here to keep us well stocked for the week. But to answer your question, the store is an hour drive. So when you do go for things, you have to stock up. It makes life out here much easier. It also helps you to improve your rationing skills."

"That sounds delightful," said Valencia. "My first real chance to feel like I am living off of the grid."

"You certainly are, my little darling," said Jim. "Living out here puts many things into perspective. It is similar to being out on the ocean for months at a time. You have to really hone in on yourself and find your own path to tranquility."

"Jim does so by making bombs and planning for the end of the world," said Carson. He had already opened another beer and was sucking it down.

"False," replied Jim. "Take it easy on that beer, buddy. That is the last of them, and you will have to switch to whiskey next. And you know you can't drink whiskey that way." He smiled at Valencia and nursed his own drink to demonstrate his self-control. "I am perfectly fine out here, and have no qualms with human nature, nor do I want to hurt anybody or isolate myself from my community. I just feel that my path out here is one to self-betterment. I exercise every day, and exercise my own right to abstain from the poisons of an overabundant culture. A good example is how people from a city like Chicago live with entertainment at a moment's notice. They never have to worry about where their stimuli will come from next. It is beneficial for me to read and work and depend solely on myself for satisfaction." Jim McNally set his drink down and watched Valencia. She looked around the room at all of his collections. He then looked at Carson and raised his glass once more to him. "And you will be able to do the same, now that I have gotten you out here. Some solace you will find, my dear friend."

Carson raised his can and looked over at Valencia, who now seemed preoccupied with the wonder of this strange, simplistic place.

"And the post office is an hour away as well, I assume?" she said.

"Yes, dear. Carson told me you are a journalist. It will be no problem for me to take in your articles any time I go to town. That is typically once a week, to check on supplies for the cabins and see what the word is on the tourism front. It should be a busy season out here. Also, I'm sure that most of our visitors will do us a favor by taking your work back into town with them when they leave." Jim leaned up in his chair and eyed her over. "You wouldn't mind helping with turnover, would you?"

"That will be no problem. I came here to help as much as I can. I just write to keep my job and my sanity," she replied.

"Outstanding," said Jim. He fell back into his seat. "Neither of us will be able to keep up with Carson here, but I think that goes for more than just working."

Carson had already broken into the third beer. "Got to settle in from all of the driving. I am sure you can understand," he said.

"I understand. Do you want me to have a drink ready for you when you are done with that one?" Jim laughed and looked at Valencia. "How is your drink?"

"Just fine," she replied. She looked over at Carson with some concern. "You should attempt to slow down some, honey."

They were set up in the cabin later that night. Valencia and Jim had to drag Carson's limp body in and put him down on the bed in their new room. It was very soft and warm under the sheets when he awoke, and she was not sleeping next to him. He looked around the room for her, but did not see her anywhere. He thought not much else of it and immediately went back to sleep. In the morning she was already up and going about the room unpacking and getting their personals arranged. He rolled over to feel that her side of the bed was still warm and unmade, so she must have slept next to him. He wondered if he had only dreamt that she was not in the room when he awoke in the night. Carson watched as she decorated the room with some of the things she had brought from her own apartment, and he could taste the metallic sharpness of bile on the roof of his mouth. His head throbbed as if he had slept with a rubber band around his neck all night. She did not turn to look upon him when he came-to.

"Good morning, Val," he said, his voice rough and grainy. He coughed and leaned over to look at the clock on the bed stand. "Only eight. I still got it."

"I have been up since six trying to get us settled in before you got up," she said. Her voice held a noticeable amount of agitation. "You are going to be productive today, aren't you?"

"Depends," he responded. "I'll have to see what Jim wants me to do. If he wants us just to get settled in for the next couple of days, then I plan on doing just that."

"Your idea of getting settled in doesn't consist of you drinking all day, does it?" She looked at him, her face upturned and pugnacious.

"Wait until I get out of bed at least before you get on me. You know that I was just unwinding last night." The man leaned up in the bed and pulled the covers down to his waist. He was in good shape for the amount of alcohol he put into his body, and she could not help but look at him as he moved about in the bed, naked to the hip.

"Unwind? You drank his whole bottle of whiskey single handedly."

"I saw him pour you both a glass," he responded in defense.

"And that was it. We watched you go through that whole damn thing, while we remained sober and steady until it came time to put you to bed."

"And then what did you two do?"

He looked at her with sullen, incredulous eyes. He was a strong, stern looking man that could never tolerate foolery from anyone other than himself. Perhaps this was a trait that made him less of a man. Valencia knew the meaning of his apprehension, but did not give. Her stature remained strong and her voice was rigid when she spoke.

"We did nothing. He showed me where all of the linens and bathroom supplies were, and then left the room like a gentlemen. He also apologized for your actions, and apologized for allowing you to drink that much." Valencia talked with such condescension that her response seemed contrived.

"I wonder where you went off to when I woke up in the middle of the night. Are we going to chalk that up to a dream?"

"We will have to, Car, because I got into bed with you as soon as we put you down, and did not get out until six this morning." She looked at him now like he had lost his mind.

It was possible that he had dreamt. It was also possible that he had not. Nevertheless, he left the conversation at that and got out of the bed and put his pants on. The wooden floor felt cold on his feet, making him want to already give up on the day—that, along with the specious activities of the night before, made him want to crawl back in bed, but his orders had been specific and immediate surrender would not be allowed. The driving force of most drunkards after a long night that yields a painful morning is either food or another drink. If one played it correctly, one could have both, and that became Carson Corbin's ambition this morning. Valencia had already unpacked all of their winter gear and laid out an outfit for him to wear for the day. He had a fresh pair of coveralls to put on over his jeans and t-shirt. Also, he had a black scarf and another overcoat to layer himself with. When they went outside they could see the northern Cascades like blue clouds lying in the hazy distance far off to the north. The ranch, nestled in between two low-lying mountain saddles, sat on a grassy plain that had now turned marsh from the spring's thaw. He could see the other six cabins for the first time and it was apparent that they were all in need of great repair. Just from the condition that they were in externally, he knew he would have at least two weeks' worth of roofing to do. Every cabin needed caulking and painting, and that would add another two weeks, and some of the porches sagged close to the ground, warranting attention as well. Carson knew that he would have to get to work if they were going to have a successful season.

"Yep," he said to Valencia. "I imagine I will have the opportunity to be productive today. These cabins are in poor shape. I wonder what the hell Jim has been doing out here."

"He has probably been getting the roads in shape for people to come out here. And he said last night that he has done a lot of interior work on the cabins." Valencia grabbed him by the hand and snuggled up against his arm as they walked the perimeter.

The cabins had been built in a row on the side of a small pond.

Next the pond stood a bronze statue of an elk with its head lowered to the water, as if drinking by some inanimate miracle. They could see the gravel road through the furrows of plowed snow and it ran downhill to a thicket of pines where some smoke billowed. Jim's cabin sat further down at the base of the hill, invisible save for the tail of chimney smoke. He liked his privacy so much that he did not want to have to see his visitors, nor they him. Carson decided to take the path down to Jim McNally's afoot. The cruiser, already blanketed with snow, looked like it had been there for years without moving an inch. There is something about the snow that gives an antiquated look to things—an equivocal distinction between earth and sky conjured from a blank canvas of white.

The path leading from the cabins was interspersed with soft snow and hard ice and the two struggled to walk it with grace, Carson especially. He could feel the hunger growing within him like something ungodly, something impure. It was a hunger that stemmed, not only from expanding his stomach with liquor, but also from his epicurean taste, a ravaging of all things satisfying; liquor to follow the meal, sex to follow the liquor, everything becoming so necessary already this early in the morning. He would have to fight it in order to get anything done. He knew that as well as he knew the taste in his mouth and the want in his mind. The ghosts of his own mental dissatisfaction were soon haunting him with every breath. Yes, he would have to fight it if he were going to be the right man for her. If he wanted to get past what he thought had already happened between Valencia and Jim. Though, that felt like a reason to give in and not fight, but he was a man, and that sort of capitulation was not for men. Strong men, with great tenacity, do not surrender to life's miseries completely. More important causes existed to fight for. He thought of these things as they traveled down the slippery path toward the smoke billowing over the hill, and they would talk to Jim, and he would know what would become of Carson's day, and he would know what would become of Valencia. These were things too certain to deny.

Michael

Mikey,

I trust that my letters have continued to reach you. It is hard to keep track without a response. I think I wrote you from Wyoming last. One hell of a journey. I am currently traveling the east coast some. Unfortunately, I have been elected to send the bad news to you. If this is belated, then so be it. You will not evade it forever. Our mother has just passed. This is the way it should be, if only to end her pain.

I really wish that I could have told you this in person, but you live by your own rules. As have I. I will be going to see our brother soon. He has got the wild idea to go down to South America. Crazy little bastard. I am sure he will tell you in his letter, and perhaps he will reiterate the details of Loretta's death. I hope that you can assume this loss with resilience. She did love you the most. You abided all of her shit, and she loved to give it. Everyone has a breaking point, and yours just happens to have padded walls. Mine has an aluminum can surrounding it. Christopher's is infested with mosquitoes the size of your arm. I would love to come see you, but we both know that it's a waste of time for me to drive there. I have done it a few times to no avail. I will await your word before I come again. Just know that we can talk about anything. The longer you are in there, the more I start to understand. Perhaps time wears you down. But time should not have the ultimate say. Just give me the word, and I'll shoot right over there, no matter where I am. I will be heading for Washington next. I believe the pony express runs out there too. You may not hear from Christopher for some time, as I am unsure of how he will get letters out of the jungle, but I am hopeful that he will bring us back plenty of souvenirs. We both love you very much, and we hope Loretta's passing does not hinder your rehabilitation.

Best,
Carson

Christopher

He had been on the river for nearly a month now and his count of days had lost its exactness. His failure to make note of each sunset had left him unaware of his time spent in the jungle. Some days had been more pleasant than others. Some days had been dreadful. The insects alone could drive a man to insanity. A fungus had started to culture on his feet and it itched and burned ferociously. His attempts at keeping his extremities dry had failed. It was always the unloading of the canoe onto unknown shores that got him. Marshland lurked inward from the banks, stretching for miles on either side of the river, buzzing with insect life and shrouded by creeping saurian as he had passed abandoned villages. The buildings now slowly sinking into the ground from which they had been assembled like some eerily post–apocalyptic wasteland. He witnessed burnt huts sitting in ashy rubble—the color of soot intermingling with the verdant flora waterside, surreal and dreamlike. It was as if he saw the future of the entire forest in small intervals as he passed; the chopping of trees, the building of cabins, the eventual destruction of the cabins, nothing but ruin. And he thought of oil. What it would cost this great land. What would men do to succeed in such a place? He wondered now what had happened to these villagers as he went deeper into the forest. The paths of men hidden by an abundance of vegetation. He watched scavengers sail overhead. They had been following him for the past few days. His discarded scraps of paca giving reason to trail if animal or man.

After pulling around a wide bend in the river with great haste and strength Christopher caught a glimpse of something moving slowly on the shore ahead. From a distance he could not decipher the origin of the creature flailing there, but the figure started to materialize as he drew near. It was a small boy with one arm waiving. He was very brown and naked there. He was moving frantically on the white sand. Christopher could now hear the boy's wild screams and started to

143

paddle toward him. As he drew closer, he could see that the boy was not alone. Several bodies surrounded him, lifeless, along the bank. And then he could see the splattered spectra of color on the sand. It was blood. The white of sand and brown of dried blood had become one. Something near a dozen bodies, and the boy. He had not the will or want to count. Something so common to man becomes so unrecognizable when met in surprise and ignorance. The boy himself looked to be in horrible disrepair. His one arm not waiving was tied in a shirt. Blood had perforated through. Christopher could tell that the boy's arm had been broken. He drew closer still. The young American picked up the paddle, pulled it into the cabin, and took a deep breath to gather his thoughts. He looked to his right, nothing but jungle—to his left, the same. He closed his eyes. Opened them again. The boy was still there, screaming. He was closer now and could see the boy's eyes grow wide with fear. The boy dropped his arm and ran for the woods.

"Hey!" Christopher yelled out to him, but the boy did not stop running.

Christopher pulled his canoe onto the bank and looked around at all of the bodies lying swarthy with blood. Horror welled within him. He walked the scene and looked at the now immobile objects. He could see an order to the bodies, something distinct. He had to ruminate over it in his mind and inventory it thusly before he could understand. After turning over a few of the bodies he could tell the pattern in which they had been killed. It was a single shot to the forehead. The distinct matter in which this act had been performed now became clear to him. They had been aligned in a row from shortest to tallest—in a direct line, the markings etched in the sand—and had been shot one by one, directly, and left on the beach. He had never seen anything like it, excepting pictures depicting genocide, war, the horrors of mankind. It'd been done in the fashion of a firing squad. It was execution. And what of the little boy? Were these his family members?

Christopher knew not what to do. He sat on the bank for a while and stared out at the river. He thought about Sacristo and his family and tried to imagine what, or who, had caused this massacre, and then he thought of the little boy with the one waiving arm. Christopher had entirely forgotten about him once he saw the bodies. The horror of this poor lot, now forever without breath or action, had clouded his mind. He took his pack from his canoe and went off into the jungle.

Every acre of the rainforest grew denser, making it nearly impossible to trail the boy's footprints through the soil. Christopher instead found a blood trail on the hands of the great leafs tracking deeper into the forest. The boy's wound would keep him from traveling very quickly, so he followed the trail by sight and tried not to fear the darker forces that now burned an ungodly terror into the back of his mind. Each snap of a twig in this dark forest now made his heart pound. A sickness grew in his stomach with each thought. The memory of the dead figures on the beach was beginning to process completely and he could see them all. He smelled the steam seeping upward from the fertile earth. He vomited a small amount of his breakfast gut into a copse of ferns and continued on after the boy.

After trailing the blood for half an hour he came upon a small village hidden deep within the forest. A few two-story cottages, typical of the architecture he had seen, stood, aligned in the shape of an open triangle, with ladders clinging to their facades. A well sat in the center. Leaning against the well was the boy, rocking back and forth, holding his arm and sobbing. The boy did not notice Christopher at first, but then perked up when he heard the man's steps creeping through the bush.

"Hey!" Christopher yelled.

The boy ran into one of the cottages and Christopher could hear the aching force of a door slam. He ran toward the center of the village and stopped to listen. He heard the metal slate used for a lock slide down from the inside of the door and connect to its metal clasp at the door joist. The young American went for the door.

"I am not here to hurt you." Christopher stood there for a time until he heard steps ascend to the top-story porch where the boy now stood holding a bow made of polished wood. It already had an arrow chambered and pulled back, the point fixed upon Christopher's chest. Christopher moved back slowly and shook his hands at the boy to let him know he meant no harm. The boy eased the action of the bow. "Please," Christopher said in a low, calm voice. "I just want to help you." He slowly took his pack and set it on the ground. He held out a hand for the boy to let him fetch something. The boy eased up even more on the bow. Christopher took his medical kit from his pack and held it up at the boy. The man pointed at the boy's arm. It was limp past the elbow where the bow rested. "I can set that for you," said Christopher. "I had to do it once for my brother. You will feel better."

The boy looked at him blankly. Christopher motioned with his own arm to show that he could straighten and set the break. He held up the medical kit once more after miming his medical intentions. The boy could no longer hold up the bow with his gimp arm. He winced when he set it down. The pain in his arm had clearly overpowered the adrenaline pumping through his body.

"Ingles," the boy said.

Christopher nodded.

"These you do," said the boy. He grabbed his arm. "All these. Ingles is by devil, thee way you come."

Christopher knelt down at his pack to show that he was yielding and motioned for the boy to come down. The boy did not move. "I don't know how much you understand, but I am not one of them," said Christopher. "I am no bad English. I do not come with evil."

"All ingles bad. You same. Ingles want fear for boy and girl," replied the boy. He was starting to whimper, either from the pain in his arm or the massacre of his village. Christopher knew not which, but hated both equally.

"I am here for my mother. I am not here for your land, or to hurt you. Or anybody else."

"Madre? You madre here?" The boy pointed at the ground.

Christopher held up a finger to indicate once again that he was getting something out of his bag. The boy flinched when he reached into the pack. Christopher brought the urn from the bag and showed it to the boy. The boy was lost to the man's display. He looked upon Christopher with a residue of malice in his eyes and shook his head.

"What these you do. These no make sense." He pointed at the urn.

Christopher unscrewed the lid, took out a handful of ash and bone, and tossed it into the air. The wind caught it and it disappeared in a white plume. "This was my mother. She died. I have brought the ashes of her body here," said Christopher. "It is ceremonial ... like what your people do for burial."

The boy turned pale. He pointed at the urn. "These, you burn thee own, ingles?"

"Some people do. My family did."

"These me family do." He set the bow against the side of the cottage and stood there for a while contemplating. He looked to the forest and then over the grounds. The boy waved Christopher on like a truculent worker in need of production.

Before Christopher could repack the urn he heard the latch slide back up behind the door and watched as it opened. The boy motioned him in and turned back into the dark room. Christopher took his medical kit in his hands and threw the pack straps over his shoulders. When he entered the small cabin he could smell the dank odor of roots drying. It was absent of furniture save for a dining table that the boy now sat upon. Several foreign foods hung out to dry on the walls, stretched over dowel rods and thick wire. In one corner sat an entire cask of corn meal. The boy stared directly at the ground without expression. He must have been losing energy from his body trying to combat the injury. Christopher looked around the room for a splint to set the arm with. Underneath one of the grain sacks sat a pallet. He took the pallet and leaned it against a wall and broke it with a couple of kicks. The boy watched him as he scrambled through the shack to assemble his medical supplies. Christopher then got a short piece of canvas cloth hanging from one of the dowels and brought it over to the boy. His first line of business was to clean the cut. He did so quickly with iodine and a wet cloth. The boy fought him little, though the bone had surfaced through the skin, as Christopher tied the wound tightly with a tourniquet made of shirt cloth and then set the arm on the wood splint and cradled it in a sling made from the canvas. The boy whined some when he tightened the strap that held the arm to the wood, but it was unbelievable, the amount of pain the boy could handle. Christopher had the boy stand up so that he could test the comfort of the sling. It was high on his chest so Christopher lowered it some while the boy fought a developing whimper.

"What happened?" asked Christopher. He pointed to the arm.

The boy shrugged with a horrified look on his face. "Ingles. Come many times for land. No for we to give. Thee land of many padres." The boy sat back down on the table and stared up at Christopher. His eyes started to fill with tears. "These won ingles, he say he tell us these las time."

"Was there a leader of the English?"

"Tree men wif gun. One wif beeg chest." The boy poked out his own chest to show some sort of physical stature. A sign of confidence or zeal perhaps.

"And he did this?" Christopher put his hand on the slung arm. The boy flinched.

"Yes, wif long end of gun, for I no let go me madre, den he break."

"Are you the only one left?"

"No, thay are more, in woods. Ingles leave all boys and girls. For we now have fear. Thay been try to teach ingles."

Christopher took the boy by the good arm to help him get back up from the table. "Come on," he said. "We should find those in the woods."

The boy fought him off. "No!" he hollered. "Thay will see you dead."

"See me dead," said Christopher. "But why?" He let the boy go and stood back with his hands up in a sign of deference.

"Ingles, I would have see you dead for me arm would no be broke." The boy stood up and started toward the door. Christopher followed. "All go dare for ingles come, stay for night. I no run, you see me."

"How many times have you seen these men?"

"No how many, seen dem from I was child, come for some times a year."

"They kill before?"

"First time thay kill. First time we fight."

"I see. But they have guns. And your arrows cannot beat guns."

The boy looked at him blankly. Outside of the cabin it was growing dark and the boy looked around to see if anyone had returned. "I seen ingles bury dead. Put sticks at thee tops of dem," he said.

"I have also. That has been the usual tradition," replied Christopher.

The boy nodded and grabbed at Christopher's pack. Christopher took it off and let the boy go through it. He pulled out the urn and smoothed it over with one hand. "These you madre in ash?"

"Yes," replied Christopher.

"We put fire to dead and put as ash for thee land." The boy handed Christopher the urn and pointed at it with an understanding look. "These how you not thee same ingles."

It did not take long for the first one to attack. He must have been a boy of about ten, but he came upon Christopher like he had nothing left to live for. The boy he'd mended had gone to gather wood when the attack began. Christopher was rearranging the items in his pack when he felt the hollow burn of a tree limb crash into the back of his skull. It took him a moment to realize what had happened before he turned to see the boy coming at him again with the switch. Christopher was able to deflect the second blow when it came. He then got to his knees in an attempt at admonishing the boy. Before he could grab the child to get him to stop, he was knocked to his knees again by a much heavier and more powerful blow from behind. He could not turn around in time to stop the second blow that caught him on his right shoulder from his side and then a small fist to the side of his head. He could feel his teeth start to jar and rattle in his mouth from the onslaught of the next few blows that struck him from what seemed like every direction. He fell to his face and the blows kept coming as he tried to gather his position to counter. There seemed to be kicks and whops from feet and tree limbs battering him non-stop, a rain of slowly fatal hits pouring all over his body. He finally got to his feet to see four small bodies working at him. He did not want to hurt a single one of them, but he had to defend himself at this point. He started by going after the tallest and strongest looking of them. It was a girl of about thirteen that he aimed for first. He grabbed her by the hair, to which she detested and screamed like a banshee, and threw her to the ground. She snarled and tried to gash at him with her nails frantically. While she was still struggling to get up he grabbed the switch from the first attacker, picked him up around the belly, and started to whop his legs and back until the boy began to squeal. Next came the worse pain any of them had administered. One of the children that had remained free from his counter strike swung the heavy end of a tree limb into his genitals, bringing him to the ground once again in immediate distress. Once he had been grounded the children piled on top of him with all they had and started to scratch and tear at his clothes like terrestrial piranhas swarming upon fallen game. One of the children started kicking at the back of his head to try and bash in his skull—a move picked up from hunting wounded game—until Christopher gathered his bearings again. This time, when he got to his feet, he was fueled by pure anger and desperation, and not a one of these children would escape his wrath if he had any say in it. He grabbed two of the children by the hair and bashed them into one another. They both fell, holding their noses and whining with capitulation. The biggest girl, and a boy that looked to be in his early teens, looked upon him with great vengeance in their eyes and began to circle him like sharks around a cove. Christopher put up his fists to warn them that he was in the business of boxing them down. The boy attacked first with a horrible scream and, without hesitation, Christopher stopped him cold with a right jab to his forehead. The boy fell down instantly and remained on the ground without making a sound. Next came the girl, who was the most ravenous and bloodthirsty of them all. Christopher could not bring himself to pugilism with her, so he went on the defensive promptly. She slashed at him with her long nails in a furious haste and he was forced to back up from the animalistic mauling. He caught one of her arms as it crossed her body. He then shifted her body, getting behind her, and fell her by putting her in a chokehold. Her arms still slowly flailed as he brought her to the ground until she could no longer breathe, much less try to attack.

By the time Christopher reclaimed his stance, the boy returned with the stack of wood and dropped it when he saw the bodies of the children heaving and squirming on the ground. A pleading look formed in the glassy lenses of Christopher's eyes and he breathed heavily. The boy could see that the children had been the initial attackers by the looks on their faces. The look of bloodthirsty revenge is much different than the look of defensive aggression. Christopher heard the boy say something to them and they started to get up slowly. The boy's voice got louder and he motioned the arm that was set in the sling and the children looked back at Christopher in disbelief for a moment. The older girl hissed at Christopher, but the boy yapped at her and she settled. He then pointed over to the wood that he had brought. They started for it slowly. The little boy that had attacked him at first was whimpering when he left, and the boy he had knocked out still looked in a daze, the regeneration of his conscious mind yet to regain cogency. The girl, leisurely to get up.

"I told you, thay want for to see you dead," said the boy with his proud new sling across his chest.

Christopher wiped some of the blood from his lip and then reached into his pants to tug at his genitals. "Angry little bastards," he grunted. The boy could not make out what he had said. It was best that way. He helped Christopher come to a seat on a stump near the fire pit dugout at the side of the well. This village was somewhat smaller than Sacristo's, but the architecture was better conceived, the village itself more succinct. "Is that all of them?" Christopher pointed to the children gathering wood and then outstretched his arms to pantomime that he meant everyone left in the village.

"Todos?" the boy asked.

"Yes," replied Christopher.

"No, not all. Just thee brave."

"How many more?"

"Two times more," he replied. "Thay mostly all little." The boy lowered his hand to a short distance from the ground. "Do you have fire?"

Christopher went through his pack and furnished a box of matches.

151

The boy gathered some twigs and tinder to start the fire at the base. Christopher bent down to help him. The boy made fire very similar to the way that Christopher had been taught to, a sentiment he did not feel that he could express. The man nodded at the boy, an approving zeal worn on his face. The others came back with armfuls of tinder, still looking at the man with contempt. The oldest of the boys seemed to have the best grasp of the English language.

"What is it that you do here?"

The injured boy put a black pot on the fire, the contents of which sizzled, and then portioned it out to the other children, who tore into it like savages new to using canines. He continued to stir the pot of the gruel and handed a saucer to Christopher. Christopher nodded and the boy began to fill the small saucer with the stew, a sinew inundated concoction. Christopher tasted it to be polite. It was quite possibly the worst thing he had ever tasted.

"I came here to bury my mother," he replied, and thus indulged the child.

"Why do you come to our land to do so?"

"I needed to go somewhere out of place, in order to handle the burial process. It felt like I could not let her go just anywhere. I wanted something to feel sacred about it."

The boy looked at him with a dumfounded curiosity and then looked about the village grounds. "You carry her body with you? I do not see a body."

Christopher got up from the stump and went over to his pack. He took out the urn, unscrewed it, and brought it over to the boy. The boy took it in his hands and looked down into the vase. By the light of the fire he could see the ash inside and he felt it with his fingers.

"She is powder now? Did you burn her?" He handed Christopher the urn.

"No. I did not. That is something others do for you, if you choose not to bury them in the ground, you can have them cremated and put to ash."

"We burn our dead," said the boy.

The boy with his arm in the sling nodded at Christopher. "I tell him these. I tell him we are same in these."

The other boy looked at Christopher and shook his head. "We are not the same." The other children seemed to agree.

"I did not come here to be the same," said Christopher. "I came here for myself, not to take anything from you or your people."

"That is something hard to believe from the ingles."

"You can believe what you want. I am not here to represent my own people. It would do no good ... but I do need to know this," he paused, "are there any wounded children in the woods where you went to hide?"

"Wounded?" asked the boy. "What does this mean, wounded?"

"Hurt," Christopher motioned with his arm. He pointed at the boy's sling. "In need of medical help."

"No," replied the boy. "He was the only one who fought them off. He is very brave." He looked over at the boy.

"And what is his name?" asked Christopher. "I never got it."

"We are without name," replied the boy. "For we are one."

"Well, I count five of you right here, and not a one of you looks the same as the other."

The boy gave him a disappointed look. "We do not see it this way. If we want one's attention, we want all's attention. If I call for help on something, I do not choose just one person. I call and see who comes, and who comes is my brother. Who comes is my friend. We do not choose just one, never do we choose just one."

"But tribes downriver give names to their children," said Christopher.

"We are not like other tribes. We are our own tribe, and we know nothing more."

"And will you be the leader from here?"

"We will all lead, and we will take up the jobs of our parents. We will take back our land from the ingles."

Christopher set his saucer on the ground. Steam still skimmed off of the surface of the uneaten gruel. He asked the boy with the sling to hand him his pack. The boy grabbed it with his one good arm and brought it over to Christopher. The man picked through the pack for a time until he found the book he had been searching for. He thumbed through the pages "I doubt that you can read English, but there are several diagrams and pictures here to help you." He handed the oldest boy the page and pointed at some of the pictures on it. "This should help give you an idea of how to set traps for large game, or other things. Also, there are several different spear types that you can make from things you find in the woods. I imagine these were the things your parents would have taught you."

The boy took the page in his hand and held it low so that the firelight danced on the pictures. From what Christopher could tell, the boy approved of the information that he had been given. He folded up the piece of paper and handed it around for the other children to see. They salivated over their chance to see the object, though the images were too advanced for them to understand. Christopher imagined the eldest boy could make due with the pictures and diagrams.

"You make these things?" said the boy.

"On a smaller scale," replied Christopher. "I have been able to catch game in traps similar to these. I think they will work if built on a larger scale. It could be helpful for hunting game, or in setting up defenses against men."

"Defenses?" The boy spat, then smacked at two of the children now fighting over the piece of paper.

"Yes. A way to fight off men without being near them. You could set these up all around your village and hope they snag intruders." Christopher pointed out to the darkening jungle beyond the village. The boy looked at him with evident speculation. "To catch them," iterated Christopher.

"Then what, once we catch them ... snag them ..." said the boy.

"Not up to me. Kill them if you have to, I suppose. Whatever you have to do to keep your lives." Christopher got up from his stump and went over to the boy with his arm in the sling. He checked the wrapping once more and asked him if it hurt. The boy said he felt fine and that the arm would heal on its own. "I can't stay. It is already getting too dark," said Christopher. He took the matchbox out of his pack and gave it to the boy. "Take these. It will make survival easier."

He looked toward the clearing that he had come through.

"Will you no stay," said the boy in the sling.

"No. I have to get on. I cannot help here. This village is in ruins." He surveyed the children's faces, now sad and rejected looking. "There is nothing more that I can do for you. There seems to be no law, no justice for the wrongdoings. If I do not get on, then I may not make it back."

"Does this mean you will be going home?" said the oldest boy.

"I still have more to see."

"There is no more to see if you have seen this. You have seen a village lose so many. Lose all men and women, and now there is nothing but kids. How much more to see, ingles?"

"I would like to stick around this country long enough to see the success of your people." Christopher tried to touch the boy's shoulder, but he shied. "You could lead your people to a better life, if you find a way to fight back."

"And what do you have to fight for, ingles?"

"That has changed over time." He thought. "I used to have to fight for my family, and then I learned that they could fight for themselves. I fought for others some, but never gave it my full effort. Now, I fight for myself. Nobody will ever have to fight for me." The boy looked at him blankly. "I will never have to fight like you will. I know that."

"And you will not stay and try?"

"It would do no good. I do not plan to stay here for any length of time, certainly not the time it will take for you to entirely rebuild your village. I can promise that I will do my best to keep those men away from your village, if I am allowed the chance. There is little else I can do."

The boy nodded. "They will not harm you when you leave," he said. "They are not brave."

"Will you?" asked Christopher.

"I have no need to harm you. You are passing like snake in the bush, or bird in tree. You have no devil in you."

The boy stared into the fire. The other children gazed at him in his trance. He looked as though he witnessed the massacre all over again, as if projected onto the face of the embers, as if he could see his father tied to his mother in line with the other village leaders, led out to the beach where they were blindfolded and shot one by one. Their pride leaving its physical form and attaching itself to some posthumous itineration—the blood still fresh on the beach. Concomitantly, the other children hid in the woods sucking their thumbs or whining in their sibling's arms.

"You need a leader. No one will be able to follow hope without one strong boy or girl. It is the way of humankind. You need to know this to survive," said Christopher. He started off for the jungle.

"We will survive. We have always survived," replied the oldest boy.

"Not all of you," he reminded them. "This is beyond me. I am sorry."

The children looked for Christopher's silhouette, now formless outside of the fire. Their appearance, beaten and disgruntled, a horrifying sight for anyone with a moral compass. He feared that his soul would forever be cast from the gates of celestial euphoria for leaving these children to survive alone, but he was not invested in the likelihood of their survival, and therefore, was rightfully exempt from being their savior. Not every man was made to be a savior, and Christopher Corbin knew that of himself very well.

"Bury those bodies in the sand," said Christopher. "And mark them, to let them know that you are not leaving. And to let them know that you will remember what they have done." The children nodded with a pleading blankness. They knew not where to go from here, but they would have to go it alone. They sat gazing into the fire as Christopher turned away and headed back for the beach.

By the light of the moon, he could see well enough to find where he had plowed through the forest in search of the boy. He hiked for some time in wandering darkness by feel of the brush for a similar trajectory as the one he took entering the village. All the while he thought of the capabilities of mankind and the darkness that lies within and the amount of fear that some have to live with because of other humans. He then thought of how horrid existence could be—something he had never thought about before. It is hard to imagine something so foul when hiding behind the comforts of a pampering society. He thought very hard about the duties of these young children. In this, he fought any oncoming sorrow. Perhaps he was cowardly. Timorous in dealing with terror. For it is a very real part of human existence, as long as other humans are solely concerned with their own success.

He made his way back to the canoe later that night, avoiding the bodies on the beach. He had no aspirations to obsess over their presence and the presence of the evil that did exist in the jungle he now traveled. And how long would he continue to travel if things remained in such a horrible state? How long would he be able to make it, knowing the hatred and fear of his kind in this country? What was his purpose out here? He thought of these things as he skidded the canoe along the beach, continuing to avoid the bodies, but could not avoid the smell. And it was once he hit the water, and started at a slow paddle, that he leaned over in his seat and whimpered softly in his hands. The moon in full glow. The water rolling slowly and quietly along the banks where centuries of footprints had been washed away forever, no trace left of any creature, just the water's natural flow.

Michael

Michael,

I will not be sending any more letters for some time. I am not sure how long I will be gone, but my path is one that I feel I must take. Loretta is dead little brother. Let it soak in and then do not dwell on it. I will take care of the disposal in a proper manner. I will be taking her ashes to Brazil. From there, I will travel by river and spread her remains. That is truly living for the day. As for you, I have given up on trying to find you. You have not found yourself, nor will you even attempt the search. If there is one thing I would like to say to you before I leave, it is this:

The world will never become what you want it to be. The hurt, the dishonesty, and the failures are always there. The hope of seeing change take place overnight is fantastical. What you must do is live for the beauty of the earth and the challenges of manhood. Face them and grow, and give back to the earth what you have gained from its elements. Do not hide behind closed curtains and false comfort. If I have learned one thing, it is that we do not live on balanced time. Time lost cannot be regained. Live to better each waking day. Do not degenerate and shrivel down into your fears. Grow like the spring and life will be generous in its pleasantness. If I can say one thing about mom, it is that she lived each day to the fullest, even if it was to benefit from someone else's loss. She lived each day by its thrill. You should take consideration of that, for you are your mother's child. I will write when I return.

Chris

Michael Corbin had been considering leaving the hospital when she came in without her work uniform on. Today she wore colors he had never seen her in before. A bright blouse and paint-stained pants. She must have come in on her day off to see Dr. Smothers.

Nevertheless, she had made the effort to come by his dorm, and that was a stimulating thought. "Outstanding, Caroline."

"Beautiful morning," she responded.

"You look nice," he said. "Are you having your day off?"

"Yes. Could we sit?"

Michael watched her where she lingered there in the doorway. He got up and pulled out the typing table chair for her to sit in. "Here," he said. "You like this one, don't you?"

"Yes, that is fine, thank you."

He sat opposite her in his day-chair. "What are you doing here on your day off?"

"I have come to tell you something that is difficult for me," said Caroline. She rested her hand on his lap. He stiffened a little.

"What then?" he said.

"I am going to have to leave you as a patient. Our relationship has gotten to be too strenuous for me, and I believe that you rely on my presence too much. It is stunting your rehabilitation. I feel that your volatile nature surfaces more often when I am around. Also, I believe that some unhealthy feelings have started to develop on my behalf." Michael tried to respond, but she stopped him and demanded that he let her finish. "It is not that I feel you to be incorrigible, but I have a hard time giving my full attention to my other patients while tending to you. Can you understand that?"

Michael felt a strange relief growing within him. He did not expect this to be his reaction if she had ever abandoned him. He wondered what it was that made him feel this relief. It had become toiling always trying to impress her. It did seem like she kept him there sometimes, like their visits had become a fixation for him. What did this mean now? "What does this mean now?" he said.

"Starting tomorrow, you will have a new nurse. Her name is Connie. I have talked to her all about you. I have told her that you are a great patient, and that you will never intentionally cause harm. I had to tell her that you might get a little sardonic at times, but it is just part of your charm." She was pursuing laughter, but did not receive it. "You have been one of the most interesting patients I have had in all of my time here. I would love to continue on as your nurse, but I feel that I couldn't handle it if you gave up on my watch. I could not go through it again, and you scare me the most out of all of my patients. You remind me so much of my father at the end. If I can eliminate anything stressful in your life, then I am obligated to do so, and I feel that I have become an unnecessary stress on you. I honestly hope the best for you, and will continue to see you from time to time, but I will not directly handle your rehabilitation any longer."

She smiled at him and waited for him to speak. His blank look did not break. She turned, slid the chair back under the desk, and walked toward the door. Before going out, she turned back once more to give him a chance to speak. No words came from the stoic man, for he was now gazing out of the window with jaw tight. She went out with some hesitation and slowly closed the door behind her. All that she had come to say had been said, and he seemed to respond to it well enough. She could sleep well on that thought.

When Connie came in to meet with him the next morning she found that he had gone. His furniture and paintings were still there. *Donations* written on sticky notes on these items. What he had taken with him were his street clothes, the typewriter, and his correspondence. The ward attendant had allowed him to leave in the night. They could not keep him against his will. He collected the rest of the month's fee from the clerk and managed to catch the midnight bus out of town. He would make decisions on his own now. He would be a man. He would be a hawk. He would struggle now. He would be tired. He would give up. He would be a mouse.

Carson

He had only been four hours on the job when he noticed that he had driven all of the posts into the hillside. His hands were raw from the constant jeer of the post-driver and as he rubbed them he surveyed the hills stretching the horizon. A teal wave of ridge and peak. Sun hitting the coastal grasses, making them flicker softly. He set the spool sideways over the makeshift rod at the front of the ATV and stretched the line out to the post and pulled it tight around the iron. Then he let up some slack on the line and started unreeling the spool by hand at the front of the ATV. Once he had enough line out of the spool he got on the ATV and drove across the mountainside, down the row of posts, to where he had started. The line of posts that he had driven intersected another fence running perpendicular. Carson pulled the line tight with the puller and secured it around a post fastened to the other fence. He checked the line to make sure that it was tight and then proceeded to putter down the line and fasten each post to where the line ran against it. Once he reached the end of the posts he repeated this process twice more with a second and third line.

By the time he had finished building the new fence, the day was closely approaching night. He could hear the bugles bellowing out of the timber as the elk stalked with their large chests heaving. Carson tried to mimic their calls. He drove the ATV slowly over the hills and it sputtered and grinded at the axels. The hillside had already grown cold and Carson changed into a dry thermal for the ride home. He wondered what Jim had Valencia doing. He then wondered if there would be a warm meal and a warm drink ready for him when he got back to the cabins. He drove down through a glade where water speckled in the grass with an august, twilight gloat and the insects were all out and zapping the air with their shrill calls. The ATV drove much smoother once the weight of the posts had been lifted, but it still bogged down into some of the thicker patches of mud degrading the cattle path. Carson fought a wet patch of land by shifting the vehicle into low and throttling it with consideration. The ATV sashayed through the sinkhole, lurching large globs of mud from the spinning tires, until he caught traction on dry ground once again and puttered smoothly back to the trail. He had considered taking one of the ranch mules, but the strain of the posts would have overwhelmed the animal. He thought about the pack mules that worked in the copper mines and how much they were able to haul. Men were much easier on animals these days. They were much easier on themselves as well.

Nearing Jim's cabin he could see a pool of light stretching the ground. He tried to get an image of his own cabin from the bottom of the hill, but the timber cut his visibility. He slowed the engine and threw the rig into neutral. Walking the ATV the rest of the way, he came past Jim's window with the ATV at his side and could see two figures in a chair next the fireplace. At first glance the images looked formless, as their embrace had blotted out any identifiable body part, but upon further glance, he could make out the arms and legs and hair. Two legs outstretched and touching the ground and then a bare back running down to a backside, now straddling the legs, and more body. The figures were moving slowly. He walked past the window and only caught a glimpse. He paused, thought for a moment, and did not return to the window. Only did he return the ATV to the shack to begin his slow march through the snow to the cabin that he knew would be empty.

He was a long time walking through the snow when he came upon the maintenance cabin. The light was on. He thought that she must have left it on earlier in the day, before she went down to Jim's cabin to fuck him. As he got closer he could see movement in the window. There was someone in his cabin, going through his things, or trying to sabotage the work he had done. He went for the porch slowly and tried to look in to see who was there. It was her. Valencia was there cooking on the stove top. He wondered how it was possible that she could have been two places at one time. Then he looked at the color of her hair and the shape of her body and felt abashed at his own mistrust. He would not tell her what he had seen, or what he had thought. It would not be of any benefit for him to tell her of his thoughts and his worries. He had to forget the thoughts that surfaced after seeing the figures in Jim's cabin. He wondered what he would say to her. He knew he would be on fire with pugnacious energy. It would have almost been a relief to catch them, so that the act could vindicate his fears. He had thought about it many times since they had arrived at the ranch. Carson was not the type of man who liked to share what he had. He was also not the type of man to be bested by any other man. But he felt that if he had caught them, he would have a reason to give into his depression and sink deep, deep down with reason; he could be considered the victim, and then could justify his self-destruction. Yes, that was a thought. But now he watched her in there—and he started to dislike her even more for a moment. He turned and looked out upon the silhouette of the sky now made palpable by the mountains. The bugles still came from the woods and the calls of wolves curtailed the bugles and then the sound of insects grew louder than even the most distinctive of animal's calls. Carson sat down in the snow for a while and drew shapes in the drift while she cooked away in the kitchen. Where did this envious paranoia come from? Was she the one to blame for him feeling this way? Of course she was, absolutely, it was her ... there was nothing wrong with him ... nothing wrong at all.

Later on that night a herd of cattle treaded their way up the hillside to eat the coastal grass that had gone to seed on the western slopes, and had been stopped by the newly erected fence. A few of the heifers started to bawl in the night until one girl started to move back down the line of the fence and the others followed. There was still a patch of open land that had not been fenced yet, which the group of heifers found and filed into and commenced eating the coastal grass until their stomachs became full and bloated by mid-morning.

Michael

Watching water flood the metal rims of windows where people with strange shelters walk around in puddles of concrete and come off and on my bus—there is a little boy with no parents sitting in front of me, but I swear that he may be placed here to watch me—he is so out of place here, but he cannot keep from turning around and looking at me—he must know something about me ... or he has been put here to watch me—I think I want to return, but I will not, I do not know where to go, or what to do—I need help— where are you brother? I want to find you, I hope this finds you—I am deciding now where I am going ... off of the ocean, Christopher once made me think about it ... they have apartments by the ocean and jobs for a man like me—my money, I have enough for rent to not worry, some salvation—I will find peace by water and cloud, by seagull and wave. When will he be back brother? Who will look for me? Find ... find ... what am I doing? My God I fear it. I will ... find me by the ocean. I will be just fine on my own ... find me brother when I send this, if I am still here, if I still make it.
   M.

Michael Corbin got off of the bus at 3:30 a.m. in some coastal city now dark and faceless. His first thought fell upon finding a place to sleep, and at this hour, his only hope was to curl up on a bench at the bus stop. He had been the last one off of the bus and found that this was the last city on route for Greyhound number 276. Michael Corbin was a loner now. He would have to fend for himself. The world does not take pity on those with cowardice, nor those with unresolved mental hardships. He was once again a piece of the demanding world. He listened to the waves crash into the beach and he thought of what would happen when the sun came up. There was something soothing about the waves, and that he was alone, and that he could hear no other sound save for the waves once the bus puttered off, and the fact that—for what he knew—this could be the end, and that this could be a beginning. He was able to start to appreciate some of the things he had neglected for the past few years; the memory of his brothers, the memory of his father, and even that of his mother—newly deceased—but now just a memory, no longer a burden—living on behalf of their sins. Michael Corbin started to weep silently and with great joviality. It was as though something inside of him had awoken and shrugged off the worrisome fibers that enveloped his humanoid carapace. He felt light again and the waves moved there too, inside of him and beyond. Deeper down where his being resided, he felt the waves allay his fettered soul, his tacit innards. The greatness of a moment such as this was beyond compare. No one to see or hear his joy. He had escaped his own inner jail cell and had taken the path of his brothers and the men before him.

When he awoke, he had fallen from the bench and lay flat on his face in the sand. The sun was up and people had already started walking the pier. Michael could hear the gulls' loud squawk overhead and still the low sucking sound of the ocean. He was unable to tell when he got off of the bus in the night, but there was a row of quaint buildings along the shore where people were already out drinking coffee and reading the morning paper. He could see the buoys floating with an inanimate serenity against the horizon and the sky was a soft gray—one that beckons the coming of a light morning storm. Michael Corbin dusted the sand from his mouth, his jacket and pants, and started out at a nervous walk toward the pier.

The day had already started to swell with humidity and Michael took off his jacket, folded it neatly, and placed it into the roll-around suitcase he carried behind him like a small child with a wagon. A German Shorthair chased seabirds on the shore and an oil liner hummed in the distance past the breakers. The air was surprisingly clear, not smoggy or inundated with the scent of sulfur like many other American beaches. He came to the very end of the pier and could see below where the water ambushed the rocks of the bay, the stilts of the pier strong enough to withstand the water's barrage. He had not an idea of where he was. It did not matter to him. Michael found himself climbing onto the banister that ran around the pier, and which was the only thing separating him from the grand drop below where certain death resided amongst the pointed rocks and breaking seawater. He stood on the second tier of the banister and only peered out upon the horizon where the sun had attempted its break into the morning sky like an egg yolk coming out of the white. He watched an eagle glide on the wind with straightened wings exhibiting the existence of free sail and it too moved out of sight.

He followed the dock back in the direction of the bus stop where cars drove slowly in the early morning fog. There was a café at the end of the pier with a porch that opened out to the beach. Some patrons sat in beach chairs with their feet in the sand, mimosas perspiring on the tables. When he came upon one of the patrons with a newspaper in his hand, he read the title to find that he was in North Carolina. An appropriate place for him to be, he thought. The patron looked up from his paper, smiled, and offered Michael the sections he had already finished. Michael declined with a calm shake of the hand and proceeded to look for a place to sit near the sand. He found an empty table and set his belongings in one of the chairs and sat down where, he too, could rest his feet in the sand.

A mousy looking waitress came out with a platter of mimosas. Michael watched her fumble with the plate. She nearly dropped the drinks on one of the customers, but recovered quickly. Her face became very flustered and Michael could see that she had a twitch in her right eye that worsened with her embarrassment. He watched her recover, apologize repetitively, and then walk back into the café mumbling. She was very strange indeed.

When she came to get his order she stopped and stared at him for a while without talking. He could tell that she was having a difficult time addressing him. Finally, but with evident difficulty, she stuttered out the words, "You hha–haave a tt–tired face … very tt–tired."

He smiled at her the best he could, but did not know how to respond. Her nervousness was beginning to make him nervous as well. He adjusted in his seat like a tortured, ungainly child fidgeting in a shopping cart. He then looked at the menu in her hand and asked for it softly. She handed him the menu and scurried back away from the table, neglecting the customers who were now shaking their water glasses at her.

Michael sat and stared at the menu for a time until he came to the conclusion that he did not want to deal with the hassle of ordering, eating, paying, and leaving, so he decided that he would sit on the beach until his hunger was such that he could stand it no longer. When the waitress came back, he had gone. She followed the tracks in the sand that his suitcase had left and could vaguely see his small silhouette rocking slowly on the beach. His hair was very blonde and it danced in the wind. She continued to look out for him for the rest of her workday.

He took up residence in a beachside apartment that cost a small percentage of what he had been paying at the ward. It was a two-bedroom unit with a single bathroom and large bay windows that opened out to a porch overlooking the beach. There were no other tenants, nor could he hear a sound at night save for the waves. No one around to hear his screams during the night. That was very pleasant. Michael Corbin spent most of his days inside. He was able to go to a few furniture stores and have what he needed sent to the apartment. This afforded him a bed, reclining chair, and a desk table for his typewriter. He found that he was able to type some in the mornings and quite a long time at night. The tortured being was now rehabilitating himself in his own way. Every day he feared complete mental breakdown, but that time did not come. Michael consulted with the only pharmacy in town and they sent word to his doctor for his medications. Like a drunk scrambling through his pockets for change, Michael checked in at the pharmacy every day until he had his prescriptions. He did not believe that he was safe without them.

It had become clear that his proximity to the sea was more rehabilitative than anything he had experienced at the ward, even more so than Caroline. He'd found peace with his new living arrangement and he found that it was no longer a burden to wake up and that it was no longer a burden to go outside. He now walked the beach daily. He even started to visit the beach café a couple of times a week and developed a rapport with the waitress there—for she was evidently fighting her own battles. Most of their communication was composed of mimicking body languages to mirror approval and he watched her as she served dishes. Sometimes he would not enter the café. Only would he sit in the sand near the porch to watch her. She did not seem to mind. There were days—very few of them—that he had the courage to sit down and order from her—it was always her—he would ask for her if he did not get her. She did not seem to mind. Michael Corbin would say very little—he did not know what to say—he would order, comment on the birds or the other people, and they would sling glances back and forth by-and-by. He did not tip her. He did not want to pay her directly for their communication. She did not seem to mind.

Michael Corbin had not received any mail to his knew abode, but he had called the hospital to have them direct his things. He had read all of his letters to date. He felt that he had changed very much—he felt that he had become a man.

One day, as he sat on the pier, he got a glimpse of her. She was wearing a white dress, not her usual waitress garb, and no shoes. Her hair was very blonde, almost white, and he could see that she was heading toward the pier from the beach. He tried not to stare at her directly, but it was quite impossible for him to do so. She did not seem to notice him when she walked past him to the end of the pier. This concerned him immensely, but he had to fight the feelings as they came—these were the measures he had to take to rehabilitate. He watched her look to the horizon. Her hair flittered so beautifully in the wind with the sun sparkling through it. He continued to watch as she climbed up on the first rung of the pier banister, and then the second. What was she doing—he thought—she was just doing as he did before—to get a glimpse below—to feel things in a different way—and then she continued to climb. Michael found himself coming from his seat on the bench and went at a healthy gait toward her. She now had one leg over the banister and the other straddling the other side. When he came to her and grabbed her by the waist she turned to look at him with confusion worn on her face. His look of worry seemed to bewilder her.

"What...d-uh-dd-you think you are d-uh-ddoing?" she said with her stuttering tick.

"What the hell are you doing?"

"Sitting on t–tt–the pier t–tto--watch the waves."

Michael recollected himself and let go of the grip he had on her. He stepped back and looked at how she was sitting on the banister—how could he have suspected—he wanted to turn and run away from her as fast as he could, but his legs were now frozen. "I have to apologize."

You c–ccould have just c–come and said hello," she said to him. "Sc–sc–scared the hell out of m–m–me."

"I do not know why I would think that. Why I thought you would do something. I was scared for you for the moment." Michael looked at her apologetically; she did not seem to mind what he had done.

"I'm n–nnot ss–ssuicidal." She laughed.

"Good."

They found themselves awkwardly making it through a conversation that day on the end of the pier and he thought intensely about some of the things she had said as he walked back to his apartment that evening. He also did not know what to think of himself and he wondered if he had been a hero, or if he had overreacted. Either way, he had been able to communicate with her because of his forthrightness. And that was something he felt that neither of them minded.

The sun was still suspended in the sky when he came to sit in his recliner facing the ocean. The sun's break now left a glassy sheet on the calm waters and he could see a rowboat with a fisherman inside. The man was dragging a single line behind him as he rowed with both oars. It was a beautiful life the man seemed to be forever living out there in that rolling calm. What of his past and how he got to where he was—Michael wondered if he would ever have the strength to take up fishing again—and if so, would he be any good—and if so, would he ever spend time on a boat with his brothers again. Michael Corbin could see lightning striking far off on the horizon. It was soothing, and he was very warm and very calm in this new world he had created for himself. And despite all of this, he still feared losing his mental progress.

Christopher

He had seen enough of the country, and after leaving those countrymen and women behind on the beach, and the children, he did not want to experience the terror any longer. The terrors of this world are of such immensity that it is hard to imagine how so many have never experienced them, terrors that drive men and women to unfathomable action. To do things they never thought they would do. All the same, this world is made up of these events, these terrors. The world is harsh, and continues to be, as long as humanity insists on displaying animalistic tendencies. There is little worse than war, and war has many faces, and they are all the same in their resolve. And this was the way of his people in this foreign country and he now knew that he would have trouble surviving much longer with these natives.

He had come into a draw in the river where it split with turbulent water skirting in both directions. The split to the north looked slightly less testing, so he steered in that direction. Once he crafted the boat north he could feel the water sucking at him from behind until the boat started careening in reverse. No matter how fast he rowed, he could not get the craft pushed out of its southern ambition and was rendered defenseless in a matter of minutes. The first jolt came quickly from below, a boulder, and almost tipped the craft completely over, but Christopher was able to recover. Preoccupied with keeping the craft balanced, the man was unable to realize that the river was careering toward an empty pocket of space ahead where the river and the sky met and there was very little greenery to be seen past the line of the river. Another jolt came from the white-capped water now stabbing upward at every turn in the river and it was much more powerful than the first. He pulled in the oars and grabbed the sides of the canoe to hold it as steady as he could, his navigational intellect now useless, and recovered the canoe again. Without any water coming in through the bottom of the canoe, he felt confident that the craft could make it through if the current desisted. Another boulder rocked him from the port side, swirling the craft around so that he was now facing ahead, and that was when he felt the terror start to materialize within him. It was at this moment that he realized he had no choice in the matter, and that there was one certain resolution to the matter presently at hand. He looked to the sides of the riverbank to see if there were any roots or hanging limbs that he could grab, but there were none. The water had been too violent for any divine debris of salvation to have survived. He did not know yet how far the drop would be, but it would mean the end of his journey by canoe. Christopher quickly grabbed his pack and held it at his side to await the drop—for it was imminent—and he watched a long tree limb race beside his canoe, as if to out race him, and watched as it rolled, toppled over end, and was gone from site. And it was he who was next on the river's chopping block when he met the edge of the waterfall and began his uprooted journey from the stern of the canoe. He could see it all so clearly, the sediment rushing through the white cascade of water forever rushing downward, and the bow of the boat trembling slowly at the edge of the fall until it too up-ended and spewed over. He could feel his gut start to lurch once he shifted upward in his seat (he held his feet on the now upright end of the bar in front of him and was at one point standing on it) and the first thing he could think to do was hold to the pack and take it down with him (but not allow him to sink with it–never sink with it–it will float- I will need it.) And once he got to the apogee of his final point with the canoe, he kicked himself from it—pack held tightly in his arms—and floated away from the rushing water and the spiraling canoe. He did not want to land on it, or under it, or anywhere near it. He held tight to the pack, as if it would save him, a makeshift parachute, but he too floated down along the cascade. The water spraying him all down his backside from behind. This was the end of his war in this country; this was the end of his war with himself. He could not think of a more terrifying or profound way to go if this were to be the end. It would not be the end. There were still paths to follow. Paths of the marching men, as they walk through the forests to the end of the world, and he would go with them to their end. He would go on the backs of the marching men.

III.

Carson

As he stood holding the diaphanous little bag up to the sky, the gray matter residing inside collecting fragments of sunlight, he watched the clouds settle in the west. He watched the cattle traverse the hillside slowly. She smiled at him and sat the hill to let him go at it alone. From the hill they could see the Dodge, flat and aberrant in the parking lot below. They had now come back around to the north side of the mountain and it was a short distance to the peak at this point.

"You coming?" Carson asked Valencia.

"I think I will stay," she said, breathing heavily from the steep incline.

"You just don't want to finish the last bit of hike over the shale," he replied laughing. "It gets awful steep up there."

She gave him a scowl, remembered why they were there, and then smiled again. "Go on. I didn't know her. This is your journey."

Carson looked down the ridge of the mountain and could see a few elk prancing through the aspens. He could see the river's form on an adjacent hillside and watched it flow down to a lake below. Valley all around wild with sagebrush and young pines. Valencia took a swig of her water bottle and offered it to him. "Do drink some before you go," she said, handing the bottle out to him.

He waved her off, patted the water satchel at his side, and turned to start up the hillside placing the bag in his pocket. Carson could feel some of the bone fragments rub against his leg as he climbed and the mountain had quickly turned to shale once he started for the peak. He had to go at it on all fours. The crest of the mountain was loose and he fought the rock, sliding down the shale, to the edge of the peak. He swore he could feel the bone digging into his leg.

He cursed the mountain, the bag in his pocket, the heat of the sun, and the aching in his bones as he continued his scramble up the mountainside. Once he reached the top he came upon rigid ground. The beauty of the land more apparent than before. He had climbed the highest peak in the range. Everything below shimmered with verdant greenness. Endless lakes stretching beyond the valleys. He looked down to see if he could still see Valencia. He called out for her, but she did not respond. His singularity, conclusive.

He took the bag of Loretta's ashes from his pocket and held it up to the sky once more. "It is very difficult to say goodbye to a parent." He looked over the edge of the peak. A yellowtail sailed below and its squawk came resonating from the mountainside like something archaic and beckoning. "It is now my duty to assume a true emotion. What is gone is gone, and your soul has parted from your physical body. No longer will we have to worry about you or your hurt, and we can live without the fear of finding you in a desperate state. Here, I have piece of you. A piece I did not want the responsibility of parting with. I hope that you would like where we put you." He paused for a moment, trying to collect a meaningful thought, but found that he hadn't one. "This is not for me. This is for Christopher, and poor Michael. You could have done more for us … Gone forever."

Carson untied the bag and held out the contents. The wind took the white matter within seconds and there was nothing left following the small plume of ash as it encountered the air, then the shale below. It's possible that he may have heard a faint echo.

The young man considered himself, Valencia, and his shame more so than he considered the death of his mother in the end. Carson remembered how his father had told him of women. He remembered how the man's words were filled with a speculative understanding of his own thoughts as they formed into his speech. He had said that women were of the nature to not forgive men. He'd said that women always acted as if they had forgiven, but it was not so. No, women were of the nature of harboring injustices, and that they justified their own actions by regurgitating those injustices. They would spout off your wrong doings to cover up their own. Carson thought about that, as he always had, and then thought about how sad of a sentiment it was. A very bleak, bleak outlook on the world and women. Apart from this, he had the same outlook on some things that his father did. He could not help it, it was just so. As he had been taught, it is too much work making a monster of one's self, and living with an acceptance of that beast within. It is truth and it is forgiveness of those harbored injustices that beats the beast. The will to better, to not wallow in self-pity—diffidence—doubt, is what ultimately cures the sickness. Carson knew that his time spent doubting, giving in, giving up, had to end if he wanted to have a restful life. Some cannot help the restlessness, but it was what he strove to beat. To satisfy the urges, to slake the allure of giving up on it all, was always something there in the back of his mind, but it would not be so any longer. He knew that for certain now. Carson looked once more upon this great land, and with resolve, he turned, checked his footing, and started back down the hill to where she would be waiting for him underneath the shade tree.

That night they made love in the calm darkness of their cabin. She whispered to him and made him feel slightly embarrassed. He was silent, but determined, and they brought each other the same joys. Later that night Carson sat up in bed with a twilight-sobriety, one that brought his most hidden thoughts to the surface. Once he kept himself from drink his thoughts cleared, and it was at night that he harvested the thoughts that were usually muddled by inebriation. He remembered things he wished he had never experienced, as well as things that were rather pleasant. He listened to her snore and roll around. She was very restless when she slept. He thought about Christopher and what he had seen and done while he was in the rainforest. It had been two months now without a word. He would send out detail to the authorities if another week went by without word. Valencia would do the same for him if he had been out for too long. But then, Carson had not the ability to take care of himself as well as Christopher did.

Christopher

Horatio Cornish and his two guards usually went out trawling their Johnboat by mid-afternoon. An American-made seventy horsepower engine, bolted to the back, powered the vessel and it whined past the coves, alerting the natives that Cornish was near. Because of this, the men were often met with a barrage of arrows that fell like raindrops across their bow. Regardless of this danger the men powered through the river cutting up a wake that flooded the surrounding banks. Horatio Cornish's men carried large automatic rifles and it was not uncommon for them to shell off a couple of rounds into the jungle to scare the natives. Their present task was to check the coordinates of a patch of land supposedly rich with oil. A bushel of flags and ground markers rolled around in the hull of the boat. One of the men had a sport-dog with him and it paced the hull and lapped up water as it sprayed from the boat's wake.

"Damn quiet out there today," said Horatio over the engine putter and the pelting sounds of the water against the boat.

Both men nodded with their rifles and one of them grabbed the dog by the collar to calm him. The dog stopped, panted loudly, and then continued pacing the boat with his tail wagging.

"You boys have no idea what a pleasure it is for me to know and affiliate with men who enjoy money in this country. The pride of your people is hard to break. Do you get that?" The men just nodded, keeping their eyes to the jungle.

"Of course you do. We will break every last one we have to, if it takes it. Look what I can accomplish by myself. Enough families removed that I can finally catch a break. It is a beautiful thing. It was the best of times for me, the worst for your countrymen. You boys see? We could cut a path right along the water's edge here, and run her all the way out to Momma river." Horatio was directing his actions with his hands. The men did not turn to watch him, though they nodded in agreement. "This lead better produce, or I will be forced to fire my inside man. Or have one of you take care of that messy business." The dog came up beside Horatio and licked at his bare leg. Horatio patted the dog on the head and then pushed him away. "Get this boy a leash, Hobak," he said to one of the men. Hobak nodded, but did not move. "Goddamn guys all the same. Barely know a lick of English."

They came upon the canoe now overturned and resting atop some bushes riverside. "What in God," said Cornish.

They sailed over to the bank and looked upon the metal craft now blown out at the hull. "That damn boy. Must have got turned around in one of the cutouts." He flicked his hand out to signal the man to keep going. "What a shame. Would have been nice to have a feller around that could give some conversation." They continued down the river looking for other items that could have been left behind in the crash, but found nothing.

When they came upon the great waterfall the dog did not take his eyes from it. He stood with both paws on the edges of the bow at Cornish's knees. "Great God," he said. "We are clear at the bottom of this plot here." He looked at the man who was steering the engine and motioned for him to cut it to the right of the stream. They cut their wake at a good distance from the falls and came upon the bank. The pack lying on the shore. "I bet you *that* has something to do with it." The man pointed up at the waterfall and laughed. "Hell of a way to bite it." They disembarked the craft and the dog leapt out and started sniffing the rocks. Hobak picked up the pack, went through it, and began throwing items out pitilessly until he came upon the urn. The vase had not a single crack in it. Hobak held it up for Cornish to see. Cornish motioned for him to throw it over. Hobak obeyed the command and slung it at the man. Cornish caught it, unscrewed the lid, looked at it for a time, and then smiled widely. Hobak and the other man watched as Cornish turned, took a steady stance, and then heaved the urn across to the other side of the bank where boulders lay erect and dark-gray in their terrestrial abodes. The black pot hissed across the stone and the ash inside exploded out and then disappeared into the water. Cornish smiled and rotated his shoulder. "I need to work on my pitching. It is getting a little rusty at my age. You men can't get to where I am without a few broken vases and scattered ashes." He laughed wildly and his eyes grew heavy and sparkled with childish joy. The men held no noticeable emotion and then turned their attention to the dog, as its yapping had overtaken the sound of the waterfall. "What the hell do you think he's got?" said Cornish. The men went off after the dog.

The young man had been able to drag himself quite a distance from the shore when they came upon him. He had completely lost the use of his legs after plunging feet–first into the pool below the falls. Cornish checked his pulse. "He's breathing." He told the men to come closer and drop their guns. They did so and took the man in their arms and carried him all the way back to the boat. The dog followed along, yapping. Cornish smacked the dog away and it whimpered for a second and then continued in full pursuit. "I'll be damned, you boys. That crazy son of a bitch made it. I'll gather his things. See if there is anything in there that we could use. Get him on in the boat there."

Michael

He knew that he would not make it to the bathroom by the time the vomit came and was forced to release the contents of his gut onto the wooden floor at his bedside. This was the worst part of the transition. He felt reliant upon it most days, though his headaches had subsided some since the beginning. It was easier to sleep now, but the vomit was the worst. It seemed as though his body was trying to expel every resource it had in order to entice the mind to give it what it wanted. And what it wanted, it had been given for entirely too long. He was weaning himself off of his medication. Some nights, like this night, felt worse than others physically, but he did not mind the physical ailments if his mental strain was attenuated. He hadn't had another seizure since the last one at the ward.

He forced himself to walk the beach in the afternoons and had forced himself to write out his thoughts daily as well. Michael believed he was growing stronger, but at this very moment he felt very weak and vulnerable. He made it to the toilet with still some bile left to emit. A very sour tasting lurch followed, and then a series of dry heaves. The sucking of the commode and the action of the tank drowned the soft whirr of the tide and calmed him as he hugged the porcelain. When he had finished he went to the mirror and cleaned some of the leftover regurgitant from his cheeks and rinsed his mouth. With the light on and the door shut, Michael Corbin looked at himself in the mirror for the first time as a strong man and smiled. He told himself that he had become a man and that he was stronger than the provocation of his body. Sometimes it felt as if he was regurgitating his former—and that with each flush, another timid layer was thusly dissolved. His face had never been clearer. He no longer wore that pallid grimace he had seen so many times before, that grimace that looked like a great injustice trying to escape false imprisonment. His hair had grown long and very blonde. Because he could grow no facial hair, an abnormality at his age, his face had a boyish charm. His communication had not improved greatly and it remained difficult for him to carry on a conversation without becoming irritated. Michael could not seem to completely get his point across, and he did not value other's opinions. That was something that would never come to change. He did not mind the thought of being alone forever. To him, people were there to test his stability and nothing more. They existed as a part of his rehabilitation. He tested himself daily to produce maximum results, and achieving maximum results meant that he went an entire day, functioning around others, without incident. And those were certainly triumphant days for Michael Corbin. He would overcome it all in a natural way. That is what the mousy waitress had told him that day on the pier. She had tried once, but she was a failure. She had always been a failure—and why should she not be a failure at that—and people do not need the approval of others to be functioning adults. She had not been medicated. She had made it ten years since she tried and she knew there were many more years to come. He had stopped his medication and he felt balanced. He deserved that.

He could see some wrinkles start to form at the corners of his eyes and did not mind the look of them. Age carried wisdom. The justification for erratic behavior. The man, waiting out his days until senility was accepted. The lines on his forehead symbolized that time inching closer. For you see, Michael Corbin was not a man that feared death. Life was what horrified this man. What a thought that was—that waking up seemed more terrifying than never seeing the light of day again. Age had become something of a goal for this man—to see how many years he could make it last. He did not mind getting older. He accepted that, the older he got, the more of life he had conquered. Michael felt the lurching in his gut once more, but held it back and swallowed the sour saliva surging in the back of his throat and felt his way back to bed by the light of the moon and climbed in slowly and wrapped his arm around one of his pillows and savored every sleeping breath that did not hold vomit for the remainder of the night.

One day as Michael walked the pier he noticed a fishing boat pulled up on the beach. Two men without shirts walked the beach, and he could see them pointing to the boat. He could see from the pier that these men carried large poles with them. They must have been sport fishers. Michael wondered what the men were offering. He went back down the pier to the entrance of the beach. The men stalked the beach at a distance of a quarter mile from him and he continued to watch them as he walked in their direction. They seemed intent on showing off their fishing vessel in its of-nothing-stellar condition. When Michael came upon them one of the men turned and smiled at him, showing very few teeth. The other man followed. "Well, what we got here? Looks like a hell of a fisherman."

The other man looked Michael over. "You ever been on a sport fisher, bubba?"

Michael started to feel nervous at approaching them. He looked at the boat and then at the men and shook his head. "No," he said quietly. "Is this supposed to be one?"

"Is this sposta be one said'm." The other fisherman said aloud. "This'n here boat damn near chase all dem fish out the water."

The two men seemed a haggard lot, but they had one possession to quantify their worth. And because of that, there was a god possibility that these men were good fishermen.

"Ever caught a marlin?"

"No," replied Michael. "I have never been sport fishing."

"Now's the time to start then, bubba."

One of the men motioned for the other man to get something from the boat. The man went and then came back with a boating vest.

"Here's your type-2 P.F.D.," said the man. He threw the float at him.

Michael had not agreed to anything yet, but it did not seem to stop these men from trying to get him on the boat. Resistance would be too much of a chore at this point. The man who had kept calling him bubba showed Michael how to fit the float and then yelled at the other man to keep at the people walking the beach.

"What does a trip cost? I have little money," said Michael.

"This is a test venture," said the man. "Me and Henry are just testing our idea of leading fishing expeditions."

"And what does this cost?" Michael repeated.

"You dense, bubba? It's a trial run. Couldn't expect you to pay, unless you wanted to throw in a tip for gas. But we aint letting you keep the fish or nothing."

"Fair enough," replied Michael. "And how long a venture will this be?"

"Long as you want, bubba," said the man. "Or as short as you want, depending on what kind of fisher you are. I can see you may be one of them impatient types, but we'll try and change that." The man smiled at Michael and then looked over at Henry who had now gathered a young married couple and was fitting them in their vests.

Michael could see that the man with his wife was uncomfortable as well, almost as if he needed to urinate, and the woman had already started taking pictures of the boat, the fishermen, and her uncomfortable looking husband in his ill-fitting orange life-jacket. Michael wanted to retreat, but that would cause a considerable amount of stress. He felt it best to stay and ride this one out. The two men loaded the passengers one-by-one and Michael was the last to get on. They set him up at the stern and had already rigged his pole and dropped the outrigging to the sides of the boat. The craft now bobbing in the water like some winged marine animal. Henry had Michael take a seat in the anchored chair in the middle of the stern and took the line and fastened it to a clip on the outrigger and sent it out on the line, mid-mast, on the outrigging.

"Yawn't have to do a thing but reel that sucker in once she catches. Aint bad, huh?"

Michael tried to grab at the handle of the pole, but Henry stopped him. "Leave 'er right there in that groove. Won't need to pick 'er up until she catches. See that line?" He pointed at the line on the outrigging. Michael nodded. "Watch for it to jump, then, and only then, start to reel. Clip this here back." Henry showed him the line release and pushed it back to show how the line fed and then clipped it back into a locking position. "Never put yer hand in there. Click her on back and start to reeling. We will do all the rest."

Michael watched Henry go around the port side to the front of the boat where the couple sat in the two anchored chairs at the bow. It was apparent that Henry was the dockhand and the other man was the captain. Michael could see the captain climb the latter over the galley cab and make his way to the tower where his dials, wheel, and throttle were housed. The man looked down at Michael and shifted the hat on his head. "You ready to pull in a healthy one, bubba?" He smiled, without waiting for an answer, and turned back to the controls.

Henry was already wading out into the shallow sea by the time Michael turned back around to the stern of the boat. The man stood waist high in the water floating the fishing vessel by hand deeper into the sea. The boat had been tied to an anchor buoy and floated with ease away from the shore. Michael watched Henry climb back up the ladder at the stern. He came back onto the boat dripping wet, wearing nothing but a soaked pair of cut-off jeans. He was a very sun-bitten and wrinkly man with very dark skin, as dark as a Caucasian's skin could be, and his hair was sandy and very blonde. Michael noticed something very distinctive about the man. He emanated freedom, or calm, Michael could not decide which, but he became envious of the man. He became very much so envious of the man.

The captain cranked over the dual engines after Henry gave him the signal and Michael could see the bubbles start to surface from behind the boat. The vessel started out in reverse to pull away from the bank, and to avoid the sand, until they hit the shelf and the boat started to thrust to the left while drifting backwards. Once they straightened out and started to head for the reef directly, Michael watched the shore and buildings start to fade into a blur that held neither face nor memory. The wake shot out in two jet streams behind the boat and there yawed two diaphanous sheets of green and white. He could see the yellow flicker of a fish already embracing the cuts in the water and watched as the line bobbed on the rigging, but it held, and the pole jounced lightly with the boat cutting its path across the deep sea past the shelving and sand. Michael could hear the woman at the bow cheering frantically, and he could hear her say, "Oh darling, isn't this great. Tell me you love this. Tell me I had a great idea."

Michael could hear the man mumble back to her. Though he could not see them, he could picture what the two looked like up there; the woman taking pictures with great excitement and the man clenching onto his hat whilst trying to avoid the glare of the sun and the woman. Henry continued to pace the boat, opening the compartments in the hull and cutting fish. The water was incredibly smooth and the birds had gone from sight. Michael could smell the diesel burning off under the stern and could see black plumes of smoke coming up from under the swimmer's platform and the bobbing motion of the boat actually soothed his empty stomach and he thought for a second that the line tugged, but it had not. He turned, looked up to the tower to where the captain stood steering with great acumen, and called out to tell him that he thought the line jumped. The captain turned around and looked at the line and then shook his head and pointed to the rigging. "Has to come clean off the outrigger, bubba."

Michael shook his head and turned back to watch the line bounce and skim over the top of the water's surface. Michael thought that the line was getting nipped at the entire time because of the present action on the surface of the water, but the line never dropped from the rigging. He enjoyed this activity very much. No one forced him to do anything but sit and study the water as it panned out all around, and the sky stretched, a light blue, and the sun hadn't grown indefatigably brilliant.

They had been out for more than an hour when Michael heard the yells coming from the bow of the boat. He got up, made sure that his pole remained secure in the chair slot, and went around, portside, to see the woman yanking fervently at the pole while her husband sat back in the chair, reeling with the best of his ability. Their lines had been cast out on the port and starboard sides and ran at a good distance from the boat's hull. The man's line had slipped off without his notice and the captain had to holler down at him to swivel his chair and make at the fish. The man reeled in quickly and pulled back to snag the slack. He then let up. His wife continued to tug on the pole. "Let go of it!" he yapped at her. She continued to stand near the pole, as if she were helping in some vicarious way.

"Reel her in, Jake," she said with great elation. "Catch your first real fish."

The man pulled back on the rod again. "What the hell are you talking about? I've caught plenty." He leaned back in the chair and pulled the slack completely out of the line. "You should have seen the yellow fin I caught down in the Keys. Fought a lot harder than this one."

"Well ... reel this one in, then. Here, let me take a snap at it." The woman tried to climb up in the seat with him but he backed her off.

"Now get out of here, Rome. You are going to get yourself hurt if you get caught up in this thing."

Henry gently pushed past Michael to get to the couple. He eased the woman back down in her seat. "Yes'm I believe he's right. It aint safe for you to fight at this thing with him. You will get yours. You jest sit and wait for 'er."

The woman sat her command and started to reel her line in slowly. Jake kept at his. Michael and Henry watched. The captain was cutting the draw of the water to give the man a better fight and had veered some away from the direction they had been heading. Michael looked back to check his line, but it had not snagged. Rome's line was the next to slip. It started to spool out of the reel with great haste and she started at it excitedly. Her face turned to show a pallid apprehension. Henry rushed over to where she sat and eased her back in her chair and flipped the lock into place on the reel.

"Now keep them fingers outa the trap there and just reel 'er in. Easiest thing you'll ever do."

The woman's apprehension eased and she started to reel in the line with a dedication comparable to that of her husband. She mirrored Jake's actions, making sure to keep her fingers clear of the line. The couple continued to fight side-by-side with their fish fighting back at them equally. Michael checked his line again, nothing. The captain began to holler with a jovial zest. "Reel 'em in. Reel 'em all in! We said we could pull every fish out of these waters. Hot damn, reel 'em in."

Henry had brandished a long fishhook from one of the compartments in the hull and now paced the port side of the boat from where the man's line shot out into the ocean. Michael could now see a great fin switching back and forth in the glassy waters below the boat. He saw the tint of yellow flicker in the water and the fish had shown its heaving belly and then submerged below the surface. It must have fought back up and out of the water at least four times by the time Henry got to it with the hook and rendered it defenseless. With one heaving motion, Henry drew the fish out of the water and plopped its seizing body onto the deck and went directly after it with his pliers to pull the hook from its mouth. Blood trickled down the sides of the boat and then sprayed across the deck where the fish flopped violently wallowing in it. Henry told Jake to open up one of the compartments in the hull. He did so, exposing a container of ice, and Henry swept the brilliant marlin into the icebox with the end of the spear. Jake slammed the door down on the fish. "Damn, that was a big one. You see that, honey?" The woman did not answer him, as she presently fought her own fish. Henry repeated the process on the other side of the boat, pulling up a slightly larger marlin, and by mid-afternoon they had two catches on ice. Michael returned to his seat and watched his line bounce without releasing. He was positive that he did not want to catch a fish. He did not want to have the spotlight put on him. The boat ride, alone, was sufficient entertainment for young Michael.

The sun had fallen halfway above the horizon by the time the captain decided to turn in and the sky was far from the shore and Michael watched the clouds turn pink from the back of the boat. They had come up with five fish in total between the couple and one line that Henry put out. Michael's line continued to bounce in the water trailing. Not so much as one snag all the way back. Henry came around to the stern and checked the line once more before bringing it in.

"Sometimes they jest smell the diesel. You'll have a better'n next time." When he reeled in the line he found that the lure had been completely taken and all that remained were the weights. "I'll be dipped in shit. I wonder how long this here been dragging."

Michael just smiled and shrugged his shoulders. "No matter," he said.

"Well this is just bout the damndest thing, man. You probably never even had a chance. You got to come out once more. It'll be on the house, honest as all."

"I will not be losing sleep over it, Henry. I am quite satisfied, considering the fact that it was not my fault. Though, I will greatly consider your offer for one more free ride at a later date."

"Good then." Henry reeled the line in completely and clipped the rigging back onto the reel. He looked back up at the captain and hollered to him. "What do you say we take these folks for a drink, cap?"

"Fine idea," said the captain.

Henry fixed his gaze back on Michael. "You in?"

Michael said sure and Henry yelled out at the other couple.

"Oh, yes," the woman said and turned to her husband. "Jake, we must go with them."

"Yaa man," said Henry.

"We have had a long one," replied Jake.

"Nonsense ... bubba says he will come. You guys come for one drink," hollered down the captain.

"No fisher passes on a drink," said Henry.

"On me," said the captain.

Jake accepted and the woman clenched to him tightly and kissed at his neck. He was keeping his neck crooked backwards to tempt her more, though he wanted her to settle. Michael could smell the salt coming off of the waves.

The boat puttered past the breakers and skimmed the shelf some distance from where Michael had met them. They passed Michael's apartment and coasted around to the end of a cove and began to slow. They turned and were now creeping in to a marina inside of the cove. One stretch of pier floated on anchors with several boat slips etched into it. It was a long dock, shaped like a horseshoe, and all of the slips pointed outward to the open coast with a floating bar and restaurant directly in the middle. The horseshoe opened out from the coast and curved inward on both sides, stretching closer and closer to the building. Michael could see well-dressed couples walking the docks by post light and fishermen strung up their catches, gutting the fish and discarding the entrails off the back of the boats. As they puttered closer, Michael could see a few attendants handling people from the boats. The captain steered the boat wide, close to the docks where people watched the boats come in, and thrust the portside engine and then completely turned off the starboard side. The boat, softly and smoothly, drifted sideways and ended up directly on the buoys cleated to the

186

dock. "Get off eer," said Henry. "Cap and I'll go get 'er cleated up. Geet us a place ou'side."

Henry opened up the cab door at the back of the boat and ushered Michael off. He then called for the couple to come around. Henry helped the woman down the steps to the galley and then tailed behind them until they were all on the swim platform. Michael went first. A tall, slender man, wearing sandals, shorts, and an open shirt, helped them out of the boat and waved off Henry. "We'll geet 'er all tied up," he hollered out. "Get me a beer, wouldya. An one for the cap." The captain had turned on the other engine again, puttering the boat back out of the horseshoe, to enter the slips from the opposite end.

"I thought this was on him," said Jake.

"It is the least we can do," said the woman. "They gave us such a wonderful day. It was such a wonderful day, don't you think?"

She looked at Michael. She had a slim, attractive form. Her entire body was long and slim and she had a very exotic looking face. He had not seen a woman that looked like her before. "Yes," he muttered. "It would seem reasonable."

"Look at that, Jake. He agrees with me. As should you, if you had any brains about you." She laughed and hugged him strongly at the waist. He wiggled some to free himself.

"Jake Mitchell," he said and put his hand out for Michael to shake. Michael returned the shake with his limp, tepid hand. "And this is my beautiful wife Rome."

The woman put out her own slender hand and their shake was much more agreeable. "Rome is quite a name," said Michael. "People that name their children after great places must have the feeling that they have not accomplished enough. It is most likely that they have feelings of inadequacy. An inadequacy they think will somehow be vindicated by having a child that is larger than life. Do you think this is so?"

The man and woman looked at him for a moment until Rome burst out in a heinous laughter. "You are a treat!" she said. "This man here has quite a wit to him, doesn't he."

Jake smiled noncommittally and nodded his head. "Yes, Roe, he is something." Jake turned to the restaurant and looked for the bar. "I will be getting a drink. What will you have?"

187

"Soda water," replied Michael.

"You don't drink, hon?" asked Rome.

"No. It is idiotic for me to drink. I have very little self-control."

She smiled at him as if he had meant it in a salacious way. "Well neither can I, but that is all part of it."

He did not return the smile. "Just soda water."

"I will have the usual, hon."

"Soda water and a Russian," he said aloud. "And a double whiskey for myself. What do you think the mates will have?"

"Get them Budweiser. They seem like Budweiser men."

"That is a strange assumption," said Michael.

"How do you think so?"

"What determines someone's type of drink?"

"Well, for instance, Jake is a whiskey man. I am a White Russian girl. And both of those men are non-lite, American-beer drinking men."

"That is very specific. But you are still generalizing an entire group of men based on their appearance."

"You want me to tell you what kind you are … don't you?"

"No."

"Come on."

"I do not drink, so it would be pointless. Just as pointless as this conversation."

She was not listening to him. The only word she would comprehend was the word yes, for she was very used to hearing it. "I know what you are, regardless of whether or not you drink. I promise you that."

"Fine," he said. "Let's hear your judgment about me."

"You would be a Brandy man, if you were so inclined as to drink."

"I have never had it. What does that say of your perceptibility?"

"It means nothing. And that is because I am still right. You said yourself that you do not drink. And do you want to know how I figured you for a Brandy man?"

"How's that?"

"We met a man once off of the coast of Stewart, in Florida, that was a Brandy drinker. He never did give us his name, even though we had gone on with him for three days, or so. We never asked it—I guess because we felt awkward about not getting it the first day, but he never gave it up. He never offered it when we first gave him ours. Like you, Mister … I still don't know your name. And that is how I know you are a Brandy drinker. Same way I know those two fishermen are Budweiser drinkers."

"It is based on past relation to things then?"

"Yes."

"That takes a good memory, does it not?"

"Not if they are just rash generalizations about people." She laughed, turned, and saw her husband struggling to bring over the drinks. "I will be right back. Get us that table right there." She pointed at a small, round table right at the edge of the dock.

Michael watched her as she went to assist her husband. He thought that it was completely useless talking to her. If only to dream about her, to never see her again after this night. He sat at the table and pulled out the two chairs next to him. When they returned Jake took the outer seat so that Rome sat in the middle. He handed Michael the soda water and set down the two Budweisers across the table. Rome already had her drink in her hand and started sipping at it. Jake took his drink carefully and sipped it with abstemious restraint. It was evident that he controlled his consumption while Rome drank freely and without concern. It was interesting to evaluate their relationship based on this little bit of information—for those who are without love are always studying it.

"Don't you think he is a Brandy chap, Jake?"

Mr. Mitchell looked at Michael, the soda fizzing in his glass. "I would say Gin and Tonic."

"Oh, you are no fun. You don't remember anything. That … or you aren't making the connection that I am."

"Once again dear, I have no idea what you are talking about."

"You don't remember Stewart, and that nice fella whose name we never caught?"

"Still, I do not know what you are talking about," replied Jake.

"Come now. Don't play me. We went with him to that little bakery, and in the evening you two smoked cigars outside of the hotel, at the pool bar. You remember the man. He had very white hair. He was a very big man."

"Mr. Cordell?"

"We did not know his name, remember? Don't you remember me saying that I wish I would have gotten his name that entire time, but he never offered it?"

"I remember, but I knew his name. He told me, later on the first night."

"Why did you never call him by it? And why did you let me go on like I did about it?" She turned sour on him.

"I imagine it was fairly comical to me at the time." He smiled and sipped his drink once more. "Come on now. What is three years ago anyhow? I thought you would have forgotten about it."

"I haven't. But do you see what I mean by this man being a Brandy chap?"

"Not entirely. Mr. Cordell was not as reserved as this man here." The two of them were talking as if Michael was an attraction in a glass box at the zoo. "He is too slouchy and sloppy to be a Brandy man. Something like that takes elegance and an urbane presence. No offense, sir. Anyhow, what *is* your name? I don't believe we got it yet."

"It is unimportant what my name is," replied Michael. He took a long gulp of his soda and looked around for the two fishermen.

Both the captain and Henry were at the bar now, talking to some women they seemed familiar with. They ordered two more beers and brought them over. Henry waved at Michael. Michael nodded his head. When they came up to the table they brandished a Budweiser each and Rome looked at Michael and smiled. "One for two," she said. "Bet I could get you drinking Brandy, if I had the time to do so."

"No need to worry about having time for that," replied Michael. The young man came from his seat and set a five-dollar bill on the table. "That should cover the soda and the two beers they got for you." He outstretched his limp hand for Henry to shake. Henry met it with a firm, yet slimy hand. Michael followed up with the captain. "I very much enjoyed myself this afternoon, but I am afraid that I must start out for my apartment."

"Nonsense," said the captain. "Stay and just have a talk. We can float you back to your place at any time."

"I must get on. These two will make fine company."

Rome and Jake did not stand. Jake nodded his head and held up his whiskey to the man. Rome glanced at him with a pleading look on her face. "Where is your apartment?" she asked.

"Two miles. A straight walk along the beach on the other side of this marina. Should be no more than I normally walk in a day."

"You sure you won't oblige us, bubba?" said the captain.

"I'll seek you out for my next fishing trip, do not worry," said Michael. His stomach was starting to become queasy and his head had begun to throb. "It will be best for me to go home. I have things that I have to do. Have to do things." He could hear himself start to repeat his words. His legs even started to shake.

"We won't stop you, bubba," said the captain.

The group commenced to talking once he left and he feared that they instantly fell upon berating him in his absence. Nevertheless, he had made it through the day, an exciting day at that, with little trouble, and he felt once more that he was gaining strength.

Walking home along the beach he started to wish that he had caught a fish. It would have been nice to memorialize the day with a more momentous event. To defeat something other than himself. To do what his brothers and forefathers had done for centuries. Something he had only done once or twice in his life. Before going home he thought that he might stop by the café in the hope that she was there. The walk was not bad. He could stand going for another couple of miles with the way his legs felt now. He could consider being awake for some time yet to come.

Carson

He sat the hill behind the cabins and watched her hang clothes on a wire line. She wore a short sundress that curled up when she bent over to wring out the clothes in her wash bucket. Carson was taking time for lunch on the other side of the hill where he could look over the cabins and the road. Presently, a soot-gray jeep climbed the hill toward the entrance of the ranch. It was the postman. The jeep came to the entrance and Valencia turned and looked at Carson. "Do you think we have anything?"

"We haven't had a single thing sent since we got here," replied Carson.

"Do you want me to run down and have a look?"

"Nah. I'll get it."

Carson came from his seat on the hill, put his food scraps in his lunch pail, and shuffled down toward the road. He kissed Valencia on the forehead and threw his lunch pail on the porch. He looked across the pond at a visitor couple painting abstracts of the mountainside on matching easels. He waved over at them and they returned the greeting. Jim had allowed many naturalists to visit the ranch to paint, take photos, or gather flora. Some would end up staying a night if they hadn't finished their work and, due to Carson's efforts, three of the cabins were now in livable condition.

He walked the gravel hill down to Jim's cabin and watched as the jeep turned around at the shop and headed back down the road. He could see a big crate in the back of the jeep and the driver's head bobbed side-to-side going down the road. Carson went through the small post box bolted to Jim's cabin on the west side. There were several bills from the lumberyard and supplies store, as well as a small package of materials. He had not seen anything with his name on it until he came to a letter that had been forwarded several times. He read his own name, then Michael's. The letter was post marked from somewhere in North Carolina that he had not heard of. Carson could not believe it when he first saw the name and the location. Without further thought, he ripped into the envelope and pulled out the letter.

Valencia continued to toil over the laundry when he came panting up the road. She watched as he rounded the porch. Some dust gathered at his feet, a visual image of the man's own magnetic propulsion, and he headed for the cabin door. She yelled out for him to stop. He halted at the screen door.

"What are you in such a hurry for?"

Carson came around to the side of the porch and looked out at her with the sun breaking across his face. He smiled widely and waved the letter at her. "You know what we got?"

"What is it?"

"A whole damn paragraph in writing," he said.

"Wow," responded Valencia with a facetious regard. "Someone must have been feeling ambitious."

"It is from Mikey, smart ass."

"What!" she replied with much more enthusiasm. "He's decided to write you back from the institution?"

"From the looks of this, he is out and on his own. And he is in North Carolina no less."

"Is that good, Car?"

Carson looked down at the letter, leaned over the banister, and then looked out at the couple painting. He slapped the letter on the porch railing and then stiffened. "I hope so. He is a weak boy."

"He is a man now, one capable of functioning in society. You have to see that."

"It's been an awful go at it for him, though."

"Well, for now, we are happy ... yes?"

"Very much so. I am just a little scared."

"Not you."

"Yes. But we cannot waste time. We must go to him."

"What about everything we have here?"

"I am going to start packing the cruiser now."

"And what about the work?" she responded with unfaltering

responsibility.

Carson turned and propped the screen door open with a split log. "We have done enough for the volume of visitors he gets." He shuffled some of his things together from the porch. There were two folding chairs, a pair of boots, a long knife, and a few jackets sitting out to dry. "I would be surprised if he even needed all three cabins that are done, and I already closed in all his cattle, so he won't be out on acreage labor. We will have him send our last check in the mail. He will understand." Carson continued to gather his things rampantly. "We have worked together several times. He has always outstayed me. He knows I am a runner. I got the bulk done, and in good time, so he won't be overwhelmed when we leave. I promise."

"Do you not plan on coming back here? I have grown to enjoy it very much, and my writing is going so well."

"Do you want to stay?" Carson stopped his shuffling and looked out at her.

"What do you plan to do once you get there? You can't just sit by his side the entire time and watch him. You will get bored of that soon enough."

"I don't know what I will do, but I have to be by him."

"I understand that, but that does not leave much hope for me. I just moved my life here for the season. I can't just up and move somewhere else. I am getting into a groove here."

"And because of that, you don't care about my brother's well-being?"

"I do, but I also have to think of myself. Can you not go visit him for a time and then come back?"

"He needs me."

"But, how much does he actually need you around?"

"More than you do," said Carson. He went back into the cabin and came out with a few tote bags in his hands and went to her at the clothesline. He started picking off his clothing and proceeded to shove the clothes into the bags.

Valencia tried to calm him as he frantically tore the clothes from the line, but he did not concede. "I cannot just uproot myself once more.

You have to understand that."

"I do!" he said. He shoved her out of the way and gathered more of his clothes. "You just stay here, and you can fuck Jim and be just happy and fine while I deal with my responsibilities."

"Where is this coming from?" She had started to weep.

"I cannot do this with you right now. I have to get on and see my brother."

Valencia grabbed him by the arm without restraint. He stopped his narrowed propulsion and looked upon her now furious face. This was the angriest he had ever seen her. "You listen to me. I will not be pushed this way or that for you, if you will not consider me for a single second. I have listened to you gloat about your qualities, and heard you whine about your insecurities. Humans were not made to give so much without receiving an ounce of appreciation for it. I know you have to do what you think is right, but I will not take your calumny. I do not care how much I feel for you. I will not take it. Jim has been a good boss to us, and that is all. I would like to think that you could respect him as a friend. And respect me as an honest woman. But it is apparent that your distrust is inescapable. I have to stay here and finish out the season, because I made a promise to do so. I will fly back east when I am done, if you have not grown restless of the Carolinas and your brother by that time. I have seen the good in you, but I will not be torn anymore. I do not deserve your mistrust." She soon let go of Carson. He looked at her wildly, as if she were no longer human. His eyes switched back to his gabardines on the line, now hardening in the sun. "Are you listening to me? Did you hear me?"

He grunted and pushed past her again, plucking his clothing from the line. "You just made it easier," he said.

She could hear him crashing around in the cabin for a while until he had gathered all of his things and loaded up the cruiser. As he slowly pulled away, he looked out of the rearview mirror and saw her sitting the hill with her legs buckled and knees sideways on the grass. She was not weeping. Valencia Marie Mott watched him leave with a blank look on her face, and he could see her one raised hand come up and linger at her cheek for a time until he started down the hill, and she went out from sight. He was now left alone to travel cross-country to a new adventure, a new life. He felt justified in his goings, but somewhere in his mind he knew that he was no great hero—nor tragic victim—he was a restless man that could not outrun the shadow that torment cast over his life. He dealt with these thoughts by turning up the radio and he began to count the miles until he would end up on the coast to find his brother.

By the time he arrived in North Carolina he had been two days without sleep. It was night and the stars were all out and the moon was one open and unblinking eye without pupil. His first stop, a small bar overlooking the sea. He ordered a whiskey neat and sat to watch the waves roll in. They were beautiful and very sentimental to him. He was by rights a Carolina man, and now he would stay for a time to come. Maybe he would get a job working on boats or forming canoes. He had good mechanical knowledge and a propensity for wood-crafting. These attributes encouraged his travels, for these were qualities that he could go anywhere with. He held the envelope in his hand and read over the address. He asked the bartender where he could find the apartment complex and the man replied that it was very close, no more than a few blocks away, and even faster by beach. The man asked him who he knew that lived there.

Carson sat and nursed his drink for a while and watched the waves crash and the couples strolling about. He thought of what he would say to his brother. He hoped to God that Michael was still there. The whiskey had started to make him feel tired so he went next door to the café. There, he ordered his first real meal in three days. He ordered a coffee with Baileys. His waitress was a mousy looking girl and he found her stuttering difficult to comprehend, but he tried to be patient with her. He even asked her about the apartments and she said she knew of them. She said she knew someone that lived in them. He paid his bill and asked for the girl to draw him some directions. She did so, and he tipped her and asked if they had a bottle of wine that he could buy. She gave him their best Merlot, and he asked her to open it for him before he headed off down the beach in the direction of Michael's apartment. He asked for her name and she said it was Cheryl.

There blazed several fires along the beach as he walked and drank from the bottle of Merlot. He could make out the forms of men and women embracing by the fires. Dogs barked and he could hear the streetcars going down along the beach and then away as they turned to go downtown. A plane scraped overhead and he could hear the long sucking noise coming from the turbines. When he reached the rows of apartment buildings he could see all of the darkened windows, mere blank slates in the middle of their white facades, save for one window on the end that remained alit. He could make out a tall piece of furniture in the light. Carson had already finished half of the bottle by this point, but had not felt the presence of the alcohol until now. It was with much gravity that the possibility of seeing his brother for the first time in several years hit him. He sat the beach for a while and looked upon the glowing window and counted the apartments until he came upon that very one. He conferred with the map that the waitress had drawn and counted the apartment numbers from their physical presence before him. Michael was still awake and active it seemed. Carson finally made it back to his feet and stumbled up to the window. When he got closer he could see a stretch of bay windows on the other side of the apartment buildings, and through them he could see into the room, but could not see Michael. He pressed his nose up against the glass and cranked his head to the side to get the best view of the apartment. He saw Michael sitting, hunched over at his typing desk. The loud clacking of the typewriter. Carson tried to open the window. Locked. The man decided instead to carry himself back out to the beach and sleep until morning. He would sit down with Michael and tell him everything that he had wanted to tell him for as long as he could remember. He knew his brother's convalescence was possible, and now came the time for Carson to bear witness to his brother's metamorphosis.

Christopher

When he came-to he found himself tucked into a bed in some dank infirmary swaddled with mosquito netting. The pain that he felt in his head was immeasurable, and thusly, was commensurate that of the pain in his legs, which he could no longer move. He tried to move his arms, but the bed sheets held. He was trapped. He wiggled his arms enough to loosen the sheets from the bedside. No longer trapped. He looked around to see if any one else occupied the infirmary, but found no one. After looking around the tent he could tell that he had been taken to the American camp. All of the medical supplies and crates were in English. An IV ran to his right arm, the liquid lingering there mid-drip, and he could see the morphine patch applied there too. He wanted so badly to scream or cry, but was paralyzed so much by his pain that he could not. He remembered the fall and then the great cracking sound of his knees once he hit bottom. He remembered swimming to the bank and clutching the sand. He remembered crawling into the forest after he heard voices in the bushes opposite the stream. Christopher assumed that he had passed out from the pain some time shortly after that, and now he was here. He did not remember how he had gotten here, or who had found him.

Christopher slept soundlessly when Hobak came in with a tray of food. The paunchy brown man checked the boy's fluids and switched his patch to a lower dosage of morphine. Christopher woke and looked him over with one lazy eye. Hobak stretched a bed tray across his lap. Christopher did not move. The man set down his silverware and nodded at the boy, told him to eat. "Beans and rice. Is soft."

Christopher tried to move up in the bed, but could feel his own weakness paralyzing him. Hobak went over to his side and raised the bed for him. This hurt slightly, but the pain eased once he got acclimated to this position. "Thanks," said Christopher. "Where am I?"

"Down river. You are safe here. Cornish kept out for you."

"Cornish is here?"

"Only American who lives this forest. You see those?" Hobak pointed to the crates.

"Yes. I read them. Does he know how to administer medical treatment?"

"I do not know how you say this," replied Hobak.

"Is he a doctor?"

"In his way, yes. You will be made better."

"What does my canoe look like?" Christopher laughed a nervous, but thankful for salvation, laughter. It hurt his sides very much to do this, so he stopped. He had a few broken ribs, he could tell.

"Boat?"

"Yes."

"Gone. Holes all in it, and it is how you say ... " Hobak made a churning motion with his hands.

"Twisted?"

"Yes," snapped Hobak. "Very twisted and dead. You are lucky to not be."

"I am relief-ridden," replied Christopher.

"Yes."

"And where is Cornish now?"

"He is come."

"Cornish is coming here?"

"Soon. Yes."

"What about my things, did you find them?"

Hobak looked at him speculatively, as if to dissect the words individually as they left his mouth.

"My bag. Mochila?"

"Oh yes. He is come with mochila. Bag, yes?"

"Yes. Bag es mochila."

"Very good," said Hobak. "You know the espanol?"

"Little, very little. You seem to know English more than I know Spanish."

Christopher was talking slowly so that Hobak could understand him, but Hobak still struggled. "Very good," he responded. "He is come now and you will rest very well."

"Let us hope so. I am Christopher, y tu?"

"Hobak." The man bowed slightly and then checked the fluids once more. "And the pain, is okay?"

"I will manage."

Hobak looked at him dumbly.

"It is okay."

"Very good," replied Hobak. "I must be go."

"That is fine."

Hobak shook his head and smiled. He set down a small shot glass full of murky liquid next to the tray. "Is good for pain."

Christopher waved to the man the best he could. It was not long after Hobak left that Horatio Cornish came into the dark infirmary, brown faced and affected greatly by the humidity, the bag around his shoulder. Christopher watched him set the bag on the floor next to the bed. He pulled up a seat next to the boy. Cornish, a very strong looking and well-kept man with hands the dimensions of primate feet, was sweating. Christopher could see thick beads of water on the man's moustache. His face long and challenged. Horatio Cornish clenched his jaw nervously.

"How are you doing, boy?"

Christopher tried to move up in his bed. Mr. Cornish leaned over and adjusted his pillow. Christopher nodded.

"Are they broken?"

"Your legs?"

"Yes," replied Christopher.

"Yes," he said, seemingly apologetic. "And you have a broken rib or two."

"Or two?"

"Two. I was trying to be optimistic."

"It is hard to be optimistic about a medical certainty."

"Out here, you have to be optimistic to survive," said Mr. Cornish. "But it is lucky we found you when we did."

"It would seem so."

"And you crawled your ambitious self all the way out of the water and into the forest. It was a smart move."

"I'd heard some movement surrounding me after the fall." Christopher looked very heavy and tired. "A panic and adrenaline driven move, I suppose."

"Yes, you were in very bad country."

"It has become more and more hostile as I have traveled."

"That is the way of the land. The things that happen beyond the watchful eye of our tourists. It can be horrifying."

"I have seen awful things. Things I do not believe these people are capable of," said Christopher. He coughed, held his side, and asked for some water.

Mr. Cornish handed him a satchel and Christopher drank from it. The cool water ran down his throat with little ease. "These people are capable of much more than you think. They have automatic weapons in some places," replied Cornish.

"And who has supplied them with these things?"

"It is hard to tell."

Christopher coughed again.

"The government may have supplied some. They are a twisted, backwards lot, you see." Mr. Cornish got up from his seat and took a spoon from the tray. He laved up a small amount of beans and rice and offered it to Christopher. Christopher shook his head. "Not hungry?"

"It would hurt too much going down."

"Understandable," said Cornish. He placed the food in his own mouth and chewed on it crudely. "Mighty fine grub. You should try it when you get to feeling well. You will need your strength to get better."

"I will manage," replied Christopher. "Did you do this medical work yourself?"

"I am afraid not. I have very little time for trivial matters."

"Trivial?"

Horatio Cornish's face turned sour on him for a second. He then considered Christopher's weakened condition and softened some. "Let me apologize. It is more so that I am not capable of such work. I have men in my camp that handle emergency situations."

"My health is no trivial matter."

"Do not work yourself up. It will only get the best of you. Believe me when I say that … but let us not talk of that any longer. Let us get back to what you have seen here," he paused. "I believe that you have no need to be here for any greater length of time. Once we get you well, I will send you off in one of my ships to the city to see you out of the country. Do you understand?"

Christopher looked upon the man and then stiffened up. "I can't immediately answer that."

Horatio Cornish smiled and then picked up the man's bag, looked through it, turned militant in face and stature, and dropped it on the other side of the tray where the young American's legs lie broken. The pain went streaking up through his entire body. Christopher whined in pain and tried to move, but could not. Mr. Cornish riffled through the pack and brought out the man's clothes, books, and supplies. "I trust everything is in here for you to travel back home?"

Christopher continued to whine and then settled down. "Move the bag!" he said in great pain.

"Oh, I am sorry. You must forgive my manners." He shoved the things back into the pack, digging down onto the man's legs, then picked it back up and placed it on top of the food tray. "Go ahead and go through it yourself. You will find whatever was left after those savages trounced through it."

Christopher's pain started to desist, save for the occasional spur of white-light heat that screamed up into his chest. He looked up at Horatio Cornish with his eyes full of water.

"Do not pout, it is unbecoming of an American."

"What is your game?" said Christopher.

"No games. But you will not stay here. You have seen and done enough, believe me on that. Any further activity here would be detrimental to your health."

"You have seen the bodies, haven't you?"

Horatio Cornish tipped over the bag for the boy to look through. "Go on, look!" His voice was growing increasingly pugnacious.

Christopher looked through his things to find that some of his books had gone missing as well as the urn. He fell back down on the pillow and sighed.

"Something gone?"

"My mother's remains."

"Strange," said Mr. Cornish. He paced the room back and forth and then went to look out upon the camp to see if there were any of his crewmembers in earshot. He then came back and sat next to the boy. "Your pack had been compromised when we came upon it. Same as your canoe."

"I can understand the canoe," said Christopher speculatively. "But I fell with the pack. I should have never left from it."

"What could you do? You are lucky to have lived. If you had not been so ambitious as to crawl from eyesight, you might have died."

"And you found the pack this way?"

"We put some of the scattered contents back in it. No *remains*, whatever that would look like."

"Ash and bone in a black urn."

"I see," said Mr. Cornish. "And now that it is not here, do you still wish to stay in this country?"

"I came for my mother, much like yourself. I came with ceremonial ambitions, but now, a different drive keeps me here."

Horatio Cornish could tell that fear subsumed the young man's voice, but he was unsure as to what extent this fear would manifest.

"Yes, your memory serves you well. I did come for my mother, more so for my oil, but my mother all the same. My father lives in the country, mind you, so he demands some of my attention. And what will you do now that you have nothing left of her?"

"I haven't the inclination to consider myself done here, though the dangers concern me greatly."

Horatio Cornish stood up once more and looked out of the mosquito netting. He leaned down and whispered in Christopher's ear. "You know who your enemy is, don't you?"

Christopher pulled his head away from the man. Then he looked at him starkly. "I have a very good idea."

"Top notch," said Mr. Cornish. He moved away and then sat back down.

Hobak came in with another satchel of water to give to the boy and Horatio Cornish addressed him directly. "Hobak!"

"Sir," replied Hobak.

"Can you not see that I am dealing with the boy?"

Hobak looked at the two of them blankly. Cornish ushered him away with a motion of the hands. Hobak retreated. Cornish looked back at Christopher. "It is his people that riffled through your pack and lost your mother, understand?"

Christopher coughed again and then reached for the satchel that Horatio Cornish held. Mr. Cornish yielded the bottle. "How did he come to work for you?"

"He is one of the good. He likes money. Do you? Like money … "

"Does it seem like I do?" replied Christopher.

"I cannot tell. Most of us with a money lust have a lust for adventure all the same. It is hard to determine what fuels a man. I imagine you must need money to pay the man to take you back home, mustn't you?"

Christopher was still inventorying his pack as they talked. He looked in the side zipper where he had kept his money, only to find none.

"Something else?" said Cornish.

"My way out. The natives could do little with it, though. American currency can't be that valuable this far inland."

"Believe it or not, we do some trading. I am sure that I could seek out your money if that is what you wish." Horatio Cornish smiled.

"Judging by the things I have seen, I don't think I want you to do that."

"What do you mean by that?"

"I was told of what your men have done in this country. It has given me much to consider. I am tempted to stay in the country long enough to find some type of authoritative body."

Horatio Cornish stood, came over to the man on the bed, and slammed his fist down on the tray. The food burst from its container, the dispersion of thick matter, beans and rice, stains on blanket and floor. Mr. Cornish was vile indeed in his proceedings from this point. That was his nature, and little else resided within his soul. Christopher had known his vileness from the start. "Is it?" he said. "And how do you mean to survive?"

"I could find a way. Find the right people to see to it. What could you do to keep me from that?"

"Your legs, for one," said Cornish.

"They will heal," replied Christopher with an understood diffidence.

"And who will make sure of that? You are not ignorant."

"Do you have the guts to kill me?" asked Christopher.

"I don't need guts to kill you. It is so easy to kill in this land. You are no better than the natives to me at this point."

"Did you come here with the sole intention of killing and making an abomination of our country's image?"

"Americans are of singular efforts. No one works together, do you understand? There are rivals and there are enemies, the people you use and let go, and the people who just get in your way. It does not matter who you are. This all happens in repetition."

Christopher lay still in his cot, for he knew that there was little he could actually do. The pain in his legs had started to subside with the morphine's efforts. He looked upon the man as he had not seen him before. He had changed. The land had changed. Very much had been soured and degraded for Christopher now. Christopher had tried very hard to find peace in this land, but had only gone further and further down and onto a more gruesome path than he had ever imagined traveling. And now, looking upon Horatio Cornish, a man who now called the shots, giving up on the battle seemed imminent. The last thing he saw before it all went dark and cold was Horatio's smile and then the thick needle enter his arm, and the liquid disappeared from the vile.

A very real dream followed the darkness. He felt alive in it and he had the use of his legs. He trailed Sacristo. Other children followed behind. They passed small villages where grown men hid behind the buildings. The children had now taken over the land. Naked, tyrannical beings wearing large leafs for hats. Rain falling. The ground softening. They continued to run past the villages. Men forever hiding and women looking upon the men with shame. The forest darker than ever, a maelstrom of clouds circling in the sky, the trees uprooting. The children ran with their naked parts dangling and they called to him and told him to follow. They were heading to a great opening. Grand meetings with others who had been coming from the woods all the time. When they all met in the middle of the clearing they looked to the sky and watched everything as the sky started to vacuum it up into its vortex. Christopher and the children remained. Cottages could be seen in all directions, and they too heaved up into the sky until there was nothing left but Christopher, the children, and the clearing. It was beautiful and unlike anything he had ever seen before. And when he looked down, Sacristo's hand was wrapped around his finger and he was looking upon him, and Christopher looked around to find that all of the other children's eyes were upon him. A generation of children with their eyes upon him, and they walked to the edges of the land where, on the backs of the children of this land, dreams of lives former continue forever in traditional procession. There was no death, nor life, only a continual march to the ends of the earth.

When he awoke from the dream he felt rested, but not restored. He knew he had not escaped the nightmare, for he could still smell the rainforest. This time he was moving. He surveyed his new surroundings. He was in a stateroom in a cabin. A ferry cabin from the sound of the water against the walls. The slow churning he could feel underneath the bed seemed a good indication. He now rested in a much larger bed and the IV had been removed. He felt for any patches on his arms, but found none. The morphine would wear down soon. His legs had been set in two thick casts. Immobility definite for some time to come. Christopher knew that Cornish had sent him off to the city. He heard all sorts of movement overhead from what he presumed to be other passengers. A knock came at the door. He did not answer at first, but then it came again.

"Come," he managed to say.

Another American-looking man came in. He wore a white suit and a cabana hat, a typical arrangement of clothing for any man traveling South America in the later stages of his life. He took off the hat and came around to the side of the bed. He stood and looked Christopher over. He was a very old and tired looking man. Veins protruding from his forehead. He was soft looking, caring. He mutely motioned to the chair next to the bed to ask if he could sit. Christopher yielded. The man sat, put his hands in his lap, and looked at Christopher with great consternation. He reached out his peach colored hand. Large brown freckles all over. Veins larger than bone. He took Christopher's arm in his hand and rocked it back and forth. The old man checked his watch and then placed his bony forefinger and middle finger on Christopher's wrist. He counted for a few seconds and then let go. "Steady beat," he said. His voice was very strained from years of cigar smoke. Christopher could smell it on him. "The pain will have to be managed with less medication. Is that something you can handle?"

Christopher nodded his head.

"Good. It's a shock that you were not overdosed. Practicing gorilla medicine out here does more harm than good most times. Do you know where you are? What has happened to you?"

Christopher could not find the voice to talk, so he nodded again.

"Good. Mr. Cornish said he found you in very bad condition upriver. He brought you to this ferry and gave us the orders to get you sent home. A very poor job they did in setting you. A very poor job indeed." The man shook his head in recognition of his own superiority as a medical technician. "We will be a few days traveling to get you to a pilot. With a day's rest, you will be able to enjoy the ship in a chair. You can see the beauties of the forest in comfort. How does that sound?"

Christopher did not respond.

"There is very little I can do for you. You will need medical care immediately upon your arrival to the states. We simply do not have the supplies here to fix what they have done. I wish things were different, but they are not so." The man had a very genuine look about him. "This has been an awfully nice retirement for me. I get to practice medicine occasionally. A sick tourist is not uncommon … Very minimal stuff. The ferries always give me a state room, and I can go up and down the river." The man chuckled softly. "I am yet to have seen a boy in your condition."

Christopher said something, but the old man was hard of hearing.

"What was that, son?"

"The natives?" said Christopher.

"Yes … "

"Do you help them?"

"Certainly not. It is best to not to meddle in their affairs."

"They need the help," said Christopher. He was now very tired and found that his energy to speak lessened by the minute.

"I agree, but I am not the one to do it. I take on very little medical work these days. I am much too old to have the energy for that."

"Then who?"

"Excuse me," said the old man.

"Who will?"

"They are their own people," said the old man. "Let me explain this to you the best way I know how to." The old man cleared his throat and readjusted himself in the chair. "This is an entire race of people with a complete set of their own rituals for doing things. I do understand that we have advanced medical technology, but these technologies would negate the generations of medical practice this race has cultivated. People live their land. They will always live their land, and with our presence, they will become dependent on our ways of practicing. I am all for helping others. I truly am. I have eight years of medical school to prove it … as well as forty years of practice … but that does not mean I am willing to change the internal structure of an entire culture to expand my practice. At one time, I may have been so naïve, but it is not so at this age. Any impact we make here must be minimal … be it for the good, or the bad. Some days I hate myself for being here, but I worked hard to earn an exotic retirement. So, here I am. And here you are." The old man paused and wiped some specks of dirt from his pants. He smiled at Christopher. "So, if we go up and down these rivers, only to enjoy the beauty of the land, and do not abscond with too many of their fish, so be it. We contribute enough to them to pay for our disturbance. That is a part of living … paying your dues. And a part of death is not becoming a bother for others. Whatever your reason is for being here, forget it. Put it behind you. Tourism is a very petty game, son." The old man shook Christopher's arm again. "So … we will have you up and about the ship in the next few days. You can say your proper good-byes to the land then, and be off to the states for a proper examination. You are not a boy of this land. If you were, you may have escaped this fate, am I right?" He laughed. The old man came from his seat slowly and walked toward the door. He turned back and smiled at Christopher once more before he put his hat back on. Christopher waved one hand. As the man was leaving, he turned and looked out from the open door and then turned back to look at the young man. Christopher acknowledged that he had something else to say.

"Oh yes, I have another pearl of wisdom." He looked at Christopher with great, blue eyes. "It is unwise to stop your course when you see things that are not of your concern … a proper burial ground perhaps?" Christopher moved up in the bed at the man's words. "What people do in this country is their own prerogative, and not the concern of some picaresque boy's heroic adventure. So, go on, get feeling better. And get yourself to a proper doctor in the states." The old man flashed his stained teeth once more and then exited the room.

Christopher lay there for a time, his face swelling up with some internal flame that he could not extinguish. He thought of what the old man had said. The darkness just kept growing darker. He could stand it no longer.

The old man had gone from the ship by the time Christopher was able to get out of bed. A few of the crewmembers dedicated themselves to the young man's care and helped him in and out of his bed and brought him a wheel chair and continued to bring him his meals when he called for them. By now Christopher knew that any further investigation would not bear fruit. These men were without authority. He had gathered from the captain that they were headed for a main port and that his pilot had already been sent for and that his journey to the states had been arranged and paid for. It did not matter what he had to say upon returning. Everyone involved knew that these crimes would go unpunished.

In the afternoons Christopher sat at the stern of the ferry and watched the river float behind. He watched the water slowly drift away. He saw landmarks he had passed before and looked to the jungle to see if he could spot a native, but he saw none. He looked for Sacristo and the men of his village. Nowhere to be seen. Christopher wondered how long the children would last on their own. He could do nothing to save them. That was a realization he had accepted in his travels. Thoughts of his father's death, and that of his mother's. He'd paid her fair goodbye and had lived for a single moment of clarity—a single moment of truth. Truth, a derivative of the good and the evil—trailing the truth was that something that traveled down the river and out in the open, and it was something that blew in the wind—and it was something that could be heard through the trees during the time of day when the stars first start to shine and all that exists starts to settle—or begins to prepare for the night ahead.

Michael

Michael,

I will be brief. Unsure of your condition, but I have seen the worst and have put Loretta to rest. I have now become positive of my need to settle. There are things you will never even see in your dreams. You do not know what is out there. You find a peaceful life and live it. My hopes are that we can share our experiences one day. It is quite unbelievable out here. I am to return to the states within the week. I have sent word to Carson so that he will not worry. I will be returning broken. Things could always be worse. You understand that, Michael. One thing; things could be worse. You take that and hold on to it. Will try and visit.

Chris

Once the showers started mid-morning the two men had to walk underneath the awnings to escape the rain. The ocean was active now and some young boys and girls were out with boards trying to catch the surf. On days like these the shops all along the beach wore clear tarpaulins to shield patrons as they sat and drank, awaiting the calm. The boards along the boardwalk held slicks of water mirroring the men's reflections as they walked. Michael led his brother to the Cadge Wharf, a small bar near the pier. A long rock quarry ran out on the other side of the pier and a great light from the lighthouse spun in its casing, leading boats through the rain. Some shirtless vacationers walked the boardwalk in the rain without shyness—they welcomed water from any source. "You would not believe my surprise, finding you like I did this morning," said Michael. He looked back at his brother.

"Understandable. Are we almost to the wharf? I have an awful headache."

"Drinking is no good for you ... never has been. We are almost there."

"I was nervous that I would not find you in good condition," replied Carson. "And, by God, it has been so long."

"It has." Michael almost slipped trying to hurry.

Carson grabbed hold of him and corrected his balance. He was a very finicky walker, very tight and uncomfortable in his gait. Carson could not tell a difference in the man he saw before him. He seemed very similar to the boy he had always known.

The Cadge Wharf existed as one of the only buildings that did not have outside seating. It was quite dark and desolate when they entered, and the bartender was an older woman who looked as though she might have held other jobs that required a flirtatious demeanor. Michael pulled his coat back onto his shoulders once they got into the building. Carson's hair had been coated with rainwater, but he did not mind. "Go on, get what you need," said Michael. He went to a booth with a window overlooking the sea. Carson went to the bartender and ordered a glass of beer and yelled out for his brother's order. A soda water. Carson ordered him a beer, despite his request, and when he brought the two glasses over, Michael looked at him in disbelief.

"Did you get a soda water for me?"

"I thought you would want a beer," replied Carson.

Michael's face twisted and he began to squeeze back out of the booth.

"Hold on now," Carson said. He set down the beers on the other side of the table. "Where are you going?"

"Home. These are things I cannot stand." Michael was determined to leave. Carson put his hand on his shoulder to calm him.

"No, no I am kidding. Sit, sit." He eased him back down into his seat. "Wanted to get myself two so that I don't have to get up, even for a second, once we start talking."

Michael looked at him with a sour face. "Soda water. That is what I want, and I do not want alcohol. Do not be dense."

"Fine," said Carson.

When he came back to the booth with the soda water, Michael was breathing on the window and making shapes in the fog with his finger.

"You know that they have to clean the window now because you are doing that, right?"

Michael did not turn to look at his brother. He etched out a picture of seagulls gliding above a curvy shoreline. He traced the lighthouse and a beam of light.

Carson sat and shoved the glass over and then drank from his own. Instantly, his eyes lit up. "Much better."

"You looked dead when I found you this morning," said Michael. He had not looked away from the glass.

"That's better than the other scenario. Your letter left a lot to the imagination. What a problem you have of forming cogent thoughts on paper."

"Just stop!" shouted Michael.

"Hey now."

"Did you come here just to tell me how poor my letter was?"

"I came to see you. It's been a hell of a long time. You know it was hard on us, with you being a recluse in that damn ward. I didn't know what to expect, from the sound of your letter ... "

"It is what I needed. Do you understand? I could not be around any of you."

"Sure. Sit down, Mikey, calm yourself."

"I hope you did not come here with the intention of sending me back."

"I wouldn't dream of it. Sit down! God damn, boy, sit your little ass down."

"Then what is it? Have you come to scold me for neglecting to take action in response to mother?"

"You told me to come, you ignorant little shit! I will not allow you to throw one of your tantrums. You are a man, by God, act like it."

Carson reached his hand across the table and grabbed Michael's wrist. Michael settled, breathing heavily. He looked very uncomfortable. The bartender called out to ask if everything was alright. Carson said it was fine—said it was a spat between brothers, nothing to worry about. Brotherly arguments are justifiable.

"And I dropped what I was doing, and possibly lost the only girl that will put up with me, just to be here. You calm your squirmy little ass down before I have to take you out of here. Do you understand?"

Michael recoiled back into the booth and nodded his head like a small child. "Yes."

"Good. You know I love you very much, but I am not very keen on grown men acting like little children."

"You are that way."

"How do you figure?" he took a long pull from the beer.

"With your drinking, you will throw just as big of a tantrum if someone won't let you at the bottle. I have seen it in you. I saw it in Eugene."

Carson looked down at his now empty drink, smiled, and then switched to the other glass. "You may be right. But you are a damn fool. I can take care of myself."

"Can you?"

"Absolutely. I made it this far on my own."

"On your own?"

"Yes. I am a traveler, a slave to another. I can do it alone, unlike you."

Michael looked at his brother with a condescending reality surfacing. "What about the girl you abandoned?"

"Detachment. Do you see? I do not hold on to everyone, clutching like a crab."

"Then you will only live in loneliness and shame, Carson, and that shame will turn into depression. You feel that you can handle it alone, but that will grow tiresome too." Michael put his hands to his head to rub his temples and began to twitch with apprehension. Carson patted his shoulder.

"You okay? Calm yourself."

"No, you must know. You must know, or you will be like him. These are things I must tell you. I must tell you ... "

"Okay ... okay ... Calm yourself."

"You will find your end like Eugene. You will! You will!"

"Stop shouting," whispered Carson.

"You should live with the luck you have. You can face life without the obstacles of anxiety, and this makes you invincible. And that is what will be your destruction. You see ... I cannot beat the anxiety within. It is what makes me weak. You are just as weak, but you reserve your shame. It will come to the surface one day, brother. Believe me on that!"

"Alright boys. Y'all gone have to get out now. I can't take this shouting anymore," said the lady at the bar.

"Come on," said Carson. He tipped his drink back and set a bill on the table. He waved to the lady. "No matter about this. We will be getting on along now."

The rain had started to dissipate when they exited the Cadge Wharf and some of the shops were already rolling back their tarpaulins. A speckle of sunlight started to surface in the sky amidst the seabirds and bulbous clouds. More young boys and girls went about their water sports, catching waves now, and the light in the tower still turned. An old man dragged a small boat onto the shore with one hand. A large mackerel in the other. The sand had turned a dark brown from the rain and lines of seaweed stretched, clumped along the shore, from where the tide had receded. Bikinied girls strolled the boardwalk and Carson eyed them. He checked to see if his brother was also, but Michael's glance was fixed on the cafe near the pier. The mousy waitress was out rolling back the tarpaulins from the porch.

"Want to go there?" asked Carson.

Michael shook his head. "No. I will be fine. Let us sit."

Michael walked out across the hardened sand and made for a spot near the café. From this distance he could watch the beach, the café, the lighthouse, and all ambulatory bodies wandering the pier. He sat and commenced to dig his feet in the sand. Carson sat next to him and started to dig in himself. He nudged Michael with his shoulder. "You going to be okay?"

"Yes ... I feel I must tell you these things. An introspection and a fear."

"I appreciate your concern, but you have to work on your delivery. You seem normal enough to me, until you start getting worked up. How are you doing with your meds?"

"I stopped taking them."

"Really? How long?"

"For some time now."

"And how has that been going?"

"It has been grounding, losing a dependency. It has made me very sick at times, though."

"Mentally?"

"Physically. I will always be mentally sick."

"That is no way to change." Carson continued to watch the girls walk the docks as they went out to the pier.

"Maybe, but it is a necessary realization. I handle my problems better knowing that my battle will never end."

"That is hard to figure."

"I am sure that it is hard for you."

"Sure," said Carson. "So … what about that stuttering beauty over at the café? You got your eye on her yet? Town this small, you'll have to call 'em quick."

"Fuck, Carson. Why do you have to talk like that?"

"Sorry. She does seem nice. That is a good thing"

"I suppose."

"Do you know her?" asked Carson.

"As well as I can. I saved her from killing herself once."

"That is a start." Carson laughed.

"She wasn't going to do anything, though."

"They never are."

"It is much different than that."

"Have you," Carson looked at Michael sincerely, "tried to do anything to yourself?"

"Times of failure."

"Since you have been here?"

"No."

"That is a thought, no?"

"I believe it is."

"Good."

A few children ran past them carrying small sand buckets and tiny shovels. It was a little brother and sister. The brother had the lead and the sister trailed behind him at a good pace. Her little blonde pigtails swayed back and forth and she screamed for him to slow down. The little boy picked up his pace and started outrunning her by a greater distance.

"Chris is coming home," said Michael.

"I'll be. I sent word for him. I have not heard from him in quite some time."

"Sent me a letter."

"I bet you were swarmed with those."

"After neglecting them for so long, I was," replied Michael.

"Get to them all?"

"Yes. It helped my rehabilitation."

"That is why we wrote them, to give you a taste of the real world."

"I missed it some. I hated it mostly."

"Here you are now."

"Yes."

"I heard you clicking at the typewriter last night."

"You chose to pass out in the sand instead of come in last night?"

"Yes."

"You are a strange man."

"Says who?" Carson smiled. He kicked his foot slantwise in the sand, the old comfort of packed sand between his toes returning. "What are you typing away at?"

"Just thoughts."

"Anything earth shattering?"

"No, nothing that would be worth reading."

"I don't believe that."

"You did not write it."

The two children stopped at the pier. A loud shout rang out from the other end of the beach. Their mother was calling them back—they had gone too far. The little girl did not seem to hear—she just watched what her brother did and followed his every move. The boy started coming back, away from the pier, and the little girl followed closely behind with her eyes zeroed in on his little back, and then they were gone and out of sight further down the beach, away from the pier, where birds gathered and picked through the shells washed ashore.

About Matthew Chase Stroud

Born in Granbury, Texas in 1988, Matthew Chase Stroud was educated there in the public schools and worked summers as a ranch hand and mechanic. He went on to the University of North Texas, where he received a Bachelors degree in History. During his time as a student, he spent his summers in Montana, Florida, and New Mexico. His fascination with the outdoors, the American working class, and cultural diversity has inspired his unique, yet relatable, characters. He currently resides in Tucson, Arizona with his wife. He will be attending the University of Arizona in the fall of 2013 for a Masters degree in Library Sciences. To date, he has written three novels and a large collection of short stories on his Olvetti typewriter.

BLACK ROSE writing™

CPSIA information can be obtained
at www.ICGtesting.com
Printed in the USA
FFOW03n0819270214
3900FF